Clouds
and Rain

ZAHRA OWENS

Dreamspinner Press

Published by
Dreamspinner Press
4760 Preston Road
Suite 244-149
Frisco, TX 75034
http://www.dreamspinnerpress.com/

Clouds and Rain

Cover Art by Anne Cain annecain.art@gmail.com
Cover Design by Mara McKennen

ISBN: 978-1-61581-832-7

Printed in the United States of America
First Edition
February, 2011

eBook edition available
eBook ISBN: 978-1-61581-833-4

To Carol for helping me out with an inspirational location for this story and to the rest of my "reading group" (of which Carol is a very active member) for helping me figure out everything else.

—1—

HE NEEDED the job, it was as simple as that.

He'd worked in supermarkets and even waited tables, which he wasn't very good at, but this job sounded like it was made for him.

> WANTED: ranch hand, able to handle young, untrained horses, not afraid of mucking out stables and mending fences

He'd grown up around horses, lived on a stud farm all his life, so he could do this with his eyes closed. Room and board wasn't much, of course, but it did say that there would be a nice bonus after the horses were sold, and that was six weeks from now at the local auction, according to the lone clerk and carrier of the post office. He didn't have anywhere to go, so six weeks of work and staying in one place sounded like something he could handle. He wasn't a big fan of cold Idaho winters, but he figured in six weeks time, he could make his way to the coast and better weather before the snow arrived.

The postman dropped him off at the main gate to the Blackwater Ranch at the start of his post run, and Flynn hauled his duffel bag over his shoulder before walking up the dusty road toward the main house. It looked deserted, although there was a dirty, dark-green pickup truck parked under an apple tree; still, when he knocked on the door of the ranch house, nobody answered. Determined to find the owner and because he didn't want to walk all the way back to town, Flynn sauntered toward the barn, passing a few unhaltered horses in a small corral. He saw a few more in a higher paddock as well, but other than that, it was eerily quiet.

The double doors to the barn were open, so he walked inside and was greeted by a large brown head sticking out of its enclosure. Flynn held out his hand and let the horse sniff it, then stroked the white patch between the animal's eyes.

"Got a boss around here, beautiful?" he asked the horse, then smiled when the animal obviously didn't answer. Nobody else did either, so Flynn walked on toward the end of the barn, peeking into the stalls he passed but not finding anyone there either.

"Guess he's working somewhere else," he told himself until a sudden voice from behind made him startle.

"Can I help you?"

Flynn turned around and saw a sandy-haired man in jeans and a plaid shirt standing near one of the stable doors he'd passed earlier. There was a black sheepdog with a white muzzle sitting next to him.

"Yes, ehm, I'm here about the job?"

"You must be pretty desperate if you're willing to take something that pays less than minimum wage. What's the deal? Did you do time or something?" the man asked Flynn rather gruffly.

Flynn shook his head. "I grew up on a horse ranch, so this is better than stacking boxes at the supermarket."

"What ranch?" the man continued in the same unaffected voice he'd used earlier.

"Back east," Flynn answered, purposely staying vague. "Canada," he eventually admitted. "We moved there from England just after I was born, since we could make more money breeding horses there than in England."

"So why aren't you working on your family's ranch then?"

Flynn was afraid of this question, but he had his standard answer. "I'm the youngest of five boys. Nothing there for me really."

GABLE didn't answer immediately; instead, he watched the young man. He was sure there was more to the story and he knew he'd find out if he hired him. Not that he had a lot of choice, really. The local boys found better-paying jobs at the bigger spreads, and not a lot of strangers passed through town. If he didn't say yes to this guy, he'd have to work the ranch alone this season, and he wasn't doing a great job of that so far.

"So what can you do?" he asked, although he'd already made up his mind. Even if the kid could barely hold his own around the young horses, he'd have an extra pair of hands to do the hard labor.

"Pretty much everything a horse needs," the brown-eyed looker answered. "Groom, water, muck out their stalls, exercise them, teach them to accept a bridle and a saddle, break them in, you name it, I've done it."

Although it sounded like Gable had died and gone to horse heaven, he knew there had to be a snag. If this kid was as good as he claimed, why wasn't he working for the big boys, making much better money than Gable could afford to give him? He wasn't about to dig deeper, though. If he didn't get a move on, he'd have no ranch left and he needed the extra pair of hands.

"Good enough," he said. "Can't pay you anything right now. As soon as the horses sell, I'll make it worth your while. For now, I can give you room and board."

"That's what the piece of paper at the post office said," the young man replied with resignation.

"I'm Gable Sutton and I own the place," Gable answered, thinking "for now," but not voicing it.

"Flynn Tomlinson," the young man answered, taking a few steps forward to shake the offered hand, "and I work here."

The smile that accompanied that final statement hit Gable square in the groin. All ideas of working close to Flynn to keep an eye on him vanished, because he knew he wouldn't get much done himself if he had to look at that young man all day long. He'd eyed his cute little butt as he was walking down the barn, admired the long legs and the lean back. Of course he could only imagine that last bit, since it was hidden underneath a suede jacket and a denim shirt, but when he'd turned around earlier, Gable had practically heard his body wolf whistle. He shook his head, trying to dispel the thoughts. They had work to do.

"Let's grab some lunch, I can show you the house and then we can get right to work."

FLYNN watched his new employer take two steps out of the stable and followed him toward the barn doors. It was hard to miss how much effort the man had to put into simply walking. If the pronounced limp didn't give it away, the labored breathing certainly showed it wasn't just a physical thing. This man was in pain with every step he took.

"You should probably get a doctor to look at that leg," he said, trying to sound casual about it. "If you were a horse, I'd bring you in from the paddock and call the vet."

"Doctor's seen it," Gable answered gruffly. "Says I'll need to live with it."

Gable's tone suggested to Flynn he'd better shut up about it, but it did give Flynn some indication why the stables were badly maintained and the rest of the ranch looked like a mess. If Gable was taking care of everything by himself, and with the sort of injury that limp implied, it was no surprise. Although Flynn could only guess at what was wrong with his new boss's leg, it looked like it was a bit worse than a sprained ankle. At least Flynn wouldn't have to ask him what he could do around the place. It was obvious he'd have plenty of work.

As they approached the house, a white truck stopped next to the green one and a tall, slender woman with a blonde ponytail stepped out. The sheepdog darted past them to greet her as she opened the back and took out a large cardboard box. Flynn, having been taught to always help a lady, rushed to her side to take the heavy load from her.

"Why, thank you!" she smiled at him and then looked over at Gable. "I see you've found a helping hand?"

"Hi, Calley," Gable acknowledged her with a nod. "Calley, meet Flynn. He's going to help me out around here until I sell the horses. Flynn, this is Calley. She owns the only decent grocery shop in town and her better half is Bill Haines, who's the only decent vet in the county. She's brought us some food so we don't starve. I see you've already learned to be nice to the hand that feeds you."

"Oh Gabe, you're such a charmer." Calley smiled none too coyly, although Flynn missed the mockery in her face after she turned away from him. "Guess I'll have to bring extra food later on in the week." Flynn noticed it wasn't a question, adding to the feeling that Calley and Gable knew each other quite well.

They walked toward the house and Calley told Flynn where to drop the box of groceries, while Gable plunked himself down on the worn-out couch that was sitting in the corner of the kitchen. He put his leg on a footstool standing in front of it and exhaled deeply. Flynn didn't miss the look of concern Calley threw him, however fleeting it was, before she started unpacking the box and putting things away as if she lived there. Although if she did, Flynn was sure the house would actually look like it saw a woman's touch from time to time. As it stood now, the dishes were piled high in the sink and the refrigerator was only filled with the things Calley had just put inside it. Although she was discreet about it, Flynn saw her throw out some stuff that almost walked out of there by itself. When Gable started protesting, she was clear though. "I don't care if you poison yourself, Gable, but this young man deserves to be fed well. He's here to help you, so you'd better take care of him!"

Gable grunted something under his breath and Flynn watched the exchange with some amusement. He didn't really know what to make of it. Was Calley Gable's ex? Was that why she knew her way around the house and why she felt free to admonish him in front of a virtual stranger? He wasn't about to question any of it, fearing that Gable was not in the mood for any sort of small talk. Maybe one day his curiosity would be satisfied, but if not, well, to be honest, it really wasn't any of his business.

"Well, Flynn, I hope you can cook?" Calley gave him a concerned look and Flynn smiled it away.

"Sure I can," he acknowledged. "Grew up in a house full of boys. It was that or eat stale bread!"

"Then I'm sure you'll feel right at home here," Calley replied with a wink before picking up the now-empty box and heading out again.

After she left, the silence grew uncomfortable.

"I can make us an omelet?" Flynn suggested.

"Had eggs for breakfast, so I'll skip it," Gable answered, his eyes closed and head relaxed against the back of the couch. "Thanks," he added, almost as an afterthought.

Flynn doubted Gable had eaten anything, judging from the state of his kitchen, so he wasn't going to leave it at that. He'd seen Calley unpack all sorts of things and was sure he could whip up some sort of tasty lunch, so he opened the fridge and took out a head of lettuce, a tomato, and a cucumber. Together with the ham and cheese she'd also brought, he made sandwiches. He had to open a few cupboards, but in the end decided to wash some of the plates and knives so he had somewhere other than the cutting board to put them. The dog stayed diligently next to his owner. He was licking his lips, but had clearly been taught not to beg.

"Here, boy," Flynn called the dog.

"She's a girl and her name is Bridget," Gable corrected him. "And she doesn't get scraps from the table. She has a bowl in the mudroom."

Flynn held the piece of ham in midair as he saw the dog torn between accepting it and loyalty to her owner, so Flynn dropped it back to the chopping board and the dog relaxed. He divided the sandwiches between two plates and handed one to Gable, who opened his eyes when he smelled the food.

With some distrust, Gable took the plate from Flynn and looked at its contents. "Thanks," he muttered as he inspected what was between the two slices of rye bread, a rather forced smile appearing on his face.

Flynn had a hard time not laughing. He rarely felt uneasy around strangers, especially now he'd been on the road for more than three years, but this man was something different. He hoped the uncomfortable silences would go away after a while, or at least that the man would let him work by himself, so they wouldn't bother him too much. In any case, he couldn't put his finger on what exactly made it so hard to be in the same room with Gable. The food was good, though, much better than what he could afford to get himself in the diners he passed along the way. Gable seemed to agree, although Flynn tried not to smile when he saw Gable trying to sneak the cucumber from between the layers of the sandwich without him noticing it. Flynn, in turn, fed Bridget the scrap of ham he'd put aside while he was doing the dishes. All of the dishes, not just the ones they'd used.

By the time they went outside again to tend to the stables, the kitchen looked much better than it had when they'd walked in an hour earlier.

FLYNN really enjoyed this job.

He was pretty much his own boss. Gable didn't interfere with what he was doing, and, despite his gruff exterior, he was a quiet, calm man. They'd divided the chores up pretty much without talking. Gable did all the things he could do sitting down or on horseback. He'd take care of the saddles and bridles, fix a hinge on a door, ride around the paddocks checking for fences that were down. He'd muster the horses when they needed to be moved and Flynn would hold the gates open and make sure they were closed after all the horses had passed through. All in all, they made a pretty good team.

Flynn knew that if they wanted to sell some of their horses at auction, they'd need to train them—some of them weren't even used to a bridle and a saddle yet—and he hadn't seen much of that in the week he'd been there. He'd often seen Gable ride among the herd in the higher paddock, and had sometimes seen him touch the animals, stroke their backs, or even talk to them, but they'd never worked with the horses individually, and this worried Flynn. He just didn't know how to strike up a conversation with Gable to introduce the subject.

Gable's limp wasn't getting any better; in fact, Flynn feared it was actually getting worse. He'd suggested visiting a doctor once again and had been snapped at, then given the silent treatment for the rest of the day. As a peace offering, he finished his chores early so he could rush home and make dinner. He had yet to meet a man who could resist his vegetarian lasagna, even those who felt a meal wasn't complete without meat.

"Go and take a shower first. Dinner will take another twenty minutes or so," Flynn told Gable when the older man finally came into the house. Gable didn't answer, simply nodded, displaying his most nondescript face as he moved to the back of the house.

Flynn knew Gable preferred the outside shower, not in the least because it saved him a trip upstairs. In the evening, the water from it was at the perfect temperature, having been heated by the sun all day, but even on an overcast day, Gable would always use that one. It was just a shower head leaning against the back of the house, with shrubs planted around it so nobody could look in, at least not from outside the house. From inside, it was easy to watch him from the shadows of the back door.

Flynn had spotted Gable's naked backside on his second day there, as the older man was stripping to get washed. He'd bent down to wrap some plastic around his injured leg, but that was not what had drawn Flynn's attention. He'd been enthralled by the sinewy body, the strong, lean back, and when the man turned around under the spray, eyes closed and clearly enjoying the water, Flynn had felt his jeans grow tight. He watched Gable's hand rubbing through his chest hair and down his stomach to his groin.

This was just the sort of body that turned Flynn on no end, and he'd felt far too few of those under his hands lately. That day was the first time Flynn had rushed into the tiny downstairs toilet to release the tension. Now he didn't do that anymore. Now he knew Gable's washing ritual and knew how long it took for the man to dry off and get dressed again. Nobody ever came to the ranch, and from where he was standing Gable couldn't see him either, so he felt confident enough to insert his hand into his jeans and rub himself. When he saw Gable wipe the suds between his legs and repeat the action a few times, seeming to hesitate for a moment when he realized he was growing hard and then taking himself in hand, a soft moan escaped Flynn's mouth. Oh, what he would do to be allowed to touch that body, to be that hand, touching

Gable's cock. Flynn barely dared to touch himself, afraid he would come instantly. He watched as Gable leaned against the side of the house, arm outstretched to hold himself upright, balancing on his good leg, while he pleasured himself. Flynn could easily imagine what Gable would look like if he could help him do that and then it suddenly hit him. He wondered how long it had been since another hand had touched Gable? He didn't look like he got around much. Maybe Gable would let him be good to him one day. Maybe.

Flynn saw Gable buck into his hand and come, thick strands of white cream shooting out of his cock. There was no ecstasy on his face, though; Gable just continued his washing. Flynn closed his eyes, imagining what the older man must look like when he was actually being treated well, being pampered and taken care of. It took only a few movements of his hand for Flynn to feel the rush of his orgasm shooting through his groin as he imagined Gable saying his name. When, moments later, he opened his eyes, he saw Gable looking at him as he was drying himself. Flynn's heart stopped. He'd never planned on getting caught.

—2—

SEEING Flynn watching him through the back-door window made Gable angry, then quite turned on, despite his little release of tension under the shower earlier. He couldn't believe the nerve of the kid. Whatever happened to discreetly looking the other way? Then it hit him. Maybe Flynn liked looking at naked men? Gable continued drying off, trying to get that image out of his mind. He couldn't go there. They had work to do, and any complications in their relationship would only make things more difficult.

Difficult because Gable felt they were doing really well. Flynn was a hard worker and Gable liked the fact that he didn't have to tell the kid what to do. Any move toward him might make him run, and there was no way he'd find anyone else as capable. Also, it was clear that managing this ranch on his own was out of the question. His damn leg made sure of that, which was another reason why he wouldn't dare gamble on the possibility that Flynn might feel even an inkling of the same lust that Gable felt for him. Why would the kid want a guy old enough to be his father, even if he had two good legs?

Fully dressed, Gable walked into the kitchen, purposely not looking at Flynn. The smells drifting toward him made his mouth water, though. He'd already sampled Flynn's cooking. Simple stuff, like omelets and spaghetti, which tasted like the restaurant food he used to get in the city, nothing like what he was used to eating at the ranch, but this smelled even better. From the corner of his eye he saw Flynn crouching in front of the oven, looking at the contents. He couldn't help but steal a look at that tight little ass in those form-fitting jeans, but he made sure his eyes didn't linger.

"Looks like it'll be done in about another five minutes," Flynn said, not turning around.

"Okay," Gable answered. For some reason his heart was racing. This was ridiculous. Plenty of men had seen him naked. Why was it so weird to know Flynn had? Suddenly he felt grubby, still wearing his work clothes, so he turned around and hobbled upstairs to change.

FLYNN got up from in front of the oven and turned around. To his surprise, the kitchen was deserted. He'd expected Gable to be there, ready for dinner, like he had been every night since Flynn had arrived. He heard footsteps on the stairs, Gable's now familiar limp, and wondered what that was all about.

Five minutes later, when Flynn was putting the steaming oven dish on the table, he saw Gable enter in a clean pair of jeans and a shirt that looked like it had never been worn before.

"Is there something to celebrate?" Flynn asked. "You didn't have to get all dressed up. This is nothing special, it's just lasagna."

Gable shrugged. "It's Saturday."

"And your mother always made you get dressed up on Saturdays?"

Gable shrugged again, this time not saying anything. Instead, he pulled the kitchen chair back and sat down, then gave Flynn an expectant look that lasted mere moments, averting his eyes when he realized he was looking directly at him.

Flynn tried to ignore the awkward shyness his boss often displayed when they were sitting down to eat in the evening. He was just going to have to find a way to make these dinners a bit more relaxed.

"Want me to do this?" he asked, holding out his hand for Gable to give him his plate.

"'Kay," Gable conceded, not looking at Flynn. He waited just long enough for Flynn to fill up his plate and then dug in.

Flynn had to admit that dinnertime was always a bit strained, but judging from Gable's eagerness, his cooking was very much appreciated. Flynn figured Gable just wasn't much of a talker. For him, though, being on the road meant he'd often just had himself for company, so now he had a listening ear, he found he couldn't stop talking.

"So many women took care of us boys when Mum died," Flynn revealed, munching on his own plate of pasta. "I was the baby, so I was always around them when they were making dinner. Learned to cook all sorts of stuff, and once I was old enough to operate the stove, I experimented on them, with mixed results." Flynn chuckled when he remembered those times.

"Sorry about your mom. At least something good came out of her death then," Gable answered, momentarily forgetting his manners and speaking with his mouth full. He swallowed and then looked at Flynn, a hint of a smile on his face. "I don't think I've ever eaten this well in my own kitchen."

Flynn's heart leapt at the compliment. He tried not to show it, not wanting to do anything to make Gable stop talking. "Thank you," he answered instead. "Want some more?"

Gable handed him his plate and Flynn gave him another serving.

"Where I really learned to cook was in the city, though," Flynn continued. "Not a lot of jobs for ranch hands there, so I had to adjust my sights. The only thing they needed plenty of when I arrived there was short order cooks."

"Did you like living in the city?" Gable asked.

Flynn shrugged. "It was certainly different. And, well," Flynn hesitated, "a lot more opportunity to sow my wild oats, if you know what I mean."

"But you returned to the country?"

"I had my reasons," Flynn said dismissively. It was no surprise that the rest of the meal was spent in their usual silence.

Gable didn't speak again until they had done the dishes and were sitting outside on the porch. The sun was setting and clouds were moving in, turning one side of the sky ominously dark, while the other side was painted in reds and oranges. Gable had his busted leg up, resting on yet another footstool, and Flynn was sitting on the steps, his back against a thick wooden post that held the roof up. He wasn't directly looking at Gable but he could, without straining himself, if he wanted to—and he did steal a look now and then, just to be sure the older man was relaxed and content. This seemed to be a position they both felt comfortable with, and whenever there was no need for them to interact, the tension between them seemed to dissipate.

Flynn wasn't totally happy with the silence, though. It meant he was left alone to think, and whenever he did that, the image of Gable under the spray of the shower invaded his mind and made his body react. He tried to will himself to relax and think of other things. He simply had to face it that since they couldn't even carry on a decent conversation, making passes at each other was entirely out of the question. Besides, for all he knew, Gable was straight. Flynn had never noticed Gable eyeing him. Then again, that didn't prove anything. Flynn sighed. Life was a lot less complicated in the city. He had almost forgotten why he had been in such a hurry to leave it.

"LOOKS like it's going to rain," Gable murmured from his chair on the porch.

"They didn't say anything about that on the radio this afternoon," Flynn replied.

"Those weather guys don't know what they're talking about. Trust me. I know what the sky looks like out here just before a thunderstorm. I hope it won't spook the horses too much. Can't afford to lose any." Gable sighed and contemplated the sorry truth in his own words. If some of the horses broke through a fence and started running, there was no telling how much damage would be done. When it had been two of them working the ranch, one could mend the fence while the other rode out with the dog in search of the horses. Now he couldn't ride out too far cross-country anymore and Flynn didn't know the area well enough to do it. All they could hope was that it was just a mild summer rain and that it wouldn't do more than make the horses huddle together near the lean-to.

The throbbing in Gable's leg was easing off now that he had been sitting for a while. It was a balmy evening, the quiet before the storm, and he watched Flynn sitting on the steps, head resting back against the post with his eyes closed. Gable even thought he saw a smile on his face, yet he couldn't help but think he was working Flynn too hard. He was up as early as Gable, which even in late summer was a pretty early dawn. He worked all day, tirelessly, and never hesitated in bringing Gable some water to drink whenever he got some for himself. On top of that, he'd made dinner for the two of them every single day. Although Gable could easily get used to the royal treatment, he knew he'd better not. Flynn was a drifter and Gable knew he'd be gone as soon as the horses were sold. No use trying to hold him back.

"Think we should muster the herd from the far paddock?" Flynn asked eventually, not even bothering to open his eyes. "I could take Bridget? She doesn't listen to me like she does you, but she knows what to do."

Gable gave it some thought. Way back when he wasn't doing this alone, they'd have ridden out together and it would have taken them no more than an hour to get the horses closer to the ranch, where they would be better protected against the elements. Now he couldn't risk it. Not with his bad leg and Flynn's inexperience. "We'll just have to hope that it doesn't get too bad," Gable answered. He watched Flynn concede, and turned away so he didn't have to look at the disappointment on his face. With some trepidation he lifted his leg off the stool and gently brought it back into contact with the floor, then got up from the chair.

"You didn't used to run this ranch alone, did you? Before... before your accident?"

Gable stopped in the doorway as he heard Flynn's hesitant voice. He couldn't turn around, couldn't show the kid the emotion in his face. He found he couldn't walk on either. How could he explain to him how much he missed his companion, how much he missed being held and touched? How he missed that much more than the help around the ranch?

Suddenly Gable felt a hand on his back and he almost retreated, but despite the warm night air, the heat that emanated from it felt so good he simply stood there, needing all his strength not to turn around and pull the young man into his arms.

"No, there were two of us, but he left," Gable answered curtly, hoping his voice wouldn't betray his heartache. He took a step forward, away from Flynn. And then another, and before he knew it, he was alone in his bedroom.

—3—

FLYNN couldn't sleep. It was raining cats and dogs, and out of his bedroom window he could just spot the horses huddled together in the shed. On top of that, the conversation he'd had with Gable kept playing in his mind. Gable had clearly said "*he* left" and the overwhelming emotions that came with that admission left no doubt in Flynn's mind that Gable had meant that "he" was a lover, not just a guy who worked the ranch with him. Flynn wasn't sure if he was happy or sad about what Gable had revealed. Of course it was nice to know that Gable liked men, but did that mean that Flynn had a chance with him? He liked the man, lusted after him too, and he had to admit that he didn't mind being the transitional man, the rebound guy. He didn't believe in everlasting love anyway, and if anything came of him and Gable, he could easily stick around longer than the agreed-upon six weeks. In fact, a year or so in the same place was starting to sound nice, although he didn't really count on it. Gable only seemed to tolerate his company because of the work he did.

Despite Gable's gruff exterior, Flynn had more than once seen the tenderness the man could show, especially to the horses. They seemed to take to him naturally as he walked among them, respecting their herd mentality as well as their individuality.

After Flynn had again dared to suggest to Gable that they needed to start training the horses, Gable had given him an impressive demonstration of exactly what his bond with those animals was by picking a colt out of the herd and taking it into the corral to accept first a bridle, and then a saddle. The horse barely protested, and when it did, Gable soothed it, stood by it silently, and gave the horse the time to adjust. The colt was too young to be ridden, but Flynn felt that it was practically ready. Although the look Gable gave Flynn, almost asking him whether he was satisfied now simply by his intense stare, stopped Flynn from opening the discussion again, Flynn knew he had to test it on some of the older horses, the three- and four-year-olds that were ready to be sold.

Outside, the thunderstorm seemed to abate a bit, but the rain kept coming down in steady sheets. There was no use fretting over the horses. They were fairly calm in their meadow and it wasn't like there was space to bring them all inside; besides, they were working horses and they lived outside even during winter, albeit sheltered by a sturdy lean-to. Flynn turned away from the window and huddled into his blankets, trying to get cozy enough to sleep, but when that didn't work, he pushed his hand between his legs and touched himself. As he closed his eyes, he let the image of Gable's sinewy body invade his mind, imagining joining him under that shower. It made him rock hard and terribly turned on. His release didn't leave him all that satisfied, but it did make him drowsy enough to drift off to sleep.

TWO hours after fleeing to his bedroom, Gable was still on the bed, fully clothed and wondering what had happened to the time. It was dark outside now and the wind was blowing hard around the house, slamming the rain against the window. Why had the kid done that? Why had Flynn tried to comfort him? He always thought he'd kept his emotions in check quite nicely around him.

Oh, who was he kidding? For almost a year now, he'd managed to not think of Grant. In the hospital he'd simply decided to banish the man from his thoughts, and most of the time, he'd succeeded. Somehow, this kid brought it all back. Flynn was smaller than Grant, but he had the same teasing smile and unruly black, curly hair. Grant had been a drifter too, yet he'd stayed for a while. Could he hope the same for Flynn? He could do without the heartache of him leaving, though.

Gable just had to look around the ranch to notice how good it looked now. Flynn was a godsend. The stables actually looked like they got regular maintenance, the horses were happy, and even Bridget wagged her tail at him. Gable didn't remember how long it'd been since his house looked habitable. Actually, he did. Before the accident, he used to do the cleaning, since Grant wasn't all that house-proud. Grant had always taken it for granted that he'd have a clean house and clean clothes and Gable seriously doubted that he had ever given a thought to who had actually done all these things for him.

Gable sat up on the bed and started taking his shirt off. He winced as his foot hit the floor a lot harder than usual and cursed himself for being so distracted. He let his head drop into his hands and sighed. He couldn't let his emotions get to him anymore. He simply had to stop thinking about Grant. And about Flynn too.

The next morning Gable got up early, since he couldn't sleep anyway. He bypassed the kitchen, despite the tempting smell that was already drifting out of it, and saddled Brenner, his brown stallion, to go take a look at the herd.

It took more than an hour of walking his horse between the other animals for him to be sure they were all okay, then another two hours of riding along the fences before he was calm and satisfied that all was well and he could return to the stables.

He had just cleared the trees when he saw Flynn exit the stable block, followed by a tall, dark man. Gable turned his horse around immediately, not wanting the two men to notice him, but curiosity won in the end. He rode a little closer and recognized the stranger. Hunter owned the ranch next door, a much bigger place than Gable's, and he always came by to get the first pick of the herd. He'd buy a few horses for his wranglers and a few more that caught his eye and that he thought he could sell for a profit. He was probably here to buy some more now.

Hunter was also an incorrigible flirt, in an unassuming sort of way. Right now he was putting the moves on Flynn, and although Gable knew Hunter wasn't gay, he felt his stomach clench. Despite what it did to him, Gable couldn't look away. Flynn was smiling, possibly even urging Hunter on. Flynn was leaning against the doorpost and Hunter was standing fairly close to him, his hand resting on the same doorpost as he was saying something that made Flynn laugh.

Gable urged Brenner to gallop down to the ranch, despite how much it hurt his foot. If anyone was doing any horse dealing, it was him, not Flynn.

FLYNN knew Hunter was flirting with him and he was enjoying every minute of it. It felt like ages since a guy had paid him any attention, so he wasn't about to give the handsome buyer the cold shoulder. Of course he couldn't talk shop with him. Hunter had told him from the word go that he was here to buy some of Gable's horses, and Flynn had immediately made it clear to Hunter they needed to wait for Gable to come back, but that didn't mean they couldn't spend their time in more comfortable surroundings.

"Why don't I get you a cold beer while we wait?" Flynn suggested.

Hunter pursed his lips. "I don't usually drink before I reach a deal...."

"I told you I can't offer you a deal. The horses aren't mine. I just work here."

"Oh, come on," Hunter drawled, leaning a little closer. "You have more invested in this ranch than your labor, don't you?"

Flynn looked away, pretending he had no idea what Hunter was getting at.

"Grant wasn't exactly a stable boy here either," Hunter added.

Flynn was tempted to let Hunter continue. Without too much coaxing he'd already found out the name of Gable's ex. Who knew what else Hunter would let slip, given enough encouragement?

"You know better than to deal with the hired help," Gable interrupted after bringing his galloping horse to a sudden halt. Gable gave Flynn a stern look before he jumped out of the saddle and onto the ground. He winced slightly, but Flynn saw how he tried to hide it from Hunter by walking toward him virtually without a limp. Gable handed Brenner's reins to Flynn and then gave Hunter a quick look intended to coax him to come with him toward the house.

"Don't take the saddle off yet. We'll be going out again in a little while. Saddle T.C. for Hunter," Gable told Flynn.

Flynn simply nodded. He didn't mind being ordered around, but Gable's tone of voice was nothing less than condescending and he did take offense to being treated that way. He'd left jobs for less than this but didn't want to say anything in Hunter's presence. In any case, he had plenty of work to do, so despite his curiosity, he didn't really want to help sweet-talk Hunter.

There was no use mulling over the way Gable treated him. He *was* the hired hand, there was no need to deny that, but he didn't know if he could continue working for Gable if this was the kind of disrespect he was going to get for it. Flynn clucked at Brenner to make the horse follow him into the stable, making a mental note to talk to Gable later.

Flynn had just finished saddling T.C., Gable's paint gelding, tightening the cinch when the two men returned. This time, Flynn didn't even get a look, let alone a thank you, from Gable. Hunter nodded his thanks, but was given little time to mount his steed, as Gable couldn't seem to gallop off fast enough. Flynn watched the two of them speed off into the distance, realizing Gable didn't look like he was being any nicer to Hunter than was necessary to sell the horses.

After finishing up outside, Flynn washed his hands at the sink in the mudroom, kicked off his boots and traipsed into the kitchen in his socks, wondering if he should make an effort for lunch in case Hunter was staying. He didn't mind. Lunch was usually sandwiches and there was plenty of bread, cheese, and ham left for all of them. He just hoped Gable's mood would lighten up after the sale, otherwise he would rather have his lunch on the porch, far away from the other two.

Through the kitchen window, Flynn saw Gable limp over to the house, with Hunter nowhere in sight. He didn't turn around when Gable entered a few minutes later. He knew he'd trained him well enough by now to be sure that Gable wouldn't walk into the kitchen in his boots anymore.

"Coffee's about done," Flynn announced.

Gable's only acknowledgement was a grunt.

"Hunter not interested in buying any horses?" Flynn asked tentatively, still not looking directly at Gable. He was peeling potatoes for dinner and that gave him the perfect excuse not to turn around.

"Why? Are you that eager to see him again?" Gable replied gruffly, slamming the fridge door shut and throwing a plate on the table with a loud bang.

Flynn took a deep breath before answering. "I thought it would be good if you sold some. I'm sure you could use the income."

"Don't worry, you'll get paid."

Flynn threw the last potato in the pot for dinner and paused before speaking again, for no reason other than to gather his thoughts and prevent himself from lashing out at the miserable mood Gable was in. "You told me I would get paid and I trust you," he said calmly. "Hunter just seemed like a really nice guy and he was pretty eager about getting first pick, so I thought he might pay a little bit more than what you would get at auction. Besides, it would save you the transport costs as well."

Flynn took the heavy pot and turned around to cross the kitchen toward the sink. He barely saw Gable coming as the older man took two large steps to bridge the distance between them. One more step and he was pushing Flynn against the wall. The force with which Flynn hit the hard surface, combined with the feeling of a hand on his throat, made him release his grip on the pot, and it fell to the ground with a loud clanging noise, the uncooked potatoes rolling all over the kitchen floor.

Before he could gather his wits, Flynn saw the predatory look in Gable's eyes and then felt the older man's mouth against his in what became an aggressive, invading kiss. At first, Flynn resisted. The abruptness of it, combined with the fact he had nowhere to run, made his flight reaction kick in, but then, as he realized he was being held against the wall by his boss's sinewy frame, his body reacted. Flynn kissed Gable back, trying to convey that he wanted this too. It was what he'd dreamed about, more than once. Okay, maybe not exactly this. He was used to taking the lead, not being smacked into a wall and devoured, but he found he didn't mind at all, despite the pain that was slowly making itself felt at the back of his head. He simply pressed his tongue between their mashed lips and battled for dominance, dancing around Gable's tongue. Flynn could feel Gable's hardness pressing against his hip and he finally allowed himself to touch Gable, grabbing his buttocks and pulling him closer.

Gable seemed to hesitate for a moment, pulling back and looking Flynn straight in the eye. They were panting, hard, and Gable's icy-blue eyes were now dark with lust. He leaned his forehead against Flynn's for a moment and then pulled away completely, hobbling out of the kitchen.

Flynn leaned his head back and was reminded of the smack he'd received earlier, so he rubbed his hand over his hair to sooth the pain. He then wiped the corner of his mouth with the back of his hand and realized he'd split his lip.

Flynn looked at the state of his surroundings. He had no idea what had sparked Gable's reaction, but Flynn knew he wanted more. He was confused, though. Should he follow Gable outside? He didn't know Gable that well yet, simply because Gable never let him get close, but he did know that Gable calmed down best when he was left to his own devices. So instead of confronting him and asking him what this was all about, Flynn decided to give him a few minutes. He picked up the pot and started gathering the scattered potatoes before continuing toward the sink to wash them. He licked his lips, still tasting Gable combined with the iron taste of blood, and then replayed the last few minutes in his head again. Suddenly it dawned on him. Was Gable jealous of Hunter? Flynn couldn't help but smile. It certainly made sense, despite Gable's clumsy way of making his feelings known.

Flynn put the potato pot on the stove, ready for tonight's dinner, and wiped his hands, then made two big sandwiches and put them on a plate each. He poured two cups of coffee, added plenty of sugar to both, and walked outside with his peace offering.

He wasn't surprised to find Gable on the porch, staring sullenly out at the paddocks, his leg up on the footstool. Flynn walked into his view and silently held out the food and drink. Gable looked up momentarily and then turned away, never changing his expression.

"Listen," Flynn sighed. "You kissed me. I didn't mind one bit. Get over it."

This time Gable looked at him a little longer, then accepted a plate and a mug of coffee.

Flynn decided he'd pushed Gable far enough for now and silently settled on the porch step to eat.

—4—

THAT afternoon, Hunter returned with a large truck and a small trailer containing two horses of his own. While his wrangler unloaded them, Gable and Hunter talked about how they were going to round up Hunter's purchases.

Flynn could see them from afar and couldn't help noticing that Gable seemed nicer to Hunter than he had been that morning. The feeling continued when Gable broke away from Hunter and his wrangler to approach him.

"Think you can ride with us this afternoon?" Gable asked. "With the four of us together, it should be easy to round up the horses Hunter wants and put them in the front paddock. From there we can load them in the truck."

"Sure thing, boss," Flynn answered, unable to hide a smile. Hell, if he'd know that one kiss would have made such a difference, he would have kissed Gable the first day he got there. Then again, it might not have had the same impact as this kiss had, since this one was initiated by Gable himself. Flynn rubbed the back of his head to remind himself of the bump, which still hurt a bit. "I'll saddle Brenner and T.C."

Despite the earlier thunderstorm, the weather that afternoon was nothing short of glorious. The sky was blue as far as the eye could see, with the occasional small white cloud but nothing so big it would block the sun, and it was hot enough to ride out in just a T-shirt and jeans. As Gable had predicted, it took them less than an hour to round up a sizeable group of horses, but Flynn knew that the biggest part of the job was only just starting. Hunter would want to see each horse individually, so he could judge how easy they would be to handle, but he'd also have to assess the animal's general build and constitution. Flynn knew they had nothing to worry about. He knew the herd well enough to be confident they didn't have any weak horses among those old enough to be sold, and the ones they'd rounded up this afternoon were all suitable to be turned into good working horses. He was sure Hunter would see that too.

On their way back to the stables, after a final ride around the herd, Flynn steered T.C. next to Brenner, so he could talk to Gable without the other two men hearing.

"Why don't you talk money with Hunter and I'll show the horses?" Once the words had left his mouth, he knew they sounded a bit audacious, even though this way of working was the logical way. He probably should have phrased it differently, but then again, Gable wasn't much of a talker, and Flynn preferred to know where he stood before they arrived back. To his surprise, Gable smiled at him for a moment before nodding and urging Brenner to trot a little faster.

Flynn stayed behind, telling his body to behave. Damn, he felt like a schoolgirl on a first date! There was no way he could expect anything more to happen today, but that kiss this morning and now that smile made his heart race and he couldn't help wondering how the evening would play out once it was just the two of them again. He knew he had to get with it now, though. They had work to do first, but Flynn couldn't help wanting it to be dinnertime already.

As Flynn had predicted, Hunter was very pleased with the horses. While he and Gable sat on the fence overlooking the round corral that was also used for training, Flynn led one horse after another into it and let it walk, then trot, and finally canter. Tim, Hunter's wrangler, would sometimes test to see how skittish they were or would lift a leg and check out a hoof, but other than that, most of the horses seemed to meet with Hunter's approval. After the last horse had been shown, Hunter and his wrangler got the truck ready to load their animals, leaving Gable and Flynn alone together.

"That went well," Flynn remarked in a bid to start a conversation between them. "So is he going to take all of the horses we mustered?"

Gable just nodded.

"You don't seem happy about it?"

Gable shrugged, so Flynn forced himself into Gable's field of vision. "It's good," Gable eventually conceded, none too enthusiastically. "He's coming back tomorrow to load the rest, since he can't take all of them at once." And then a bit more quietly, "He certainly made my year."

Flynn smiled at no one in particular. It was good to see Gable a little more relaxed; he hoped it would continue. It had been a long day, though, and he was glad it was over. Seeing Gable crawl down from his perch, carefully avoiding putting too much strain on his injured foot, made him think that Gable was probably pretty worn out too.

"Why don't you go inside and start dinner?" Flynn suggested. "It's all on the stove. There's three of us to load the horses, so I'm sure we can manage."

Gable looked at him suspiciously, and for a moment Flynn thought he'd ruined everything again by telling Gable what to do instead of letting him make the decision. He couldn't take his words back, so he tried to ignore it by looking over at the approaching truck.

"I can help," Gable tried, but as they started walking, it was clear that his foot hurt pretty badly, so he conceded. "Well, if you're sure?"

Flynn nodded encouragingly, briefly touching Gable's shoulder to send him on his way. As he saw what effort it took Gable to simply walk, he couldn't help but wonder what was underneath the bandages. He'd only seen a glimpse, but for the injury to stay so painful for so long, it would have to be something serious. He shook his head, knowing it was futile to mull over it. Gable didn't want to talk about it, he'd made that clear quite a few times.

Less than an hour later the truck with the horses was en route to Hunter's ranch and Flynn made his way inside, his stomach growling. He kicked off his boots and washed his hands in the mudroom, and then made his way into the kitchen, where he found Gable standing by the stove with Bridget next to him, looking up expectantly. He paused for a moment to look at the older man and shake the indecent thoughts out of his head before walking toward him. Although he knew he had to keep his body in check, he dared to lightly touch Gable's back to alert him to his presence.

"Smells amazing." Flynn couldn't help but let his hand linger, especially when it became clear that Gable wasn't pulling away from him.

Gable shrugged. "You're the cook. I'm just the help in here."

Gable nodded at Bridget to vacate the space between them and Flynn's heart leapt inside his chest. He silently told himself it didn't mean anything and urged himself to stop expecting things to be different all of a sudden because they'd kissed, but he couldn't help himself, especially not when Gable took a fork and offered him a taste of the carrots.

"Watch out, it's hot."

Flynn blew on it and then took the offering, but couldn't help showing his discomfort when he burned his tongue.

"That bad, hey?"

Flynn gestured "no" with his hands and then opened his mouth to let it cool. "Just… hot!" He opened the side cupboard anyway and took out the rosemary he'd bought in town earlier that week. "And it needs a little of this, but other than that, they're done."

"Let's eat then."

Dinner passed almost in silence. They were both hungry and tired, so they didn't talk about the day until they were out on the porch.

"So will you need to go to the auction or will Hunter's money be enough for this year?" Flynn asked a little hesitantly. He didn't like bringing up the money side of things, because he was afraid that Gable would start talking about paying him so he could go on his way, and he didn't want that.

"We still have a few horses that are ready to be sold, so we should go," Gable answered, as usual not looking at Flynn but out at the distant fields. "Any extra money is always welcome. You never know what might happen over the winter." He paused for a moment, and Flynn was eager to hear certain things, like that it was more expensive for two people to live through the winter than just one, or even that Gable was going to get his foot fixed, but instead Gable fell silent again.

"Have you ever considered breeding horses instead of just buying foals?" Flynn asked, trying to keep Gable talking. "Brenner would probably make a first-rate breeding stallion, and you have a few good mares in your herd already."

"It's a big risk," Gable replied as if he'd thought it out carefully already. "Things sometimes go wrong and it takes a number of years for the investment to pay off. Besides, it would mean building extra stables and I can barely maintain the ones I have."

Flynn wanted to shout at him that he was here to help and that he would stay if only Gable gave some indication that he would be welcome. Instead he tried to keep himself calm enough to be more subtle. "I grew up on a horse-breeding farm. I know how to handle it. We could start it as an experiment, with just one or two breeding mares."

Gable remained silent for what seemed like an eternity. He seemed to be thinking about what Flynn had said and Flynn didn't dare interrupt him now. He'd said his piece, made it clear to Gable as best he could that he was interested in staying on longer than they'd agreed.

"The vet's bill would be astronomical, Flynn," Gable eventually said, quietly.

"But the revenue is a lot bigger too."

Gable nodded slightly and kept staring out at the meadows, which were growing darker as the sun set and a low mist started to form.

Flynn got up from the porch step where he always sat at night. "Do you want a cup of coffee or something?"

Gable got up as well. "Better not. I'm just going to check on the stables and then I'm turning in."

"I'll do the checks," Flynn offered.

A rare smile broke on Gable's face. "Thanks," he said quietly, and with a soft touch of his hand on Flynn's arm, he limped past Flynn into the house.

Flynn shivered as he was left abandoned on the porch. He hadn't expected Gable to take him to bed tonight, but he wished he'd had the nerve to kiss him again. Now the moment was gone and Gable's fleeting touch lingered on his arm, so he covered the spot with his hand in an attempt to keep the feeling there. It didn't last, so he sought solace where he had always found it: in the stables with the horses.

Brenner and T.C. were lazily munching on the extra oats they'd been given just before Flynn had gone inside for dinner, but they looked up as Flynn approached. "Hey, boys." This was where Flynn felt at home, even though this wasn't his home. He patted the horses on their necks and scratched the base of their manes.

"So what am I going to do about your master?" he asked them, as if they were going to answer him. "Do you think he wants me to stay?"

Flynn heard scratching outside the stable door and pushed it open. Bridget entered and sat herself down next to Flynn. "Well, I'm glad you could join us, girl," Flynn told the dog. "I guess we're all here now." He chuckled at the scene. "We were just talking about how to handle Gable," he said to Bridget, who perked up her ears and cocked her head. Very much like her owner sometimes did, Flynn thought.

"Come on, girl, everything seems okay in here. We'll let the horses sleep, okay?"

Flynn smiled as he watched Bridget get up and move to the door, as if she'd understood every word he'd said.

They walked toward the house in silence, side by side. Flynn checked that Bridget had enough water for the night and then walked upstairs toward his bedroom. He couldn't resist pausing in front of Gable's room to listen for any sounds inside, but it was quiet. The door was slightly ajar, as it usually was when Bridget didn't go upstairs with Gable, because Flynn knew the dog always slept in Gable's room. He watched her push it open some more to enter and couldn't help stealing a look inside.

Gable was on the bed, his naked body covered by a blanket, but only up to his waist. Flynn felt his body react to the vision of the lightly furred chest and nicely sculpted, but slightly sinewy, shoulders. He contemplated going inside, but given the interesting turn the day had taken, he was reluctant to jinx what he had gained. He leaned against the doorpost and watched Bridget settle down for the night next to the bed before heading to his own room.

—5—

As USUAL, Gable woke up before dawn. Even Bridget was still sleeping on the floor next to his bed, although she looked up as soon as he stirred. The rest of the house was just as eerily quiet.

Gable got up to pee and realized he was pretty sore all over. Although they'd had quite a busy day yesterday, he hadn't done an unusual amount of riding, so his protesting muscles surprised him. Maybe he was coming down with something, or maybe he was just getting too old for this work. He sighed, scratched his head as he returned from the bathroom, and decided to lie down for a few more minutes before he had to get dressed.

The next time he opened his eyes, there was some sort of banging going on outside and he quickly pulled on his jeans to go and take a look.

Outside on the porch he was greeted by an enthusiastically tail-wagging Bridget and a bright, mid-morning sun.

"Flynn?" Gable called out.

"Up here!"

Gable looked up and felt his heart stop. Flynn was on the sloping roof, hammer in hand, trying to keep his precarious balance.

"You look like I just woke you," Flynn shouted down, not without some amusement in his voice. "I'm sorry, I thought you were out already."

Gable looked down at his bare chest and couldn't help rubbing it, as he felt exposed all of a sudden. He didn't want to leave Flynn alone, so he crossed his arms in front of him. "Will you come down from there? You might get hurt."

Flynn laughed. "I'm fine. This isn't the first roof I've climbed on, you know. Hand me that plank, will you?" Flynn pointed at a piece of wood leaning against the side of the house, right next to the ladder.

Gable handed it up and would have climbed up on the roof alongside Flynn but he knew his foot wouldn't let him do that. His heart was still racing, though, and a little voice inside him was telling him he wouldn't feel comfortable until Flynn was on solid ground again.

"I wish you had waited," Gable told Flynn.

"Come on, Gabe," Flynn pleaded, using the slightly abbreviated version of Gable's name he must have heard Calley use. "It finally stopped raining long enough for the roof to be dry and they're already saying it's going to rain again later on today. I don't know about you, but I'm kind of tired of taking my boots off in a mudroom that is always wet."

Gable had to admit Flynn was right. The roof over the mudroom had been leaking for over a year now. If Grant had still been around it would have been fixed in no time, but now it hadn't, because Gable couldn't climb up a ladder.

"I could have asked Bill to help with this," Gable suggested, although he knew his vet friend wasn't much of a carpenter.

Flynn climbed down, giving Gable a nice view of his jean-clad ass, before turning to face him. "Bill's got work of his own to do. I'm here now, so I can do it. All part of the job." Flynn shrugged and then planted a quick kiss on Gable's mouth.

Gable stood nailed to the ground as he realized what had just transpired, and all he could do was watch Flynn disappear into the house. Instead of feeling calm now that Flynn was back safely on solid ground, his heart was beating its way out of his chest. He started to follow Flynn inside, feeling uneasy, not knowing whether Flynn expected a reaction from him. But there was no need, it seemed.

Inside, Flynn smiled at him. "Why don't you finish getting dressed? I noticed you hadn't eaten yet, so I left a slice of ham for you in the oven and I can scramble you some eggs if you like."

Gable nodded quickly and then made his way upstairs. When he returned, the aromas drifting in from the kitchen made his mouth water, just as they had every day since Flynn had arrived. He knew he'd have a hard time going back to the way things were, but he also knew Flynn would eventually leave again, just like Grant had.

"I don't know how you do it, but this is so much better than when I make it," Gable admitted as he sat down at the table.

Flynn sat down where he usually did, at an angle to Gable and with his back toward the stove. He had obviously already had breakfast, since his place was cleared. "I learned my cooking from the best."

"From all those neighborhood women you told me about?" Gable queried, hoping to keep Flynn talking while he ate.

Flynn nodded. "We would have starved without them. Not to mention my Dad and my brothers had no idea how to take care of a baby, so I was shipped around to anyone who could take me on until they grew tired of me and then someone else took over."

"Interesting childhood," Gable said after swallowing a large piece of ham.

Flynn shrugged. "I got used to feeling at home pretty quickly wherever I was and not to be sad when I had to move on. When one of those women lost her husband and she became our housekeeper, I could finally come home," Flynn added, almost as an afterthought.

Gable had to admit, it said a lot about why Flynn lived on the road. It also meant it was probably futile to think he could ever settle down. He was enjoying the fact that Flynn was such an efficient, not to mention versatile, cook, though.

"So once you were home again, you went from being the kitchen helper to being the cowboy?" Gable emptied his cup of coffee and saw it being filled again by Flynn. He didn't let him answer. "Sit. You're making me dizzy."

Flynn smiled and Gable couldn't help but think that he was making him uncomfortable, because he seemed to be shying away from the confrontation.

"I had to fight to be allowed near the horses. At first I thought Dad wanted to wrap me in cotton wool, but after a few fights, I realized he couldn't stand me being around, because I was the reason my mother had died."

"Is that why you left?" Gable asked quietly. He could tell the pain was still pretty vivid for Flynn.

Flynn got up from the table, taking Gable's dirty plate and cutlery with him and turned away from Gable to wash it in the sink.

"Don't do that," Gable said, getting up to stand next to Flynn. He took the plate from him and put it down, then grabbed Flynn's hand and pulled it out of the sink. After a few moments of hesitation Gable placed his other hand on Flynn's back and continued, keeping his voice gentle and soothing. "You're not my housekeeper. I can do my own dishes."

"I don't mind."

"I know you don't," Gable acknowledged. "But you're spoiling me and I could easily get used to it."

"And we wouldn't want that, now would we?" All of a sudden, Flynn's voice sounded harsh and unforgiving. He turned away from Gable and walked toward the mudroom, but Gable stopped him.

"I know I'm not much of a talker, but maybe it's time we talked." Although what he said was certainly true, Gable felt he needed to clear the air. He couldn't prevent Flynn from leaving, but he could ask for some reassurance that he would be told in advance when he was going to have to do without. Right now, Flynn was running away from something, though, and this something had to do with his family. Gable knew all too well that it was easier to walk away from the things in life that hurt too much than it was to face them head-on, but he was afraid Flynn was going to walk away from him too, and he couldn't let that happen.

"The honest truth is that I need you. I can't manage this ranch on my own anymore." It felt strange to hear himself say those words, and even though they were true, they were also difficult to hear.

"I'll stay," Flynn said quietly, not looking Gable in the eye. "If you need me, I'll stay. Now, there's work to be done." With that, Flynn pushed past Gable out of the kitchen.

Gable could see Flynn striding toward the stable and knew it was no use chasing after him. Knowing how much Flynn hated it when his kitchen was untidy, Gable first washed his dishes and cutlery before going out himself.

FLYNN couldn't get out of the kitchen fast enough. He didn't cry; he hadn't cried since the day his father threw him off the family property, but he'd come very close this morning. Hearing Gable say he needed him had made his heart jump, the elation almost too high to contain, but the feeling had quickly abated when Gable made it clear he just needed him to manage the ranch. He wanted to stay, but this way it was torture. Every time he was near Gable, every time the man touched him the lust boiled up inside him, but somehow, Gable seemed oblivious to what he did to him.

Flynn grabbed a bridle and saddle and stepped into T.C.'s stall. He needed to clear his head, so going for a ride to check the fences was a good excuse. On his way back he could check out one of the older mares who looked like she was going lame, and then he wouldn't be back until after lunch time. The last thing he wanted right now was to sit on that porch with Gable. They'd done enough fraternizing for one day.

After riding along the fences for well over an hour, Flynn reached the herd and found that the mare was doing just fine, so he uncoiled his rope and used it as a halter for one of the younger geldings instead. This was one that Hunter had wanted to buy, but Gable had told him it wasn't ready to be sold yet. The horse looked old enough, but maybe it lacked the proper training. Flynn was curious enough to bring it back to the corral to see for himself.

Inside the confined space of the round corral, the horse was frisky and easily distracted. Flynn made him run to ease the stress, and that seemed to calm him down. Throwing a rope in the horse's path, but far enough away from him that he didn't touch him, was enough to make the animal stop in his tracks. Flynn clicked his tongue to make the horse take notice, but didn't approach him. Instead, he turned his back on the animal, allowing the horse's natural curiosity to take over. Slowly the horse came closer. Flynn could feel him lower his head, although he couldn't see it, and then he felt the animal's soft nose nuzzle his back, near his shoulder.

Flynn carefully let his hand travel toward his back, enticing the horse to sniff it, which it did.

"Good boy," Flynn whispered.

Trying not to make any sudden moves, Flynn gradually turned around to face the animal. The horse seemed much more at ease now, so Flynn took the bridle and slipped it over the horse's head, which the horse allowed. He knew this couldn't be the first time the animal had been handled like this. He was too old for that. Maybe Gable just didn't think this horse was gentle enough?

A sudden rattling sound made both Flynn and the horse look around. While Flynn tried to locate the rattlesnake, the horse whinnied and startled, rising on his hind legs dangerously close to where Flynn was standing. In a split-second decision, Flynn rolled to the ground, away from the rattler and narrowly avoiding the sharp hoofs as the horse came down and then rose again.

A gunshot blast pierced the air and, from the corner of his eye, Flynn saw the gate at the side of the corral fly open. The horse bolted out toward the lower paddock and before Flynn could get up from the ground, the shotgun landed next to him in the sand and Gable was on top of him, his hands everywhere at once.

—6—

IT TOOK Flynn a few moments to realize that Gable practically ripping his clothes off had everything to do with the fact that Gable thought he'd been bitten by the rattlesnake and nothing to do with a sudden bout of lust. The intensity of Gable's eyes and the thoroughness with which Gable touched him, combined with the roughness of his hands and the fact he was straddling him, made Flynn's blood rush south. Once he understood what Gable was doing, Flynn simply let him continue, hoping he'd be satisfied soon, but not too soon. Gable was bound to realize how much this was turning him on.

"Gable, I'm fine," he said, without too much conviction. "Gable, stop, I'm fine," he repeated, a little more strongly.

"The snake," Gable simply replied.

"It's fine. It was far enough away from me, but it spooked the horse. I was trying to get away from the horse, that's all."

Gable was panting as he stopped to look at Flynn's face.

Flynn was a little puzzled by Gable's expression, but when he saw those icy-blue eyes turn dark, he understood. Gable had noticed Flynn's arousal. Flynn froze, afraid that if he followed his instincts to grind against the heaviness of Gable's body, he'd only make it worse. Or better, depending on how you looked at it.

But then Gable started moving.

Flynn swallowed hard. He couldn't look down, because he didn't want to break eye contact, but he was sure Gable was as aroused as he was. He was also afraid that if he looked at their groins, he would come in his pants like a virgin schoolboy. The air between them was electric, and Flynn was about to cave in under the pressure.

Suddenly Gable dove down and kissed him. It was an intense kiss, bordering on the aggressive, and Flynn couldn't help but kiss him back. This time he wanted his actions to show he wanted this too, not just his words. Gable was still grinding against him, and with their changed position Flynn could feel Gable's hard length next to his own, only separated by two layers of coarse fabric. He'd expected Gable to pin his hands down, but he didn't. Instead he leaned on his elbows and steadied Flynn's head, leaving Flynn free to move, which gave him another way of showing Gable he wanted more.

After Flynn grabbed Gable's ass and began urging him on, Gable started moaning into Flynn's mouth. Flynn knew where this would end, and he hoped that nothing would happen to make Gable pull away.

Flynn didn't care that they were out in the open air. Nobody came to the ranch unexpectedly, and even if they did, the corral was pretty well boarded up and the visitor would have to climb up it to see anything. The hard, uneven ground beneath him did start to bother him, but the fact he was hard and horny and had an equally aroused man lying on top of him made up for most of that. Their tongues were fighting for dominance, neither of them eager to break the passionate kiss, although they were both struggling to keep breathing.

Gable's long, rhythmical, grinding moves were becoming more urgent and the pitch of his moans was changing too. Flynn could feel the tight muscles in Gable's ass cheeks contract and relax under his hands until suddenly Gable pulled his head away from Flynn and, after one strong thrust and a tense shudder, the movements stopped.

Only moments later, Gable retreated completely and left Flynn behind unsatisfied, getting up faster than Flynn could react. His gait was unsteady, even more so than usual, and he had to hold on to the boards of the corral to make his getaway.

Flynn got up out of the sand too and, after wiping some of it off his clothes, followed Gable out of the enclosure. He had no problem catching up with him, but Gable pushed him away.

"Gabe, stop running. Please...."

"What do you want from me?" Gable barked at him.

"A little less aggression every time we get close to each other would be nice," Flynn answered, equally sharply.

Gable had to hold on to the barn door to keep on his feet. "What do you want me to say? That you made me come in my pants? That I would have preferred it if you'd fucked me instead of that..." he pointed in the general direction of the corral, "... that thing we did there? Is that what you wanted to hear? Or did you want me to beg you for it? I'm not like your fancy friends from the city, who know all the right words to say. I'm just...." Gable's voice turned from harsh and hurting to quiet and defeated during his rant, and Flynn didn't know what to do when he saw Gable give up like that.

"I don't need to be courted, Gable."

"I was scared that you'd been hurt," Gable admitted, his eyes pinned to some unmarked spot on the ground. "I told you not to train the horses alone. Anything could have happened. You could have fallen off and been dragged along. That horse could have seriously hurt you."

"I'm fine, Gable," Flynn repeated his earlier words as he moved closer to Gable. He was still hard and horny, still unsatisfied, although he knew that Gable was probably no longer in the mood for anything. To his surprise, Gable pulled him closer again, and this time the kiss was more loving, less aggressive.

Gable continued kissing him while he pushed Flynn inside the barn.

Flynn liked the forwardness and near-violence of Gable's kisses, although it cast doubts on Gable's earlier admission that he was a bottom. Then again, maybe Flynn was just drawing this conclusion based on the way city guys behaved, and Gable had made it clear that he had next to no experience with those kinds of people.

Gable stopped moving Flynn backward when the back of Flynn's knees hit the bales of straw stacked in the corner. To Flynn's surprise, Gable turned them around so that he could sit down on the straw and pull Flynn forward before making swift work of unbuttoning Flynn's jeans, so he could release his still straining cock. Flynn let out an audible sigh as Gable's mouth wrapped around his erection, and there was no mistaking that Gable enjoyed what he was doing.

"Oh fuck," Flynn sighed. He wanted to grab Gable's head and aid the man's movements, but then retreated, feeling it might be too much and the last thing he wanted was for Gable to stop. He eventually settled for resting his hand lightly on Gable's shoulder. This helped to steady him and prevent him from following the demand of his body to thrust into Gable's mouth.

Just when Flynn thought he would no longer be able to hold off coming, Gable stopped and let go of his cock. He didn't talk, simply looked at Flynn and pulled a bale of straw down so that there were four standing together in a square. He got up and grabbed a horse blanket off a peg, then threw it over the straw and started taking his boots and jeans off.

Flynn didn't know what Gable wanted from him, so he simply stood there, unable to keep his eyes off Gable's bandaged foot, his sinewy, slightly asymmetrical legs, and his half-hard cock.

"Do you want me…?"

Gable pressed his finger against Flynn's mouth and then replaced it with his lips.

"I'll stop if you tell me to," Gable whispered after turning Flynn around until he was standing with his back to the bales again.

Flynn shook his head and was pushed back until he fell backward onto the straw. All he could do was lie there and watch how Gable straddled him again. He wanted this, but wasn't used to being such a passive participant. In this case, though, it was like with the skittish horses. Let them come to you and don't make any sudden moves.

Gable spit in his hand and coated Flynn's cock, then reached behind him to hold it up while he slowly sank onto it.

For just a moment, it crossed Flynn's mind that he was being used by Gable, but that all went away as he felt Gable's incredible, tight heat surround him. Part of him was worried that Gable was going to get hurt, impaling himself without any sort of prep and no decent lube, but those thoughts were dispelled too when Gable's mouth opened in a rough gasp of pleasure.

Flynn knew he wasn't going to last long, but he tried to hold on, tried to give Gable a chance to get what he wanted, what he needed, and hoped that it would be good enough for Gable to want more. Right now, the enjoyment was going to be Gable's, Flynn decided. Flynn let his gaze drift from Gable's slightly pained but blissful face to the rest of his body. To his chagrin, Gable's shirt, which was still buttoned and hung low, now covered their groins, stealing Flynn's visual stimulus. He didn't dare brush it aside, since Gable was just getting into a comfortable rhythm. It wasn't until Gable casually gave him a look behind the shirt tails, when he touched his own stomach en route to his quickly hardening cock, that Flynn realized how much the sight turned him on, so he started thrusting, meeting Gable halfway, making him moan.

Gable's eyes were still closed, his face now more relaxed. The pain seemed to have been replaced by pure enjoyment and a wry smile was forming on his face. With his right hand he was slowly fisting himself in time with his rocking motions and his left hand came to rest on top of Flynn's, making Flynn realize he was caressing Gable's thighs.

The intimacy of that small gesture, that connection they seemed to be making, was enough to make Flynn's passion rise again. Maybe they did have a chance to make this work? Maybe this was going to be repeated?

Gable sped up his movements and Flynn felt the familiar tightening in his groin, signaling that he wasn't going to be able to stop himself from coming. What finally sent him over was the look on Gable's face. It was one of total concentration and total surrender to what he was feeling. In that moment, Flynn knew how much Gable had missed this. Flynn thrust up fiercely and heard Gable respond with a deep grunt before he spilled his seed deep inside Gable's tight channel. Although he was panting hard, Flynn was lucid enough to see Gable's desperate attempt to join him, his hand frantically fisting his cock while trying to keep undulating his groin. Flynn barely dared to touch more of Gable, moving his hands to support Gable's hips. Just when he thought he wasn't going to stay hard enough to continue giving Gable the pleasure he so clearly craved, Gable grunted loudly and his whole body seemed to contract as thick, white spurts of come shot out of his cock and onto Flynn's shirt.

Gable moved to one side and slumped down on the hay next to him, and lay there panting for a few moments. Then a flash of lightning pierced the sky and lit up the barn. Gable got up and gathered his jeans and boots.

"Don't go yet," Flynn asked quietly, sitting up next to Gable. He hesitantly touched Gable's back.

"It's going to rain and the shotgun is still out there," Gable responded, equally quiet. "Besides, there's a spooked horse running around sporting a training bridle, so we better let him go back to the herd."

Flynn knew he wouldn't be able to stop Gable. "I'll go." He got up and tucked himself into his jeans again. He was already out the barn door when he changed his mind and returned to where Gable was sitting. He sank to his knees, grabbing the back of Gable's head, and pulled him into a blistering kiss before heading out again.

—7—

BY THE time Flynn returned to the barn, the rain had started pouring down, so he was soaked to the skin. To his surprise, Gable hadn't returned to the house yet. He was standing in the middle of the walkway between the house and the rest of the ranch, looking up at the sky and letting the rain fall all over him. His stance was a little lopsided and Flynn could tell he wasn't putting much weight on his bad leg, so he rushed over to him.

"You okay?" Flynn shouted to make his voice heard over the noise of the rain. He wiped the water off his face and put his hand on Gable's shoulder.

Gable shook his head. "Think I overdid it a bit."

"Want to go back in the barn and sit down?"

Again Gable shook his head. "We're halfway to the house and I'd prefer to go there. It's only going to get colder and I wouldn't want you getting sick."

Flynn smiled at Gable's concern and obvious disregard for his own discomfort. "Come here," he said, grabbing Gable's hand and laying it across his shoulders so Gable could lean on him. "Let's get you someplace dry and warm."

Gable leaned heavily on Flynn as they hobbled inside. This worried Flynn somewhat, since it was the worst he'd known Gable's foot to be, so he helped him up the stairs and into the bathroom, for once not caring that they'd left a wet trail all over the house.

"So what else do you need?" Flynn asked after helping Gable sit down on the closed toilet seat.

"I'm fine," Gable shrugged.

Flynn crouched down in front of Gable. "I don't mind. Just tell me what you need and I'll get it for you."

Gable shook his head. "I'm not very good at this," he murmured softly.

Flynn put his hand on Gable's knee. "I know, but humor me. I'll go to my room and put on some dry clothes and then I can get you some too, if you tell me where you keep them?"

"In my room, first closet on the left," Gable answered, somewhat reluctantly.

Although Flynn wanted to stay around to fuss over Gable, he could tell Gable wanted him out of there, so he went to his own room to do what he said he would do and get out of his own wet clothes. He then walked into Gable's room. It was the first time he'd ever set foot in there, although it wasn't the first time he had wanted to. He found himself quietly hoping he'd be sleeping here tonight, but he knew not to get his hopes up, so he took a good look around before opening Gable's closet and taking a clean pair of boxers and a T-shirt from a shelf just inside the door. Surveying the bedroom, he noted that the bed was unmade and there was a heavy book on the side table, but otherwise the space was positively Spartan. Flynn couldn't see any evidence of there ever having been anyone else in Gable's life, but he didn't want to go so far as to open drawers and snoop around in them, although he was tempted.

As Flynn walked back to the bathroom, he could see the door was half-open. When he got closer, he saw Gable sitting there, tending to his injured foot. He was peeling away the wet bandages and revealing the carnage underneath. Flynn only just managed to stop himself gasping. No wonder Gable was in such pain. The foot looked red and tender, and like it definitely needed more time to heal. There seemed to be pieces of skin missing and some places looked thin and sinewy, while others seemed swollen. Flynn didn't know much about extensive wounds in humans, but he'd seen plenty in horses and knew this wasn't the sort of injury that got better overnight.

WHEN Gable noticed Flynn near the door, he took a towel and dropped it over his foot. He didn't want Flynn to see it and hoped it didn't look too deliberate, so he held out his hand to take the dry clothes Flynn had brought in for him. "Thanks for those. It's getting kind of cold in here. Could you get me another towel from the hall closet, please?"

Gable had to get Flynn to leave again. The scrutiny and worry he saw in the kid's face was too much right now, especially after what had happened in the barn earlier. Gable took the towel off his foot again and started cleaning out the wound. It still hurt after all this time, and running over to the corral earlier, totally ignoring the throbbing in his lower leg, hadn't helped any. The pain did help to take his mind off what had happened after that, though. The last thing he wanted was to grow hard again just thinking about how willing Flynn had been to let him have his way with him. Fuck, he'd needed it. His own hand had proven totally inadequate once he'd had a taste of Flynn, and all he'd been able to think about since that first kiss was what it would feel like to be fucked by him.

Gable closed his eyes and took a deep breath at the same time that Flynn entered the bathroom again. Startled, Gable grabbed the discarded towel and covered his groin with it. His hopes that he'd been quick enough to hide his bulge were dashed by Flynn's expression, which was a mix of surprise and unease. For a moment it looked like Flynn was going to say something, but then he didn't, and Gable was glad of that. The situation was awkward enough as it was.

"You're still wearing wet clothes," Flynn noticed. "Why don't I help you out of them and into the dry ones?"

Gable quickly shook his head. "I'm fine. I'm used to doing this alone, I'm sure I can manage."

"I know you can," Flynn replied calmly. "But the thing is, you don't *need* to manage. It's not a crime to ask for help, Gable. I'm here if you need me."

Gable didn't want to grow dependent on Flynn. He'd managed all this time on his own and he'd manage again when Flynn left. "I know, but I need to do this alone," he eventually murmured.

Flynn nodded and reluctantly left him. As soon as he'd closed the door behind him, Gable felt abandoned. Yes, he'd told Flynn to leave, but if he was honest with himself, he wanted Flynn to take care of him. He just felt that he couldn't afford to.

Suddenly a violent shiver wracked his frame and he was reminded that the wet clothes were chilling him rapidly. Gable shook his head and decided to change his clothes before redressing his foot, hoping it would help him get warm. Getting up from where he was sitting and walking the two steps to the medicine cabinet behind the bathroom mirror made the pain shoot through his foot again, and Gable cursed his own stubbornness. He gritted his teeth and persevered, leaning on the bathroom sink so he wouldn't need to put a lot of weight on his injured leg. As he opened the cabinet to take out everything he needed to redress his foot, he noticed the condoms hidden behind his spare can of shaving cream. It was at that moment he realized that what had happened in the barn was far from safe sex. Flynn had fucked him without a condom and he could only hope that this wouldn't result in any unpleasantness. Gable tried to shake the unease, both at feeling scared that they could have passed something on to one another and at knowing he'd need to bring it up with Flynn. Damn, he wasn't very good at these types of conversations.

Dressed in the clothes Flynn had brought him and with his foot carefully bandaged again, Gable limped toward his bedroom. When he opened the door, he noticed his bed was made, the blanket and top sheet neatly folded back so he could step into it. He sighed. Flynn's urge to take care of him was both a blessing and a curse. Gable had to admit it felt good. In the few relationships he'd had that went beyond one-night stands, he had always been the carer, the one who provided for his lover, never the other way around. Yet Flynn didn't seem to be able to help himself, and if anything, it was refreshing.

As Gable sat down on the bed, he opened his nightstand drawer and was relieved to see the contents undisturbed. At least Flynn wasn't a snoop. It would have unsettled Gable more if Flynn had poked around in his private places and found God knows what embarrassing items. Still cold, Gable crawled under the covers and picked up his book, hoping he'd feel warmer soon. He hadn't been reading long when a shy knock on the door made him look up. Before he could answer a more insistent one followed.

"Flynn?"

The door opened and Flynn walked in, carrying a tray, so Gable sat up, momentarily wondering if he should get out of bed. Flynn didn't give him time, though, as he walked to the unslept-in side and sat down, putting the tray between them.

"I didn't have time to cook today." A shy and slightly wicked smile spread around Flynn's mouth. "But there was soup left over from yesterday and that's sure to warm us up, so I thought I'd bring some up to you."

"I don't deserve you," Gable said under his breath, not looking at Flynn, who was sitting on his bed, fully clothed.

"Sure you do," Flynn answered with the same teasing smile. He handed Gable a steaming bowl of vegetable soup and a spoon, which Gable immediately put down again in favor of a chunk of bread he could dip into the liquid.

"Maybe you should explain to me why I deserve a really great horse wrangler and an exceptional cook when I haven't even paid you for what you've done around this place," Gable asked while he tried to get the dripping bread into his mouth without embarrassing himself.

"Because you put up with me?" Flynn tried, spooning some soup into his mouth and almost burning his tongue.

"Nothing to put up with," Gable shrugged. Part of him was afraid to open up to Flynn, but then, so much had happened between them today. Gable didn't want him to leave too soon. "I like having you around."

Flynn nodded as he continued eating his soup, letting an uncomfortable silence fall between them. Gable wished they were outside on the porch again. There, it seemed, they could just sit together and enjoy each other's company without the need for conversation.

Eventually, Flynn got up and put their empty bowls back on the tray. He seemed reluctant to leave, but there wasn't much else to do. Just before he lifted the tray from the bed, Gable covered Flynn's hand with his own.

"Are you still hungry? I can make some hot cheese sandwiches if you like. Until Calley comes with groceries tomorrow, there's not much else left, I'm afraid."

"I'm fine. The soup was great." Gable hesitated. Could he just blatantly ask Flynn to sleep with him tonight? Lord knows he wanted to. He wanted to feel that warm body close to him again. "Will you come back again when you're done downstairs?" Gable asked hesitantly, annoyed by his creaking voice. "I mean, in here," he added to clarify. He wanted to add "if you want to" but he was too afraid Flynn wouldn't want to, so he left it unsaid.

Flynn smiled a little and nodded. "Okay, I won't be long."

As Gable watched Flynn leave his bedroom, he realized he'd never been this nervous in his life. When he heard a muffled "*Yes!*" outside on the landing, he couldn't help but chuckle. And his chuckle soon turned into an uncontrollable giggle.

—8—

GABLE stopped himself from fidgeting. Christ, it felt like he was going to lose his virginity all over again. Then again, he wasn't used to waiting for a lover to come upstairs, to lie next to him in his bed. He could make himself stop fidgeting, but he couldn't stop his heart from racing a mile a minute. Flynn took forever to come back upstairs. Gable wondered if he'd changed his mind and was now in the kitchen, biding his time until Gable fell asleep. No, that couldn't be. Flynn would come and then…. Gable didn't know what was going to happen then. This was almost as bad as the first time he'd really had sex, the first time he'd gone further than just fooling around and copping a feel. Only this time it wasn't just some random guy; this time it was Flynn, and he'd developed feelings for him he had never felt before. Was this what falling in love was all about?

Gable heard a knock on the door and looked up. "Come in," he said almost immediately, his anticipation for what was going to happen cranked up some more.

Flynn peeked in and then opened the door further before stepping inside and carefully closing it, as if there was a reason to be quiet. For a moment he simply stood at the door, looking at Gable, but then he retraced his earlier steps and walked around the bed to the opposite side from where Gable was.

"Okay if I crawl under the covers?" Flynn asked a little hesitantly.

"Yeah, it's cold," Gable nodded, noticing the goose bumps on Flynn's arms now he had changed into a T-shirt and boxers. "By all means." The book Gable was reading lay facedown over his chest, and he held onto it as if it was a shield. Suddenly he realized how silly it looked, so he put it on his nightstand.

Flynn had crawled under the covers, making himself comfortable on his side, facing Gable, and he seemed a lot less nervous than Gable was. Somehow this calmed Gable down. Maybe he should just let Flynn take the lead. Feeling Flynn's eyes on him didn't help, though.

"How about I turn off the light?" Gable suggested nervously.

"I'll do it," Flynn offered, throwing the covers back.

"No. No need to get out of bed," Gable said, stopping Flynn with his hand. He reached up for a long cord hanging down over the headboard and pulled it, making the room go dark.

"Nice gizmo," Flynn chuckled.

"Bill installed it when I couldn't get around much. It's a great help."

The lightning outside lit up the entire room for a split second, plunging them into darkness right after. Gable turned to face Flynn now that he felt protected by the dark.

"Lots of thunderstorms and lightning in this area," Flynn stated with a sigh.

"The clouds get trapped here by the mountains," Gable replied. "The horses aren't too crazy about the lightning and thunder, but they love the rain, because lots of rain means lots of nice soft grass to eat. And I don't mind the clouds and rain."

"I'm sure you don't," Flynn chuckled.

"Oh?" Gable didn't have a clue what Flynn meant by that.

"'Clouds and Rain' is a Chinese euphemism for sex. 'The Bringer of Clouds and Rain' is a lady of the night, a prostitute," Flynn lectured. "Clouds are thought to be the blending of the male and female, the sky and the earth, and the rain, the climax of the union. It comes from an old Chinese creation story in which heaven or sky, the Great Father, and earth, the Great Mother, are thought of as a conjugal couple engaged in never-ending intercourse."

"You know a lot about this?" Gable fished, hoping to keep Flynn talking so they wouldn't end up with their uncomfortable silences.

"Sex?"

Gable chuckled. "Chinese."

Now it was Flynn's turn to smile. "Back in the city, I lived in Chinatown for a while and tried to study Chinese. I saw it as a way out, a way to get as far away from my father as I could, but it didn't work out that way. Although it was fascinating to read about, the culture isn't very open to someone like me, so I decided to stay here and study other stuff."

"Animal husbandry and cooking?" Gable suggested.

"The cooking I already knew, and I perfected it on the road. Sometimes being a short-order cook pays better than being a farmhand or a supermarket grocery stacker."

"I'm glad you decided to come work for me here," Gable said softly. His eyes were slowly adjusting to the dark, but he was momentarily blinded by a flash of lightning when he felt Flynn's lips against his.

"I'm glad I came here too."

"I'm…." Gable hesitated. "I'm not very good at this… this…."

"So you keep telling me." Flynn cut him off. "I don't mind." He moved closer to Gable and Gable could feel the heat radiating off Flynn's skin, yet their bodies barely touched. Only Flynn's hand lightly caressed Gable's jaw.

Flynn kissed him again, the kiss light and non-intrusive. "We can get used to it together. Unless you want me to stop, and then you just have to tell me," Flynn continued, paraphrasing the words Gable had used in the barn earlier.

"Grant and I. We…." Gable didn't know how to tell Flynn or even if he wanted to tell Flynn about the nature of his relationship with Grant.

FLYNN was relieved to hear that Gable was scared and unsure. Not that it was how he wanted Gable to feel, but it was nice to know they shared the feeling. It meant that, together, they could make it work.

Hearing Gable talk about Grant felt good too. Gable never talked about himself, and even less about his past, but after Hunter's visit, Flynn had grown quite curious to learn about Gable's ex-lover.

"Tell me about Grant?" Flynn asked softly.

Gable shivered, as if he were cold.

"I know," Flynn suggested. "Why don't you turn around and I can keep you warm?"

"You mean turn my back on you? While we're talking?"

Flynn nodded. "Sometimes it's easier to talk that way."

Gable turned around quite hesitantly and Flynn gave him some time to get comfortable, knowing he would need to be careful of his leg. He put his hand on Gable's back and caressed his shoulder blade, then his shoulder.

"Don't jump, okay?" Flynn asked gently before moving forward even more until he was spooning Gable. He placed his hand over Gable's stomach and pulled him closer to his chest, then felt Gable almost shiver with tension. "Relax, Gable. Nothing will happen unless you want it."

"I'm not worried about your reactions; it's mine I might not be able to control," Gable admitted, clearing his throat halfway through the sentence.

Slowly Flynn moved his hand to Gable's stomach. Gable's T-shirt was still preventing Flynn's hand from making direct contact with Gable's skin, so their caress was intimate, but not too sexual. "I'll take care of you," Flynn whispered in Gable's ear.

Gable took a few cleansing breaths and Flynn slowly felt him relax in his arms. Somehow the silence between them was a little easier now, so when Gable eventually spoke, it almost startled Flynn.

"Grant never slept in here."

Flynn was a little confused by Gable's confession, but he didn't want to bombard Gable with his questions. He hoped he would talk about it without being coaxed.

"We had sex. Lots of it. Everywhere you could think of, but never in a bed. Grant just… I guess it felt too permanent for him if he had to sleep with me too."

"Had to? I'm sure he didn't have to. Now 'want to' I understand. It's not like it's a chore."

Gable chuckled. "Grant was a big macho man. I can't recall the number of times I heard him boast about how many women he'd had in town. When there were other people around, he would even do it in front of me. I guess the last thing he wanted was for the other guys to think he was queer, but I know for a fact that what he chased in town was cock, not women."

Flynn was a little surprised by Gable's colorful choice of language, but he wanted to know more about Grant, so he urged Gable to continue.

"Was he unfaithful to you?"

Gable nodded. "And he didn't bother hiding it either. His excuse was that he needed it. And he needed more than I could give him."

"Hell, Gable, you didn't need to put up with that!" Flynn almost shouted. His voice sounded too loud, so he continued in a softer tone. "You deserve better than that." Flynn kissed Gable's neck and snuggled closer, resting his cheek against the back of Gable's shoulder.

"Grant didn't believe in cuddling or kissing much. And certainly didn't believe in us sleeping together. His room was your room, and if he slept in the house, it was in that bed. But the longer he was here, the more he'd disappear. I'd hear him sneak out late at night. Sometimes he was back in the morning, sometimes he was gone for three or four days, and he'd come back looking like he hadn't slept all the while he was away."

"Is that what happened when you got hurt? Was Grant not around to take you to the doctor?"

Gable didn't say anything immediately. He swallowed hard and Flynn thought he was fighting off tears, but eventually he answered.

"I was breaking in horses. In the corral. He'd left the night before and I didn't expect him back, but I needed to get the horses ready for auction, so I had to keep working. One of the big ones threw me trying to jump out of the corral and my foot got caught in the stirrup. He dragged me along for a good while until the stirrup leather broke, but by then I'd been knocked unconscious. When I woke up, I couldn't move. I hurt all over, but I couldn't figure out why I couldn't move. Eventually it got a bit better, but it still took me three days to crawl back to the barn."

"Three days? My God, Gable, and that bastard didn't show?"

"I haven't seen him since that night he left. Calley found me and called an ambulance. I guess he somehow found out what happened and just decided to come pack his things and disappear for good. He wasn't the type of guy to take care of a cripple."

Flynn squeezed Gable closer, hoping to convey that he was nothing like Grant. "You're not a cripple."

"Yes, I am. I can barely walk, I can't take care of this ranch alone any more, and...." Gable stopped midsentence and pulled away from Flynn, just enough for him to loosen his hold.

"I'm still here," Flynn said softly. "And I'm not going anywhere unless you tell me to."

"Well, maybe you should leave. There's nothing here for you."

Flynn sighed. He didn't know what to say to make Gable understand that he had a reason to stay. And that reason was Gable. "There's plenty here for me. There's a great ranch, which we can easily handle with just the two of us. I'm sure that Hunter's payment will keep us in business for another year, right?"

Gable nodded in agreement.

"And I have what I've never had before. A home, and someone here who cares for me even though he hates to admit it, even to himself. And you know, that feels a heck of a lot better than having someone who *says* he loves you, but who really couldn't care less."

"How did you know?" Gable asked, his voice sounding emotional and broken to the point that Flynn was sure he was crying.

"How did I know you cared for me?" Flynn smiled and snuggled closer to Gable again. "Your face when you thought that rattlesnake had bitten me was pretty much the giveaway, but there were other things too. There are moments when you seem to be afraid to look at me, and other moments, when you don't think I'm taking any notice, that you can't seem to help yourself and you're practically undressing me with your eyes. You have no idea how many times I've wanted to come over to you to kiss you or just touch you and you have no idea how many times I've had to hide what that look of yours does to me."

Gable sniffed and his mood seemed to lighten up a bit. "Now there's the pot calling the kettle black," he snorted. "There's a reason why I sometimes couldn't look at *you*. I feel like I've been running around with a hard-on in my jeans for weeks. Working alongside you wasn't always easy. Do you know how many excuses I've had to think of to have some privacy to release a bit of tension?"

"Like in the shower?" Flynn teased.

"I couldn't believe you were watching me. And then I realized that it was turning you on." Gable paused as if he was recalling in his mind what had happened. "Before that I could always tell myself that you were probably straight so it was no use lusting after you, but after I saw that flushed complexion of yours, as if I'd caught you with your hand down your pants...."

"You did. I couldn't help myself," Flynn admitted. Because they were so close together, the memory made Flynn's body react again. He'd hoped that the fact they were both wearing clothes would prevent that, but the images were too vivid. "Seeing you naked was already a turn-on. Seeing your hand wrap around your cock and then seeing it swell right in front of my eyes... it was like a dream come true."

"Come on...." Gable said quietly, shrugging a little. It sounded like he couldn't believe what Flynn was saying.

"What?" Flynn whispered. He ground his burgeoning bulge against Gable's ass, both to satisfy the need of his own body and to let Gable feel what he was doing to him. Flynn felt Gable's stomach muscles tense up under his hand, though. "Why is it so hard for you to believe that you turn me on?"

Gable sighed. "Because I'm damaged goods. Not to mention, I'm old enough to be your father."

Flynn moved back and pulled Gable along with him so they were lying on their backs. "Look at me," he commanded with a serious tone in his voice. "I can't choose who I like. If I could, then I'd find myself someone a lot easier and a lot less grumpy than you. And leave my father out of it." Flynn didn't wait for Gable's response. Instead he leaned over him and gently kissed him. His hand was still on Gable's stomach and slowly he felt his lover relax, so he deepened the kiss. When they broke apart, Flynn's hand had travelled to Gable's hip.

"Now I'd like to make love to you, the way a guy is supposed to make love to you. And I want it to be good for both of us."

Gable looked away. "I know what we did this afternoon was not very good for you and I'm sorry."

"Will you stop putting yourself down? What happened in the barn, happened. It wasn't the best sex of my life, but it was nowhere near the worst either. Plus, it got us talking, right?"

Gable nodded, but the expression of doubt hadn't left his face.

"Gabe, I've been on the road most of my adult life. I travel light. If I didn't want to be here, I would have left a long time ago."

A shy smile broke on Gable's face and Flynn couldn't resist cuddling up to him again. "Now will you let me treat you right?"

"Seems like that's all you've been doing up until now," Gable answered almost inaudibly. He turned his head toward Flynn, wordlessly asking for a kiss and Flynn gently nuzzled him before letting their lips meet. This time there was no urgency, simply the enjoyment of each other's taste.

Gable was almost completely on his back now, his head turned slightly toward Flynn so they could kiss, but his hips turned away so Flynn had the access he needed. They didn't break their lip-lock to push their sleeping pants down and out of the way and only separated to pull their T-shirts over their heads.

"There are condoms in the bathroom if you want," Gable whispered against Flynn's mouth after Flynn had almost finished prepping him.

"I hadn't had unsafe sex for a long time before this afternoon," Flynn replied. "I assume they tested you in the hospital?" Gable nodded slowly. "Then I think we can do without," Flynn said resolutely. "I enjoyed feeling just you this afternoon, no matter how rushed it was."

Very carefully, Flynn slipped inside Gable's tight body after positioning himself close and slicking up his erection with some lube Gable handed him from his bedside table. It was a relaxing position from which Flynn could not only gently rock in and out, but could also see the changing expressions on Gable's face... not to mention they could kiss the whole time. Flynn's hand travelled to Gable's slowly hardening erection and he caressed it lovingly, feeling a certain pride at how hard he had made his lover.

"God, you feel amazing," Gable whispered, his voice slightly strained by what Flynn was doing to him and by the twisted position he was in. He reached for Flynn, leaving his hand on Flynn's hip as if to gently guide him.

Flynn moved his hand to Gable's belly and started thrusting harder. His body was demanding he push in faster as well, but he knew if he did that, he'd come almost immediately and he wanted to make Gable come first, especially since they were moving so fluidly now, with Gable pushing back as Flynn thrust in. It felt amazing to Flynn to feel Gable's tightness, along with the way Gable's muscles were pumping his cock every time he pulled back, and he didn't know how long he was going to last.

Gable stopped kissing because he needed to breathe. His half-closed eyes were becoming unfocused and he reached down to stroke himself.

"You're making me come. So good," Gable managed to squeeze out. "Faster," he demanded, upping the tempo on his own ministrations just to aid his resolve. "Oh fuck... come with me... want to feel you... come too."

Flynn was trying to hold on for dear life, wanting to see Gable's face when he came, but it was getting harder with every thrust. Suddenly Gable arched his back and groaned. Flynn felt him spasm, but what finally sent him over was seeing Gable splatter his own belly and Flynn's hand. Coming inside of his lover's relaxing body with no condom between them was the most amazing sensation he'd ever felt.

They continued kissing as soon as they had enough breath to spare, this time with their eyes open, as if they didn't want to miss even the tiniest reaction from the other.

"We need to clean up a bit," Flynn eventually whispered.

"I don't care. Please stay here?"

Flynn got up anyway and he couldn't hide his smile. "Oh, I'll be back, don't worry." It was cold on the landing and in the bathroom and Flynn hurried back with a washcloth.

"The storm passed," Flynn said as he crawled back onto the bed.

"Guess we made enough Clouds and Rain of our own." Gable shivered when Flynn wiped his belly, and he drew Flynn back into a kiss. "Fuck, I can't get enough of you."

Flynn discarded the cloth on the floor and snuggled closer under the blankets. "Good," he answered. "Because I want to sleep here tonight."

"I was hoping you would." Gable pulled Flynn into his arms and they settled together, naked skin against naked skin.

"Just you try to keep me away."

It didn't take them long to fall asleep, content and sated. Flynn woke once, when he heard Gable curse under his breath.

"You okay, love?"

Gable shrugged. "Just the damn foot. It'll go away, don't worry."

Flynn nodded, but the worry didn't go away. He was going to have to talk Gable into seeing a doctor, and that wasn't going to be easy.

—9—

THE morning light was already creeping around the drapes covering the window when Flynn woke up. For a moment he wanted to jump out of bed, afraid he'd overslept, but then he heard Gable groan next to him and he decided to stay in the warmth of their bed a little longer. Their bed. Flynn liked the sound of that. Waking up next to the man he'd fallen in love with was amazing, and knowing that those feelings were returned made it even more special.

"We should get up. It's past eight o'clock," Gable moaned. He didn't budge, though; in fact, he seemed to snuggle even closer to Flynn, so Flynn kissed him. When they broke apart and Gable shook his head, Flynn started to fear he was retreating again, but then Gable wrapped his arms around Flynn and squeezed him tightly.

"I don't know...." Gable seemed to stop midsentence, then change his mind. "Thank you," he told Flynn.

"There's nothing to thank me for," Flynn said, pulling back slightly so he could look at the expression on Gable's face. He hoped to dispel any doubts Gable still had, but he wasn't sure he was succeeding.

"Oh, there's plenty to thank you for," Gable replied. "But we should get up. The horses are waiting."

Flynn was happy that Gable was smiling, but he realized he was still putting himself down. Flynn let it go, though. After everything Gable had gone through with Grant, it would take time for him to trust again, and the only way that was going to happen was if Flynn stuck around and showed him there was plenty to love.

Reluctantly, Flynn left Gable's embrace and crawled out of bed. After a quick wash and a short visit to his old room for clean clothes,

Flynn took Bridget downstairs to make breakfast, giving Gable the time to get ready as well. He was standing by the old stove, making scrambled eggs, when he felt Gable wrap his arms around him from behind.

"I've been wanting to do that since the first time I came down to you making me breakfast," Gable whispered in his ear.

"You should have tried earlier," Flynn replied, turning around in Gable's arms so they could kiss.

The eggs were slightly scorched that morning, but neither of them seemed to care.

Calley came by after breakfast, bringing them supplies from her store, and judging from the looks she gave Flynn, she seemed to notice the change in Gable. Flynn was happy that she didn't say anything, though, at least not until Gable was out of earshot.

"What did you do to my Gable?" she asked Flynn with a broad smile as he followed her to carry her empty boxes to the truck.

"Oh, nothing," Flynn answered. He was eager to share with someone, but he didn't think Gable would appreciate him spilling the beans to Calley so soon, especially not since he still didn't know the extent of Calley's relationship with Gable.

"Nothing, my ass," she teased. "He's darting around here like a lovesick puppy. I haven't seen him this happy…. Come to think of it, I don't think I've ever seen him this happy. Whatever you did, it seems to be working."

She nudged him with her shoulder in what seemed like a very unladylike gesture, then placed her hand on Flynn's arm and made him look at her. "You're making him very happy, Flynn, and he needs that. He deserves it too."

Flynn simply smiled at her, bursting to tell her outright, but at the same time preferring to keep it between him and Gable for the time being. Flynn was pretty sure she knew exactly what was going on, and for now, that was enough.

She touched his face briefly in what felt like a very motherly way and then turned around to get into her truck and drive away.

Flynn waved her out and then turned to Bridget. "Come on, old girl, there's work to be done!"

THEY started out as they always had, with each doing their daily chores around the ranch, but Flynn felt the change almost immediately. Before today they'd worked as two individuals and Flynn barely saw Gable before lunchtime, but now Gable seemed to seek out things to do close to Flynn. On several occasions he even asked Flynn to help with things he usually did alone, and Flynn was always rewarded with a quick kiss and a fleeting touch. Flynn didn't mind Gable looking for excuses to be near him; he could only hope that soon Gable wouldn't need excuses anymore and they'd simply work as a team, but for now, Flynn enjoyed being courted.

The day passed quickly, with a brief interlude just after lunch where Gable pulled away during a searing kiss, claiming they couldn't possibly have sex in the middle of the day. Flynn had to bite his tongue, remembering Gable's admission from the previous night that he and Grant had had sex everywhere around the ranch, at every hour of the day, but he didn't want to break Gable's uplifted spirits. It left him hungry for more, though. Lots more. Still, Flynn was pretty sure that good things were worth waiting for, and that he'd get what he wanted later, after their work was done.

That time came while Flynn was seasoning a casserole.

"I'll take a quick shower," Gable announced, smiling enticingly as he made his getaway.

Flynn had chosen that night's dish carefully. It would take minimal work, and they had about forty-five minutes of nothing to do but wait while dinner was cooking, so about five minutes after Gable left the kitchen, Flynn was watching him through the back door.

Gable had wrapped his bandaged leg in plastic and was standing under the spray of the cold shower at the back of the house, just like the first time Flynn had spied on him, only this time, Flynn wasn't going to leave him out there on his own.

"Can I join you, or would you prefer I watch you from afar?"

Gable wiped the water off his face and opened his eyes. "It's up to you, but I wouldn't mind a little... help."

Flynn couldn't get out of his clothes fast enough, especially not when he looked down Gable's body and saw his lover's cock swell before his eyes.

The water under the spray was freezing, though. "Fucking hell, this is cold!" Flynn shouted.

Gable laughed and protectively wrapped his arms around Flynn. "So you thought it was a good idea to have sex under the shower?"

"I'll have sex with you anywhere, but I doubt I could get it up now," Flynn shivered.

Gable turned the water off and grabbed a towel, throwing it around Flynn's shoulders and rubbing him intensely. Slowly the feeling returned to Flynn's skin and he noticed Gable was still hard, despite the cold water.

"You're a horny bastard, aren't you?" Flynn teased.

Gable nodded, a wicked smile on his face. "That's not hard around you." He pulled at the towel, dragging Flynn closer to the bench so he could sit.

Looking up, Gable took Flynn's cock in his mouth and sucked on it. It made Flynn light-headed to feel all his blood rush south, so he lightly rested his hand on Gable's wet hair in case he lost his balance. Gable's mouth felt amazing, and within no time he was rock hard. The fact that he could see Gable touch himself only made the heat rise faster.

"Gable, stop. Gable, please stop."

Reluctantly, Gable pulled back. "What's wrong?"

Flynn took Gable's face between his hands and kissed him. "Too fast," he managed to utter when he came up for air. They renegotiated their positions until they were both straddling the bench, but since that meant they were sitting too far apart, Gable eventually pushed Flynn down so he could straddle him.

"Fuck, I need you," Gable groaned against Flynn's mouth as he wantonly rubbed their groins together.

"Just take it slow, okay?" Flynn didn't want a repeat of what had happened in the barn. Not because he was selfish and wanted some of his own pleasure, but because he hoped that, by now, they were lovers, mates, and not just fuck buddies. Gable didn't seem to get what he meant, though.

Before Flynn could object, Gable was impaling himself on Flynn's erection and riding him and Flynn felt used. Again. Even so, he couldn't control the reaction of his body. Gable was tight and the friction intense from using just saliva as lube. The sheer enjoyment on Gable's face, the look of ecstasy combined with the total abandon in his movements left no doubt that he was giving in to his physical needs, and despite Flynn's misgivings, all these things were also having an effect on him. He couldn't deny that, even though Gable was using him, Gable's enjoyment was because of him, because of his body. He was the direct reason that Gable's cock was rock hard, jutting around every time he rolled his hips, precome beading at the slit with every movement. He was the reason for the reddened flush on Gable's chest. As Gable lifted himself slightly, Flynn's body pushed up into the tight heat and Gable groaned. He touched himself, hand firmly gripping his erection as he let Flynn thrust into him.

"Fuck, that's good. So good!" Gable called out. He opened his eyes and looked at Flynn before diving down and kissing him sloppily.

Flynn couldn't help but kiss him back, conflicting emotions fighting for dominance in his mind. Purely physically, this felt good, but Flynn missed the emotional side of the lovemaking so much, he knew his impending orgasm would not be a very satisfying one. He was close, though, and feeling Gable's still wet chest hair rub up against his own hairless chest made his nipples peak.

Gable grabbed the bench at either side of Flynn's head and pushed himself upright again before speeding up his movements. He moaned when Flynn took his heavy cock in his hand and fisted it rapidly until he sprayed his seed all over Flynn's hand and belly.

Seeing Gable come and feeling the pulsating channel around his cock sent Flynn over as well, while his hips thrust up reflexively. He closed his eyes, refusing to look up at Gable and even going so far as turning his head when Gable tried to kiss him, so he wasn't surprised when he felt the weight lift off his hips. Flynn sat up and from the corner of his eye saw Gable wet a washcloth underneath the shower.

"What's wrong?" Gable asked innocently when Flynn aggressively grabbed the washcloth out of his hands before Gable could start cleaning Flynn off.

"I need to check on dinner," was all Flynn could muster. He grabbed his clothes from where he'd left them near the door and quickly dressed before walking into the kitchen, leaving Gable behind. He couldn't work his anger out on Gable, but he was sorely disappointed. He'd expected so much more after the night before, but clearly Gable wasn't ready for that level of intimacy to creep into their daily life. Maybe he never would be.

They ate in silence, Flynn too angry to make small talk and Gable too confused to find an opening to break the wall around Flynn.

"Casserole was nice," Gable eventually dared to say while they were doing the dishes.

Flynn just nodded, feeling that he could at least acknowledge the compliment, although he was sure Gable would say pretty much the same if the dish was inedible. He was fighting his emotions, swaying between running away and lashing out at Gable. He wasn't the type to run away from a difficult situation. He didn't like his options for fighting back, though, mostly because he didn't want to accuse Gable of something he possibly wasn't aware of. He needed to find a way for them to talk, but had no idea how to broach the subject, especially because they'd already discussed it the day before, so he left it to simmer and walked outside as soon as he'd washed the casserole dish.

Gable joined him on the porch a few minutes later. He was silent, but you could have cut the tension with a knife.

"I did it again, didn't I?" Gable said quietly after several minutes of both of them staring out into the dark night.

Flynn swallowed. The fact that Gable knew somehow made it harder. "Yes," Flynn acknowledged, clenching his teeth.

"I'm sorry," Gable replied, even more quietly.

"That doesn't help me much, now does it?" Flynn answered, anger boiling up right under the surface, but he was trying hard not to let it explode. "I'm not your fuck toy, Gable. I thought that after last night, we'd both agreed we were equals? I know you have issues, but I can't do this. I can't be in a relationship where I never know what's coming next. I need a partner, not... not...." He was so angry he couldn't find the right words.

"Maybe I should just give you some space." Gable got up from his chair on the porch.

"We need to talk, Gable. Communicate. Explain things before we draw the wrong conclusions." Flynn's tone of voice wasn't soothing, though. His anger and exasperation prevented him from hiding how much it all affected him.

Flynn watched as Gable limped down the steps and into the darkness. He knew Gable would go to the stables and hide among the horses for a while, but he couldn't run after him yet, so he stayed on the porch. Just before he saw the light in the stables turn on, he heard a loud volley of expletives, but then the night grew quiet again. Flynn couldn't settle, though. Despite their fight, hearing Gable swear like that made all sorts of worst-case scenarios run through his mind. He waited for as long as he could, and then set out toward the distant light.

GABLE sat down on a bale of hay, clutching his foot. He was still cursing, albeit a lot more quietly than when he'd just tripped, willing the pain to subside. He could feel his ankle swelling inside his boot and hoped nothing had broken. He had just managed to take his boot off when Flynn appeared in the doorway.

Gable looked up but Flynn didn't speak immediately. His eyes trailed from Gable's face to his foot.

"You're bleeding."

"I know. I caught my foot on the bale and I think I ripped something," Gable replied without looking at Flynn. He was glad Flynn seemed calmer.

"It looks nasty. Shall I call a doctor?"

Gable shook his head. "No doctor."

"Gabe, you should have this looked at. It can't be normal that you're in so much pain from something trivial like tripping over some hay."

For a moment, Gable looked at Flynn's face and saw how worried he was. "I'm always in pain, Flynn. There isn't a doctor who can fix that."

Flynn put his hand on Gable's knee and crouched down in front of him. "At least let me help you back to the house?"

Gable shrugged. "I'm fine here. Just give me a few hours of peace and quiet and I'll be okay."

"Gabe?" Flynn stood up and held out his hand.

Gable shook his head. "You go back to the house."

Gable could tell Flynn was thinking about it, and eventually he trailed off, leaving him alone. This wasn't the first time Gable had stayed in the stable. It was his favorite place to think, with just the sounds of the horses and the occasional bird penetrating his oasis. His foot was throbbing, so he elevated it a bit more and rested his back against the barn door. He was out of the draft and had put on a warm coat before venturing out on the porch earlier, so he wasn't cold.

As soon as he felt comfortable, he thought back over what had happened that evening. He'd clearly misread Flynn's signs. With food in the oven, he'd deduced that Flynn had wanted a quick fuck before dinner. He had to admit to himself that was all he'd been in the mood for too. The prospect of going to bed together again had frightened him, since he had no idea what Flynn expected. In that respect it had been easier with Grant, who hadn't expected anything from him. Flynn was good to him, but the speed with which they had become close was scary to say the least. How long would it take for Flynn to realize he wanted someone younger and more mobile?

Gable snuggled deeper into his coat. He was tired and weary. Hopefully tomorrow everything would look brighter.

FLYNN couldn't sleep.

He'd reluctantly left Gable in the barn, but only because he didn't think he could persuade the stubborn man to take better care of himself.

Now it was way past midnight, and he was still worrying.

After watching the beat-up alarm clock on his nightstand for the last two hours, Flynn decided to get dressed to try to persuade Gable to come to the house again.

Outside, the temperature had dropped significantly, and even though Flynn knew that the barn was pretty warm, he was still not sure it was such a good idea for Gable to stay there overnight.

When he walked inside, he saw that the light was still on. Gable was huddled into his parka, asleep on a bale of hay, his back resting against one side of the barn door. Flynn saw the dried-up blood caked into the bandage around Gable's foot and lightly touched his toes, which were stone-cold and an ugly gray-blue color.

"Gabe, wake up. You need to come inside and get warm."

Flynn gripped Gable's arm more firmly and shook him with a bit more force. When Gable's head fell to the side, he tried to catch him and realized Gable was burning up.

"Damn! Gable! You have to wake up!" Panic in his voice, he tried to rouse his lover, but didn't succeed.

—10—

FLYNN was surprisingly calm. He had run back inside to call Calley and then an ambulance. He knew it would take a while for either to arrive, so he grabbed a blanket before heading back to the stables, where he found Bridget waiting diligently next to Gable's huddled form.

Because Gable's breathing had become somewhat labored, Flynn had an easy time checking his vitals, as the ambulance dispatcher had asked on the phone. He'd done it numerous times with sick horses, but it was far different with the man he loved. Still, it gave him something to do and helped pass the time while he could reassure himself that Gable's heart was still beating.

"Don't you die on me now, Gable," Flynn insisted to his unconscious lover after Gable stopped breathing for a moment, just as Flynn pulled him into his arms. Flynn exhaled the breath he'd been holding when Gable sighed. "The ambulance is coming and so is Calley. We're taking you to the hospital, love."

Flynn sat in the cold stable for what felt like forever, rocking Gable back and forth every time his breathing seemed to falter. Eventually, Calley arrived with screeching tires. She looked very worried.

"What happened?" she asked Flynn after taking a quick look at Gable, then at his foot.

"He tripped on a bale of hay," Flynn told her. "When he didn't return to the house, I came looking for him and found him here."

"I suppose it's a miracle it took so long."

Flynn wasn't sure what she meant. "You expected this?"

Calley nodded. "When he got hurt the first time, they were afraid they wouldn't be able to save the foot. The bones were shattered and there was apparently some problem with the blood flow. I'm no doctor, so I don't know the specifics. Anyway, when it seemed to heal up some, Gable didn't want to have anything more done to it. The first time we left him alone here, he hit his foot on a table inside the house and it swelled up again, and they told him that eventually he'd lose it, but he wouldn't hear of it. That's why he refuses to see a doctor."

Flynn pulled Gable closer and hugged him. "What are you saying?"

"All any doctor talks about is amputation, Flynn. And Gable flat-out refuses to even contemplate it. He's had third and fourth opinions. They all agree that, sooner rather than later, he's going to have no other choice."

Flynn looked into Gable's sleeping face. "Right now, he doesn't even have the luxury of choosing."

"That's what I was afraid of," Calley replied.

They both looked up as they heard a car stop in front of the barn. The flickering lights accompanying it identified the vehicle, and Calley got up from her crouching position in front of Gable to take a look. She soon had to prevent a loudly barking Bridget from guarding her master too diligently, as the ambulance team arrived with a stretcher and a bag of supplies.

"I found him unconscious," Flynn explained to them. "He hurt his foot earlier today. Now he has trouble breathing and he stops sometimes, but he starts again when I rock him."

One of the men looked at Flynn compassionately. "We'll take it from here, sir," he stated.

Flynn had a hard time letting go of Gable, but the stern look the EMT gave him told him he was going to have to. It was then that his heart started racing.

"Come on, Flynn, get into my car. We'll follow them to the hospital," Calley said, placing a compassionate arm around Flynn's shoulders.

Flynn shook his head as he saw they were carefully transferring Gable to the gurney. "I want to ride in there with Gable." He pointed at the ambulance.

"I'm sorry, sir, but the lady is right. There's no space for you. Better follow behind us."

Flynn shook his head with even more conviction. "No! I need to be with him. If he dies in there, I need to be with him." Hearing himself say the words shocked Flynn, but there was nothing he could do. He feared this with all his heart, and hoped he was wrong.

Calley pulled him closer and hugged him tightly. Then she took his face in her hands and made him look at her. "Flynn, listen to me. He'll be fine. He's in capable hands!"

"We'll take care of him, sir," the EMT said after they loaded Gable into the back of the small ambulance. "Just follow us."

The trip to the local hospital along the pitch-dark country roads was not something Flynn would have contemplated, but Calley was a more than capable driver and, despite her own apprehensions, she safely navigated them into town. The local doctor who'd been called on almost immediately gave the order to transfer Gable to a larger facility, though, so once again they were driving behind the ambulance, only this time along less-familiar but better-lit roads.

The emergency room in the city hospital was busier and quite a bit larger than the makeshift reception area in their local hospital. They were told to wait and fill out some forms, and Flynn realized he really didn't know that much about Gable. Luckily, Calley seemed on top of things.

"This isn't the first time I've done this, Flynn. Just after the accident, he was in and out of the hospital and never unless it was absolutely necessary, so I've been through this routine a few times." She put her hand on his arm to console him.

"I don't even know if he has any family," Flynn mumbled. "I don't know anything about him."

Calley squeezed Flynn's arm. "He's not the most talkative, is he?"

Flynn shook his head.

"Gable has some distant relatives back east, but no one he's in touch with on a regular basis."

Flynn sighed. "So he has no one." It was more a statement than a question.

"He has you, Flynn."

"Does he?" Flynn looked at Calley, whose face was all compassion. He gazed in the direction they'd wheeled Gable off to and sighed again. "We had a fight. That's why it took me so long to find him." Flynn didn't know how much he could tell Calley. What had happened felt very personal, but he had to tell someone and he hoped Calley could put things in perspective. "One moment he's loving and caring and the next it's like he doesn't want me around for anything else than…." Flynn stopped. He didn't know Calley well enough to go into that sort of detail.

Calley smiled indulgently. "And here I was thinking that all you men were the same."

Flynn couldn't resist smiling a little in return. Calley's easygoing manner and her compassion made him feel more accepted than he'd ever been. He'd been a bit apprehensive about it, since they'd never really disclosed the nature of their relationship to her, but he felt she understood somehow. In any case, she knew Gable was gay, since she knew all about what had happened with Grant, and Gable had told him one thing and that was that he trusted her with his life.

"I always sensed you were different," Calley said, breaking the silence between them. She sounded serious now, the teasing note in her voice totally gone. She smiled again when Flynn looked up at her, but it wasn't a humorous smile. "He was hurt badly, Flynn. I didn't think he'd ever recover, and I'm not talking about the physical side of the accident. For some unfathomable reason he was in love with that man, and it took him months to accept that he had left him. If all this is too much for you as well, I understand, but please let him down gently. Tell him and don't let him live in false hope."

"I'm not leaving," Flynn replied determinedly. Then his courage faltered. "Unless he tells me he wants me to."

"He probably will, just to guard himself," Calley replied, voicing what Flynn was thinking.

Hearing Calley say that made Flynn's confidence grow again. "I'm not Grant, you know. Whatever happens, I can take it."

"Thank God you're not Grant!" She squeezed his hand again and briefly looked at him, then turned her gaze toward the corridor they'd both been watching since they arrived, and their conversation stilled.

Uncomfortable with the silence and unused to sitting still for so long, Flynn got up from the hard fiberglass seat he was sitting in. "I need to stretch my legs. Want some coffee?"

Calley nodded. "Black for me, please."

Flynn set off, hoping he could get some information on Gable's condition while he was looking for something to keep them warm and awake. The girl behind the reception desk gave him the standard answer, telling him they were still working on Gable and that the doctor would be with them shortly, so Flynn returned to where Calley was sitting, handing her a paper cup with lukewarm liquid that barely deserved to be called coffee. They drank in silence, and after some time, Flynn felt Calley lean against him as she dozed off. He couldn't sleep, despite the fact he hadn't slept in almost twenty-four hours. He needed to know how Gable was doing, and although he was outwardly calm, his insides were playing hockey. He was certain something was seriously wrong and almost feared the moment the doctor would come out from wherever he was hiding and tell them just how bad it was.

"Mmh," Calley murmured as she startled and sat up, wiping the corner of her mouth as she opened her sleep-drunk eyes. "Any news yet?"

"No, go back to sleep," Flynn answered, trying to sound soothing in response to Calley's ever-caring demeanor. She didn't get the chance, as a serious-looking, forty-something man strode over to them then.

"You're the relatives of Mr. Sutton?" He reached out to shake first Flynn's, then Calley's hand, and they both stood up. "I'm Dr. Isaacs. I'm in charge of the ICU."

"How is he?" Flynn asked, nerves knotting his stomach so tightly he felt he might vomit.

"He's stable, but it's been quite a struggle and we're not out of the woods yet," the doctor answered, directly addressing Flynn. "It's a good thing you found him when you did."

"Can we see him?" Calley asked.

"I don't think that's such a good idea right now." Dr. Isaacs seemed to hesitate, trying to find the right words to get his message across. "He's surrounded by a lot of machinery."

"I want to see him," Flynn said in a barely audible voice.

"He needs to see him," Calley said more forcibly. "I can wait here, but he needs to see him." She took Flynn's arm to get her point across, and Dr. Isaacs nodded.

"First, I need someone to sign the permission slip for surgery," Dr. Isaacs said, standing his ground between Flynn and Calley and the corridor.

"You can't take his foot," Flynn said flatly. "He doesn't want to lose his foot!"

Dr. Isaacs held out his hand in a calming gesture. "We have no other choice, sir. He has an infection and, with the added injury, his foot isn't getting much of a blood supply. The tissue is dying and it's sending toxins to his blood stream. He went into shock, and we've had to intubate him and give him medication to support his blood pressure and his heart. He has a high fever, and I'm afraid that if we don't remove the foot, his chances of surviving this are next to none."

"But…. You can restore the blood supply! You can patch it up. He didn't hurt himself that badly!" Flynn knew he was bargaining with the doctor, but he couldn't imagine having to tell Gable that he'd lost his foot.

Dr. Isaacs looked at Calley in an effort to get some help, but all Calley did was put her hand on Flynn's back. "Calm down, Flynn. We need to think about this. Dr. Isaacs, please let us see him. I promise you we'll give you our decision after that."

Dr. Isaacs nodded, stepping aside to clear the way to the corridor. He led them through a series of passages and a locked door, which he opened with his ID card. They passed several beds toward the end of the large room until he stopped in front of one particular bed.

At first Flynn didn't recognize the man with the gray complexion, connected to more equipment than he'd ever seen, even in the movies. It wasn't until Dr. Isaacs suggested they come closer that Flynn recognized Gable. There were tubes coming out of his mouth and nose and there was a machine making an almost hypnotic sound in the same rhythm as the rise and fall of Gable's chest.

"We're breathing for him right now," Dr. Isaacs explained in a subdued voice. "In fact, we've taken over quite a few of his bodily functions."

Calley nodded, but Flynn couldn't stop staring at Gable, trying to recognize the man who was his lover underneath all the wires and tubes. He hesitantly reached for Gable's hand and then retreated when he noticed Gable's hands were bound to the bed.

"You can touch him if you like," Dr. Isaacs intervened. "They say it's beneficial for patients to be touched by their loved ones, even when they are sedated."

"Why are his hands tied?" Flynn asked.

"It's a precaution," Calley answered. "This isn't the first time I've seen him like this."

She looked at Dr. Isaacs for help, but he simply nodded and stepped back. "I'll leave you for a few moments. Please talk about signing the permission."

As soon as he was out of earshot, Flynn turned to Calley. "I can't sign for this, Calley. He'd never forgive me!"

Calley sighed. "You can't sign for it, but I can. I have his power of attorney. We need to make this decision together, though. Flynn, if we say no, he'll die, and I can't let that happen!"

"We don't know that! You said he'd been here before. You said you'd seen him like this and he pulled through last time. I can't let them hack off his leg, Calley!"

Calley pulled Flynn into her arms and hugged him tightly. "He was never this sick, Flynn. The last time I saw him like this was after he'd had surgery for his foot. He was sedated then too because he'd cracked a lot of ribs, but he was nowhere near as sick as this." She let go of him and looked into his distraught face. "We'll need to explain to him that it was a matter of life and death. That we would have lost him if we hadn't given permission. He'll understand."

Flynn knew Gable well enough to know he wouldn't understand, and judging from Calley's face, she knew it as well. He turned toward Gable and took his lover's hand. It was cold and clammy and didn't feel like Gable's at all. "We have to do this, love. I can't lose another lover. I can't sit by and watch you die without knowing I've done everything possible to save you, and although you might never forgive us, at least we'll give you a chance to live."

Flynn turned toward Calley, wiping his face with the back of his hand. "Let's do it."

—11—

FLYNN spent the next few days driving back and forth between the ranch and the hospital, since they would only let him into the ward to sit next to Gable's bed at set times in the afternoon and the evening.

At night Flynn lay in Gable's bed, trying to catch his scent and his presence, but it faded fast, so after tossing and turning all night long, he would get up at dawn to start his work at the ranch. Working hard had always served him well when it came to getting the time to pass more quickly, and making sure Gable had a well-maintained ranch to come home to was an added incentive. By the early afternoon, Flynn would drive to the city to sit next to Gable's bed.

Despite the amputation they'd given their reluctant consent for, Gable wasn't recuperating like Dr. Isaacs had predicted. He was still sedated, still having bouts of extreme fever when he would become so unstable they'd sometimes ask Flynn to leave the room so they could take care of him, and he was slowly becoming unrecognizable to his friends. During the times when Gable was calm and seemingly pain-free, Flynn would untie his hand and hold it to his face, talking to him in soothing tones, hoping that small talk about the horses and Bridget would somehow reach Gable's brain. As Flynn got more accustomed to the goings-on in the ward, he would sometimes wash Gable's sweat-soaked face and chest, what little pieces of skin weren't covered by monitoring stickers or IV bandages. It helped him to feel like he was somehow taking care of his lover, despite knowing he had to relinquish most of that task to the nurses. Under his hands, Flynn could feel Gable's muscles wasting away, and the fact he looked paler and more bloated with every passing day meant Flynn had to will himself not to give up hope.

Hope became even harder to hold onto when he arrived one afternoon and found that more equipment had been added around Gable's bed. Heart racing, he went in search of Dr. Isaacs.

"I don't think I need to explain to you that he's not doing well," Isaacs told Flynn compassionately. "His kidneys were having a hard time dealing with the toxins from the infection, and now they've shut down completely, so we needed to help them out a bit."

Flynn nodded, trying to process the information. "So the operation did no good? He's dying anyway?"

"Don't lose hope, Mr. Tomlinson. We have to give his body the time to heal itself. In the meantime, we're giving it all the help we can."

Although the doctor was compassionate enough and seemed to know what he was doing, Flynn still wasn't convinced they'd done the right thing. Especially now there was another setback. "So what will happen next?"

Dr. Isaacs interlocked his fingers and inhaled deeply. "We've put him on dialysis to help his body get rid of all the toxins that are causing his organs to shut down. We hope this will give us the chance to lower all the medication he needs to stay alive so we can slowly wean him off it."

Flynn didn't pretend to understand, but he needed to know the basics. "So there's still a chance we'll lose him?"

Isaacs nodded.

"How much chance?"

Dr. Isaacs bit the inside of his lip. "I don't want to put a number on it."

"I need to know," Flynn asked calmly. He did need to know. For days now he'd been expecting a call saying Gable had died. He needed to know what to expect.

"I think he's got a fifty-fifty chance."

Flynn nodded. It wasn't an answer he wanted to hear, but at least he now knew that it was a gamble even for the doctor who'd so diligently been there every single day to take care of Gable.

"Thank you. I think I'd better go see him now," Flynn stated softly as he got up from the office chair and walked out without shaking Dr. Isaacs' hand. He needed to be with Gable right now, spend as much time with him as he could, despite the fact he had no idea whether Gable actually registered his presence or not. It didn't matter, because he didn't do it for Gable, at least not entirely. He needed to be there for himself, so he would never again have to beat himself up for not taking the time to be with his lover in his final hours.

Flynn started staying in between the two visiting hours, and although it was a battle of wills for a few days, eventually Dr. Isaacs officially gave him permission.

In the following days, they moved Gable away from the large ward into a single room in the ICU, and although the alarms going off around Gable's bed every few minutes were driving Flynn crazy, he couldn't tear himself away from his lover's side. He found himself doing only the most necessary work at the ranch, so he could speed to the hospital to sit in vigil for endless hours. At first he counted those hours, cherishing every moment that Gable survived, but as the fever started going down and Gable became more stable, boredom started taking over and Flynn began bringing in a newspaper, which he read aloud, then a book. He became friends with the nurses and continued helping them take care of Gable as they washed him and turned him from side to side.

One afternoon, after three weeks of barely sleeping and eating even less, Flynn had dozed off, sitting by the bed. He was awakened by Gable's hand moving against his face. When Flynn looked up, at first not sure if he had dreamed it, Gable looked like he was simply asleep, but then his fingers moved again.

"Gable, love. Open your eyes for me?" Flynn asked gently. At first Gable didn't respond, but then his ventilator started beeping. Three weeks ago, this would have sent Flynn into a panic, but he was much calmer now, since this noise was not so unusual and he'd heard it before. But then Gable started coughing and pulling at his bound hands.

"Gable, calm down. You're in the hospital," Flynn echoed the words he'd heard the nurses use more than once. "Let the machine breathe for you."

This time the words didn't seem to have any effect on Gable, and as the machine protested louder, two nurses rushed into the room. They adjusted some settings on the ventilator and repeated Flynn's words as Flynn took a step back. He felt helpless as he watched Gable struggle against his bonds and against the ventilator, and he simply wanted the torture to stop. When the alarms didn't stop, Dr. Isaacs joined them in the room.

"I think you better wait outside, Flynn. I promise we'll take good care of him." Dr. Isaacs nodded in the direction of the hallway, but Flynn was reluctant to leave. He was worried something was seriously wrong and Gable had taken a turn for the worst. "He's fine. I'll come get you as soon as he's calmer."

Flynn had little choice but to walk outside. He wanted to hold Gable's hand and tell him everything would be okay, but he knew he'd only get in the way, so he walked toward the waiting area at the entrance of the ICU and bumped into Calley.

"You look like you've just seen a ghost. Flynn, is everything okay?"

Flynn nodded. "I think he's waking up, but he was fighting and trying to break free."

"That's what the restraints are for. He'd do himself a world of harm if they let him."

"I know," Flynn murmured. He was glad Calley was here, like she had been almost every day. She'd kept him fed and had kept his hopes up, even in the most bleak of times, and he was grateful that he didn't need to sit and wait for news on his own. As she was getting them coffee from the machine in the waiting area, Flynn realized that, despite all the time they'd spend together in the past three weeks, he still didn't know if there was more to Calley's relationship with Gable than her supplying him with items from her store. He couldn't believe how selfish he'd been, talking only about Gable and never showing any interest in Calley.

"You know Gable pretty well, don't you?" Flynn asked Calley as he took the cup of coffee from her.

"Oh, the stories I could tell!" Calley laughed. "But I won't. I don't tell other people's secrets. One day Gable will want to tell you."

"He's not the most talkative person," Flynn reminded her.

"I know," Calley agreed. "But one day he will tell you more, I'm sure. He just takes a long time to trust someone enough to open up. He told you about Grant, didn't he?"

Flynn nodded silently.

"He'll tell you more. Maybe even about what we did when we were younger."

Flynn thought she looked mischievous and was dying to ask her for more details, but he had a feeling she liked being mysterious and wouldn't divulge any more secrets. He hoped he'd get the chance to hear Gable tell him more about himself.

At that moment, Dr. Isaacs entered the waiting room, white coat flaring out behind him. "I think you can go back in now, but not for long. I'm afraid I'm going to have to tell you to keep the visits short from now on. Gable's still very weak and he'll need his rest, but I have a feeling he'll be dying to see you. So to speak."

Flynn looked at Calley and then at the doctor. "Do you mean he's awake?"

Isaacs smiled. "Yes, he is. We're still trying to wean him off the ventilator, and that may take some time after depending on it for three weeks, but yes, he's awake. We've given him something for the pain, but we've shut off the sedation. He can't talk, which will be very frustrating for him, but try to keep him as calm as possible, okay? He'll still be quite drowsy and he'll fall asleep from time to time. Please let him. He needs the rest. And maybe just one of you at a time?"

Flynn couldn't help but think Isaacs seemed relieved about the whole turn of events as well, and that gave him a good feeling.

"Go on, Flynn, it's you he'll want to see," Calley urged him on.

Flynn wasn't as confident, despite the fact he wanted to run, not walk, to Gable's room. "I don't know, Calley. We had a hell of a fight right before—"

Calley shook her head. "That's long past. Go on."

Flynn followed Dr. Isaacs down the corridor and overtook him just before they reached Gable's room. As he walked in, he saw Gable lying on his side, both of his hands tied to the same side of the bed and looking comfortable, with his eyes closed. He sighed, the knots in his stomach not unclenching yet, although the anticipation of finally seeing his lover awake had somewhat abated. He remembered the doctor's words and didn't try to wake Gable.

Then Gable opened his eyes. They still looked a little unfocused and it seemed to take him some time to recognize who he was looking at, but then he reacted and tried to speak, making the ventilator beep loudly.

"Shhh," Flynn tried to soothe Gable. He took Gable's hands in his. "You can't talk yet. You have a tube down your throat to help you breathe and lots of wires attached to you, but they told me that if you stay calm and try to rest, they'll be able to take the tube out soon."

Gable tried to talk again, and this time the machine beeped even louder as he gagged and pulled on the restraints.

Flynn took Gable's face in his hands and made him look at him. "Calm down. Breathe. In and out. In and out." Flynn's attention was momentarily drawn by the nurse, who was keeping his distance, as though Flynn was being given permission to try and soothe his lover. In other words, he wasn't doing a bad job, which was demonstrated when the machine stopped its irritating noises as Gable tried to comply with Flynn's demands.

Gable relaxed and dozed off again while Flynn caressed his cheek, and the nurse left his spot at the entrance of the room. It was an exhausting evening for both of them, as Gable struggled with his circumstances and Flynn jumped up every time something awakened Gable and made him gag. Slowly, he adjusted, and Flynn just had to grab his hand and nod at him to make him remember what he was supposed to do. Calley briefly dropped by to say good-bye and promised to visit again the next day, and Flynn settled on the couch next to Gable's bed until they politely asked him to go home.

Flynn was back early the next morning, after only riding out to make sure the horses in the paddocks were okay. To his disappointment, Gable still had the tube and not a lot had changed, but he was glad to see some recognition in Gable's confused eyes. Gable was sitting more or less upright and Flynn saw they'd replaced the arch that had been there right after the operation and that kept the blankets from pressing down on Gable's legs. He knew it would be hard enough for Gable to come to terms with the amputation and preferred to tell him when he could actually talk and ask questions. For now, they could blissfully ignore what had happened, and Flynn was glad to sit quietly and read while Gable rested.

Gable's room was right opposite the nurses' station, and after Calley paid them a quick visit, Flynn settled down with a book while Gable dozed. When Flynn looked up, he saw a tall man with dark, curly hair talking to the male nurse in charge of Gable's care. He didn't pay them much attention until he caught the visitor staring at Gable while the nurse was telling him something. Flynn got up from his chair with the intention of closing the door to keep the insolent man from eyeing his lover when the ventilator alarm went off and he saw the panic in Gable's eyes. The nurse came in to check out the alarm, but by then Gable had managed to pull out his breathing tube, despite being well restrained.

Although everyone rushing around had a calm, professional air about them, Flynn felt his heart beating wildly. He wanted to stay by Gable's side, but was more than a little curious who this dark stranger was and why he'd had such an effect on his lover.

"We're going to give him a chance to breathe on his own for a bit," Dr. Isaacs informed Flynn. "Let's hope he does well enough to prevent us having to put the tube back in."

Flynn nodded before turning toward Gable, who was clearly exhausted. He wiped the stray hairs off his forehead and kissed it. "Who was that man, Gable?"

"Grant," Gable mouthed silently.

Flynn felt rage building inside and rushed out of the room toward the hallway, hoping he could catch up with Gable's ex. To his surprise, Grant was still in the waiting area and Calley was talking to him.

"Grant, I believe?" Flynn called out to make the taller man turn around.

When Grant nodded, Flynn stepped forward and planted his fist into the man's jaw.

—12—

FLYNN was not a violent man, but he couldn't believe that after all Gable had been through with Grant, he'd dare to show up at Gable's hospital bed. On top of that, seeing Calley talk to Grant quite amicably made him see red.

"How dare you come here!" Flynn shouted at Grant. He turned to Calley and pointed his finger at her. "And you are no better!"

"Flynn, please," Calley pleaded, trying to keep Grant from retaliating and Flynn from lashing out again. "Stop this!"

"You know exactly how much damage this man has done to Gable," Flynn continued. "We trusted you, but I suppose it was you who told him about Gable's whereabouts."

Calley shook her head.

"She didn't tell me," Grant replied, rubbing the side of his jaw Flynn's fist had impacted with. He was still not entirely calm, but clearly trying very hard to control his temper.

"Then why did you come back here after more than a year?"

"I came through town on my way to… another job and someone told me that they'd rushed Gable to the hospital in an ambulance. I knew it must have been serious, so I came looking for him."

This made Flynn's blood boil even more. "I don't believe you. Last time he was hurt, you weren't around to call the ambulance, and you didn't even bother to say good-bye afterward, when you ran away like a coward. How am I supposed to believe that you all of a sudden grew a conscience?"

Grant sighed and looked defeated. "You have no idea what it was like."

Flynn gave him a stern look.

"People were talking behind our backs. I wouldn't have found work elsewhere if that had continued."

Flynn bit the inside of his cheek to stop himself from reacting on impulse again. "Macho man like you?" he mocked instead. "I'm sure you could have proven your masculinity in one way or another." He threw Calley a poisoned look and turned around. "Now I'm going back to where I'm needed."

Flynn took a few deep breaths and tried hard to calm down on the way to Gable's room, but he was worried about the impact seeing Grant again would have on Gable. He knew he was no coward, though. He'd never run, never leave Gable as long as he needed him. If he was honest, he was glad that he'd finally met Grant. It helped to have a picture of the man in his head; he now understood the physical attraction, but he couldn't see Gable having his way with Grant the way he'd shown he liked to have his way with a man.

He couldn't imagine Gable overpowering Grant the way he'd overpowered him in the barn, and then again by the outside shower. Grant was the ultimate alpha male, tall and overbearing, with well-developed muscles clear underneath his clothes. This, combined with what Gable had told him about Grant's reluctance to embrace the fact he was gay, made Flynn feel very uneasy about their relationship. Maybe it was a good thing Grant left when he did. Flynn hoped the man would simply keep traveling.

When Flynn arrived at Gable's room, Gable was asleep. He was breathing calmly and had clearly been made comfortable after the earlier emotional outburst.

"He's doing well," his nurse said, appearing behind Flynn while Flynn stared at his lover. "Looks like he'll be able to go without the breathing tube."

"I hope so," Flynn replied. "We have a lot to talk about."

TALKING with Gable wasn't really on the books the first few days. Although the nurses and Dr. Isaacs agreed he was doing well and would be allowed to leave the ICU soon, he slept almost all the time, and when he woke, Flynn had to tell him time and time again where he was and how he'd gotten there. Although the nurse who primarily cared for Gable told Flynn that Gable had seen what was left of his leg when he tended to the wound, they hadn't really discussed it.

When Gable was transferred to an ordinary hospital ward, Flynn knew he'd have to broach the subject eventually. He had no idea how to do that, though. Gable still tired easily and would often lie back and close his eyes when they were talking, dozing off almost immediately. It made their interactions rather one-sided, and Flynn felt intensely lonely, especially since he was still not talking to Calley.

"I want to go home," Gable stated out of the blue.

Flynn hadn't even noticed he'd woken up again, so he put down his book and moved a little closer to Gable's bed. "You can't. You're not well enough."

"But all I do is lie here and sleep. I can do that just as well at home."

Flynn sighed. "You still need your dialysis. The doctors think your kidneys are recovering, but until they do, you'll still be in the hospital three days a week." They'd had this type of conversation a few times, but Gable was usually easily dissuaded. Not this time, though.

"At least I can be home in between. I want to go home, Flynn."

Flynn bit his lips and tried to gather his courage. "You have to give it time, Gable. You were very sick."

Gable shook his head. "The walls are closing in on me here."

"You have to learn to walk again." Flynn didn't look at Gable when he said it, but the only reply he got was silence. For a moment he thought Gable had fallen asleep again, but when he dared to look up, Gable was smiling.

"I'm getting stronger." To stress the point, Gable raised his arms and showed what was left of his biceps. "I know I'm always tired, but that will get better once I'm home and can spend time with the horses and sleep in my own bed again."

Flynn swallowed. "You need physiotherapy for your leg, Gable."

"It doesn't hurt any more, Flynn. All that bed rest did some good, you see."

"Gabe...." Flynn's voice faltered. Gable was in denial, despite the fact that anyone walking into the room could see that there was only one foot tenting the sheet. Gable's other leg sort of... ended into nothingness. Flynn had seen the stump a few times when Gable was still sedated and he'd forced himself to look at it, knowing that if he had his way he'd have to get used to it, because he was going to have to look at it for a long time to come. That first time it had made him gag, emotions running high when he imagined Gable's reaction. Now he could look at it and think about it without showing much reaction, but on the inside, the fact that Gable had shown no acknowledgement of it at all still made him apprehensive. "Gable," he repeated, placing his hand on Gable's leg, just above the knee and far away from the bandaged stump.

When Flynn looked up, Gable's eyes filled with tears and he shook his head so minutely, Flynn almost missed it.

"I can't stay here," Gable murmured. "This hospital is making me sick."

"I'll talk to the doctor and see what I can do, okay?" Flynn reassured him, moving closer so he could put his arm around Gable's shoulder. Flynn didn't dare go any further. He wanted to touch his lover, make him feel loved and wanted, but they hadn't even as much as kissed since that horrible night. When Flynn retreated, Gable grabbed his hand and held him back. He didn't say anything, but there was a pleading look in Gable's eyes that Flynn couldn't resist.

"Scoot over a bit," he gently told Gable, then he crawled onto the narrow bed next to him and snuggled closer. He had to admit it felt good to have Gable in his arms, despite the fact that it made it even clearer that Gable was skin and bones and the bed was really too narrow for the two of them. "I need to fatten you up a bit," he told Gable, placing his hand gently on Gable's hollowed stomach.

"I miss your cooking," Gable replied quietly before growing heavy in Flynn's arms as he fell asleep.

Flynn did talk to Gable's doctor, and the man was polite enough not to laugh in his face. Instead, Flynn was given an explanation of why it would be very difficult to take care of Gable at home. None of the arguments were unexpected. Gable had barely been out of bed. The nurses transferred him to a comfortable chair every day, but after barely an hour he was exhausted. He couldn't even stand on his good leg, let alone make his way around the house on crutches or even a wheelchair. Then there was the dialysis and the physiotherapy he needed to get stronger so he could be fitted with a prosthetic leg. All of these things could be accomplished easier in the hospital, unless of course, Flynn could provide round-the-clock care.

Fully aware of the financial situation Gable was in, Flynn knew that the round-the-clock care would fall only on *his* shoulders, and he had neither the experience nor the energy to do that and run the ranch at the same time. The hospital bills were piling up, and although Flynn had some ideas to make money, he needed Calley's cooperation, since she had Gable's power of attorney. Legally, Flynn was no more than a temporary ranch hand, and although Calley had made sure that Flynn was paid for his work, he couldn't sell any of the horses or buy supplies for the ranch without her consent.

This meant Flynn would have to go to Calley's store to talk with her. They hadn't really been in contact since he'd seen her talking to Grant. He knew he'd have to get over what was bothering him about it, because right now Gable had to come first. That didn't mean he was looking forward to it.

With Gable being out of danger, Flynn drove by Calley's store in town before heading to the hospital.

"Well, look what the cat dragged in," Calley mocked by means of a welcome. "So what brings you here after all this time?"

"I think we should talk about the ranch," Flynn said, too nervous to engage in small talk. "And of course about money."

"There's enough to pay your salary," Calley stated matter-of-factly while she continued stacking apples.

Flynn shook his head, fighting the urge to just walk out again. He couldn't believe that, after all this time, Calley still thought he did it for the money. "I worked for nothing for weeks before the horses were sold, Calley. I think I trust you and Gable enough to know I'll get paid."

Calley smiled and looked away. "I know that, Flynn," she said softly. "It's just that... I didn't expect you'd come in here for anything else than money for the ranch. That's all I seem to be good for these days."

"We do need to talk about the ranch," Flynn started, but he really wanted to talk about other things as well, like whether she'd support him in changing the way the ranch worked and what she was thinking, chatting to Grant as if he was a friend of the family... but he didn't dare. Instead, he started handing her the oranges he found in a crate near his feet.

"So is that your financial plan?" Calley asked casually. She laughed when Flynn raised his eyebrows. "Are you fishing for a job at the store here?"

"No thanks. Between the ranch and Gable, I have my hands full."

Calley laughed again. "I would say so! How is our Gable by the way?"

"In denial," Flynn answered sadly. He shrugged. "He's getting better. His kidneys are recuperating and they're talking about him being well enough for rehab now, but he won't even acknowledge the operation. Whenever I bring it up, he either changes the subject or pretends to fall asleep."

Calley stopped stacking her oranges. "He's always been as stubborn as a mule."

"He keeps telling me he wants to come home, but nobody but him thinks he's ready for that." Flynn shifted his weight from one foot to another and then back. He wanted to ask Calley for help in convincing Gable, but didn't know how.

"I think Gable's calculating the cost of all this in his head," Calley suggested while she grabbed the last two oranges from Flynn's hands, dropped them on top of the pile, and picked up the now empty crate. "He knows the ranch is barely surviving and he's got a pretty fair idea of how big a dent his hospital stay is causing in his already tight budget, so he figures that if he comes home, he'll just manage. It was no different after the accident. Bill barely saw me the first weeks after Gable came home. Between the shop and helping Gable out...."

She didn't finish her sentence, but Flynn knew what she meant. "It's not that I don't want to take care of Gable, Calley, it's just...."

"I know," Calley replied, looking at Flynn with compassion in her eyes. "You're the polar opposite of Grant, and that makes me more than happy."

"You didn't have a problem being nice to him during his surprise visit. Despite all the grief he caused Gable," Flynn confronted her.

Calley took a deep breath before answering. "What happened between Gable and Grant was none of my business, Flynn. I know Grant hurt Gable, but I can't take sides. You have to understand that."

"I know that Grant left without even saying good-bye. Like a coward. And you're a coward for not involving yourself!" Flynn felt the same anger rise that he felt after seeing Gable's ex.

"Maybe Grant wasn't the right man for Gable and he knew that. Flynn, it wasn't Grant's fault that Gable had an accident. I don't know what Gable told you, but their relationship was nothing like what you have with Gable, and Grant is a macho man. He cut his losses, but that doesn't mean I have to stop talking to him!"

Flynn was practically seething. He didn't even finish listening to Calley, but stomped outside, slamming the door behind him. How could she protect Grant like that? How could she defend the man to him after all he'd done to Gable? Flynn paced the parking lot, trying to calm himself down. He needed Calley. Whenever he said he needed some money for supplies, Gable told Flynn he had to talk to Calley, so he couldn't deal with this without her help. Yet right now, she rubbed him the wrong way.

"I know you love him, Flynn."

Flynn heard Calley's voice behind him, but he didn't turn around. She sounded calm and amicable, but he was still unsure whether he could stop himself saying things he might regret later, so he continued looking across the nearly empty street.

"You probably love him more than he's ever been loved before, so it's hard for you to understand that someone else could feel differently about Gable. Grant didn't love Gable the way you do, Flynn."

Flynn sighed. Calley was right. He knew Grant's type all too well. For them it was all about the sex, and if commitment came knocking, they ran. Flynn wasn't wired that way. Sure, he didn't say no to the occasional romp in the hay, but Flynn always wanted more. He wanted it all. Flynn wanted the house and the picket fence and a relationship he could depend on.

He turned around and faced Calley. "You're right. And maybe that's what's freaking Gable out as well? Maybe I'm a bit too intense for him."

Calley tentatively walked closer. "I think he's incredibly drawn to you and feels he can trust you but at the same time, he doesn't know what he's dealing with."

Flynn nodded. "Did he…?"

"… talk to me about you?" Calley interrupted. "Not in so many words, but he dropped enough hints for me to know how important you are to him."

Flynn thought she looked a little smug, but then, this was the Calley he knew, always a little secretive and enigmatic.

"He does get all starry-eyed when he talks about you," Calley added. "He turns into this teenage boy whenever your name is mentioned. It's really cute."

Flynn didn't quite know how to feel about hearing Calley refer to Gable as cute. He wasn't angry at her any more, though. "So should we expect Grant back any time soon?"

She shook her head. "He has a job not too far from here, but I told him it would be wise not to show his face around you again. He said he was happy that Gable had found someone to champion him."

"Yeah, I bet he is," Flynn replied wryly. He had the sudden uncontrollable urge to get into his car and drive to the hospital to see Gable.

TO FLYNN'S surprise, Gable wasn't in his room when he got there. A quick query at the nurse's desk garnered no reply, so he walked back to Gable's room, where he found a stranger in a white uniform leaning against the doorpost.

"Craig," the stranger said, holding out his hand. "Gable's on his way back. He's determined to go home as soon as possible, so he's making his way here from the elevator."

"Walking?" Flynn asked, his eyebrows flirting with his hairline.

Craig chuckled. "No way. We're working on getting him a bit more mobile in a wheelchair, but he told me he's going to have to navigate a narrow flight of stairs in his house?"

Flynn nodded. "Not to mention four steps up to the porch and a not-so-even driveway to get there. I told him he's not ready to come home yet."

Craig smiled compassionately. "He's a bit stubborn that way."

Flynn laughed. "Tell me about it."

When Flynn looked into the hallway, he saw Gable sitting in a wheelchair halfway down the corridor, his elbows resting on the arm rests and his head hanging down between his shoulders. He wanted to go over to him but Craig held him back. "Leave him. I want him to feel how much effort even the smallest thing will cost him. It's the only way we'll be able to persuade him that it's too early to go home."

Although Flynn knew how stubborn Gable was and doubted that Craig would win, he could see the sense in what the therapist was telling him. That didn't make it any easier for Flynn to watch Gable struggle for every foot of progress he made down the corridor. Eventually, Flynn walked inside the room to wait there, and he was glad to see Gable enter through the door. He stayed back to watch how Craig helped Gable stand on his good leg and then transfer to the bed, where he laid down, totally exhausted.

"A lot of work to do, buddy," Craig told Gable after patting his knee. "Rest now."

Gable nodded and watched him leave, after which he looked at Flynn. "You're late. I was hoping you'd come to the therapy room with me so you could see how well I'm doing."

Flynn walked to the bed and took Gable's hand. "I'm sorry I missed it. I was making amends with Calley." Gable didn't say anything, and the silence wasn't entirely comfortable.

"Craig says I can go home soon."

Flynn shook his head. "Craig says you need to be patient. There's still a lot of work that needs to be done, like fitting you with a prosthesis."

Gable closed his eyes and Flynn knew he was hurting. Gable didn't respond, though, again ignoring Flynn's plea to talk. "I can't stay here much longer, Flynn. I need to be in my own house and I need to be able to see the horses and then everything will be okay, I promise."

"But you're exhausted just from pushing your wheelchair down three hundred feet of corridor," Flynn tried.

Gable pulled him closer. "But at home I know where everything is. It's MY house. Please, Flynn." He scooted over a bit, making a space for Flynn.

Flynn crawled into Gable's bed, as he'd done so many times in the past weeks, and snuggled into his arms. He knew Gable would fall asleep as soon as they got comfortable, but he liked that it made Gable feel good and it cemented their bond. He'd expected Gable to be angry with him for giving permission for the operation, even though it was Calley who had signed the papers, but Gable had been surprisingly loving, and Flynn reveled in the attention. He had to give it some time. "Are you still awake?"

"Mmmh," Gable moaned.

"Give me a few days and I'll take you home."

—13—

FLYNN picked Gable up from the hospital and drove him back to the ranch. Gable was nervous. He desperately wanted to see his house again, wanted to sit on the porch, look out over the paddocks and inhale the fresh, clear, open air, but it wasn't going to be easy. He didn't look forward to climbing the stairs to his bedroom, and he hated thinking about all the hours he'd sit waiting for Flynn to be done with his work around the ranch, but anything beat lying in that cold, white hospital room. He was surprised to see all the snow and had to remind himself he'd lost a few weeks of his life in that hospital room; time he'd never be able to recover.

Gable knew he was putting a huge burden on Flynn by begging him to let him come home, but he had no choice. He wasn't the type to be cooped up inside four walls, never had been and never would be, so his only chance of living through this was at the ranch. He just wished he knew a way to do it without Flynn. Right now, Gable knew he needed Flynn, to take care of him and to do things for him, not to mention he was grateful for the care Flynn had taken of his ranch, but he also felt like he couldn't tie the kid down. When he'd hired him, he'd known Flynn was a traveler and, sooner rather than later, Flynn would be leaving again. What was there to keep him here anyway?

Despite the fact he was tired just from getting into the truck, Gable enjoyed being driven down the country lanes and seeing the familiar trees and curves along the road. He could tell Flynn was nervous too, because he was driving extra slow and he wasn't talking. Then, there wasn't much to say anyway. Flynn had kept him up to date about the ranch while he was in the hospital, so that took care of that. He couldn't ask Flynn to leave because he knew he couldn't take care of himself yet, and he couldn't ask him to stay because he had nothing to offer the kid.

"We just need to stop at Calley's for groceries and then we'll be heading home," Flynn announced.

Gable grunted. He wasn't ready for Calley and possibly Bill fussing over him and he really wanted to get home as soon as possible.

"She's got it all packed up for us," Flynn responded. "We just need to load it in the truck, and of course she wants to look at you. It was that or ask her to bring it and then we'd be stuck with her for longer. At least now we can leave when we want."

Gable half-smiled at Flynn. He was right. As much as he loved Calley, this way they could just sit in the driveway for a few minutes and that would be it. He sighed when they drove up into the small parking area in front of Calley's grocery store, which was abundantly decorated with Christmas lights, and Calley came rushing out even before their truck had come to a standstill. She hadn't even bothered wearing her heavy winter coat.

"Come here and let me take a look at you!" Calley greeted Gable after waiting patiently for him to roll his window down. "Are you okay? Flynn's been keeping me up to date, but between the store and you needing your rest, I haven't seen enough of you these past weeks." She lovingly enveloped his cheeks with her hands and rubbed them with her thumbs.

Gable nodded. "I'm fine. Will be good to be home."

Calley looked worriedly in Flynn's direction, then back at Gable. "Let Flynn take care of you, okay? And Flynn? If he gives you grief, remember I have experience with this one being sick." She nodded at Gable and then let him go as Flynn exited the truck to pick up their box of supplies.

Gable was grateful when they went inside and left him alone. He leaned his head back and closed his eyes until he heard the thump of Flynn putting the box down in the back of the truck.

"Okay, we're on our way," Flynn announced as he started the truck again. "How does roast with potatoes and glazed carrots sound?"

Gable's stomach growled. "Sounds great," he answered quietly.

"Good," Flynn answered, placing his hand on Gable's knee and squeezing it. "I wasn't kidding when I said I wanted to fatten you up a bit."

When Flynn looked at him, Gable couldn't hold his gaze. He was too afraid of seeing Flynn's expectations in those big brown eyes of his, so he looked down at the bottom of the truck and then out the window until Flynn pulled his hand back to take the sharp bend up to the ranch.

Although his nervousness grew as they approached the house, Gable's heart almost leapt out of his chest when he saw his homestead again, complete with Bridget coming out of hiding to greet them. This was his home, the one place where he felt safe and where he could be himself; where no one questioned his lifestyle. In his heart he remembered how good it was to share this with Flynn, but his mind kept telling him that everything would be different now. Flynn was staying out of some strange sense of obligation, and Gable knew that as soon as he was able to fend for himself again, Flynn would leave and he'd be alone inside that big house. The notion hurt something fierce in his chest, but that was the way the cookie crumbled. He'd been alone most of his life, so he knew he'd be able to cope.

Flynn stopped the car with the passenger side as close to the porch of the house as he could and got out while Gable was still trying to gather his courage. Bridget leapt up to the door and, in all her excitement, licked the window, but Flynn coaxed her inside, assuring her that she'd get time with Gable later.

"Okay, let's try this," Flynn announced, opening Gable's door and presenting him with the crutches Craig had taught him to use. Gable's arms hadn't regained their full strength yet, appearing too frail for the bulky-looking but lightweight metal supports that fit under his armpits.

Gable swung his legs out of the car and accepted the crutches, slowly putting weight on his leg and trying to find his balance, while Flynn fidgeted around him. Gable saw how Flynn had tried to clear the driveway and the porch steps of snow so he wouldn't slip and had to admit he was grateful.

"I'll be fine," he told Flynn in no uncertain terms. "Just leave me be for a moment."

"But—" Flynn protested.

Gable shook his head. "Take my suitcase inside, open the door, take the groceries in. Do anything, just don't get in my way," he interrupted, irritation in his voice. He knew Flynn didn't deserve this, but he was crowding him, and it was going to be hard enough without Flynn watching him fail, so Gable sank back down to the car seat and waited for Flynn to leave.

Frustration grew as it again dawned on Gable how much effort every single action took him. All he could think of right now was that he could do with a lie down, but his bed was upstairs and he was afraid he would barely be able to make it up the four steps to the porch, let alone actually make it to the bedroom. The couch was going to have to do, and he remembered Craig's words: take it one step at a time. He had no other choice. As he slowly made his way up the porch steps, Gable saw Flynn hovering around the front door, pretending to be busy inside, but keeping a close eye on him. It was both reassuring and annoying, but at least Flynn was doing what Gable had asked and was giving him some space.

The steps were tough, but Gable managed to make it to the top without falling. He had to stop to catch his breath, though, and as he looked at the door, he caught Flynn staring. Gable looked away and tried to distract himself by straightening his back and taking another step. When he looked at the door again, Flynn was gone, but as soon as Gable crossed the threshold, Flynn was right by his side, closing the door behind him.

"You must be exhausted. We got a...." Flynn stopped mid-sentence as Gable wavered, seeing the bed in the living room. It was a Spartan-looking single bed, neatly made up with unfamiliar-looking sheets, and it was standing next to the wall, underneath the window that overlooked the paddocks and the barn. Bridget was sitting next to it as if she'd been instructed to look like a Norman Rockwell painting, but her tail betrayed her excitement.

"I was afraid you might be too tired to go upstairs the first few days, and if not, you can still use it for a nap during the day or just to rest," Flynn rambled. "It's Calley's and she let us borrow it for as long as we need it. You need it," Flynn corrected.

Gable nodded. He was annoyed at having his incapacitation thrown in his face, but on the other hand, the bed looked very inviting right now, so he hobbled his way over there and sank down on it with a heavy sigh. He looked up as Flynn took his crutches from him and put them against the wall, then took some extra pillows and started arranging them around Gable.

"Flynn, please," he pleaded, grabbing Flynn's hand to stop the kid from fussing over him. "I'm fine. The bed's fine. Just give me a little time to rest. Don't you have work to do out there?" Gable pointed toward the barn.

"I did all that this morning," Flynn answered, hovering uncomfortably around and finally deciding to take Gable's shoe off.

"You must have gotten up at the crack of dawn!"

Flynn smiled. "It was still dark, actually."

Gable, still holding Flynn's wrist, pulled Flynn closer so he had no choice but to sit down on the bed next to him. "I think you could use some rest too."

Flynn hesitated and then snuggled closer so Gable had no choice but to put his arm around him. "I want you to feel good here."

"I do," Gable whispered, his face half-buried in Flynn's curls—which, Gable noticed, were growing quite long now, as if they hadn't been cut in months. He could inhale Flynn's sweet scent and closed his eyes, enjoying their closeness without the risk of getting caught by nurses or doctors prowling the corridors of the hospital. He was dead tired and felt himself slowly drifting off to sleep.

"I better get started on dinner, so you can have a rest," Flynn said, interrupting Gable's slumber.

"I kind of enjoyed having you near me," Gable tried, but Flynn had already extracted himself from Gable's embrace and was getting up from the bed.

"Only kind of?" Flynn asked teasingly. He started walking toward the kitchen and then turned back. "You'll be asleep by the time I leave the room. Lie down and rest."

Gable could only nod, knowing Flynn was right. He'd barely swung his legs up on the bed when Bridget laid her head to rest next to him. Stroking her soft fur, he felt his eyelids grow heavy.

When he woke, he was covered in a blanket and his head was resting on a pillow. He was sore and cramped up, but no more than usual after sleeping, and delicious aromas were drifting in from the kitchen. "Flynn?"

"Be right there," Flynn called from far away.

Gable let his head fall back to the pillow and smiled. He was home. "I'm home," he whispered to himself, listening to Flynn puttering around in the kitchen, and realized he enjoyed the feeling so much it was making him emotional. He shook his head and stretched a little before sitting up on the bed and swinging his legs over the side. That's when it dawned on him that he couldn't reach his crutches, which Flynn had conveniently placed too far from the bed to be any use to him. He wasn't about to let that stop him, though. Holding onto the side of the bed, he hauled himself up and, balancing on his one good leg, he turned around. Somehow this all felt familiar; being in his own environment, his body remembered what it was like to do this from the last time he couldn't use his bad leg. Supporting himself by holding on to the bed, he hopped closer to where the crutches were, but he misjudged his own weakness and felt his knee give out. It was enough for him to lose his balance, and he shouted out as his hip crashed to the hardwood floor.

Within seconds, Flynn was hovering over him. "Gable! Are you okay? Can you move? I said I would only be a minute! Dinner's almost ready and I didn't want it to burn. I thought …."

"You thought what?" Gable hissed. His side hurt and he barely had the strength to move, let alone drag himself up from the floor, so he stayed down. "Let's mother the cripple a bit? Make him feel even more helpless than he is? Let's put the crutches on the other side of the room so he doesn't feel tempted to move even a finger when I'm not there?"

Flynn reached to help Gable up, but Gable swatted his hand away. "Just… leave."

"But you need help…."

"Yes," Gable spat out. "Thanks for shoving that in my face. Does it make you feel all butch that I need you for everything? That I can't as much as take a leak without asking you to help me? Do you feel like a real man now you're in charge of me?"

Gable felt the anger bursting out of him. Flynn was standing over him and he couldn't get up. Flynn was still holding out his hand and Gable only had to reach for it to be helped, but he'd rather lie on the floor for the next few hours than be shown yet again how helpless he was. *"Leave me!"* he shouted at Flynn, the power of his voice sapping the last of his strength, after which he dropped completely to the floor.

Flynn hesitated. Breathing heavily, he took a step back and straightened up, then turned around and walked out.

—14—

FLYNN paced the porch outside, afraid to go any farther. He had tears in his eyes and knots in his stomach that were ten times worse than the ones he'd had when he brought Gable home that morning. He knew it wasn't going to be easy, but he'd never expected Gable to shout at him and push him away. Not this soon. All he wanted to do was help Gable and make him feel happy to be home, and yes, the ulterior motive was that he hoped Gable would get better soon so they could start the rest of their lives.

The head nurse at the ward where Gable had stayed had warned Flynn about this sort of behavior, though. It wasn't bad enough that Flynn felt guilty as hell for being part of the decision to sign the agreement for the operation; it was also just a matter of time before Gable would hold it against him, and maybe that time had come. Had he expected it to be easier? Had he underestimated the wall Gable had built around himself all those years? A wall that had only been reinforced by his injury and by what Grant had done to him? Flynn didn't know what to think. His resolve to stay was faltering. He couldn't leave yet, though. He'd never forgive himself if he left Gable to fend for himself in the state he was in.

Flynn just couldn't figure out the push and pull. One moment, Gable was loving and needy. They cuddled and were kind to each other, even if it didn't go further than that. They still hadn't really kissed since the night of their argument, at least not like lovers did, on the mouth. They'd exchange the sort of kiss a parent gives a child—on the cheek, the temple, the hair—but it was always more caring than passionate. Flynn missed their lovers' kisses, but he was patient, hoping that one day when Gable felt stronger, they'd kiss again. Right now, the tenderness they shared felt like enough.

But what he couldn't understand was how Gable would always turn on him afterward. At the hospital, Gable would pretend to sleep, shutting himself off from Flynn, but he'd never shouted at Flynn before.

Feeling himself calm down a bit, Flynn sat down on the top step of the porch, where he used to sit before he and Gable had become intimate. He looked behind, toward the chair and footstool where Gable would always be then, but it was empty now. During the long days when Gable was struggling for his life in the hospital, Flynn would come back home in the middle of the night and sit on the porch for a few minutes, telling himself he'd made the right decision. Seeing the empty chair always made his eyes well up. He couldn't lose another lover, that had been his motivation, and even now the thought of Gable dying, despite the fact he was well on the way to a complete recovery, gripped Flynn's heart. Splitting up was one thing, but he couldn't stand the thought that Gable could have died.

What Flynn really wanted to do was walk back into the house, pick Gable up off the floor, and tell him exactly how much he loved him, but if he'd learned one thing, it was that Gable felt stifled by the love he showed him. Calley had made it clear to him; Gable didn't know what it was like to be loved so much and he couldn't deal with it, so Flynn was going to have to continue doing what he was doing now. Showing Gable he loved him instead of telling him. Keeping his distance when he really wanted to be around Gable twenty-four-seven and the only way he knew how to do that was to take care of him, of his house and his ranch, and to cook and clean for him and make sure he had everything he needed. Christ, he sounded like a housewife. Was that what he was?

Flynn got up quickly when he heard the floorboards creak, and he saw Gable appear on his crutches in the doorway. "Do you need anything?" Flynn asked. It wasn't until he saw Gable raise his eyebrows that he wiped his hand over his face and saw it come back quite wet. Flynn sniffed. "Sorry. Was thinking too much."

"Food's getting cold and that's a shame," Gable replied. "It smelled really good when you were cooking it."

Flynn nodded and walked past Gable into the kitchen. He was sure he could salvage some of it so they'd at least have a decent meal.

Gable was slow to follow him, but Flynn tried hard not to help. It wasn't easy, but he managed to prevent himself from pulling Gable's chair back or keeping Bridget from running in front of him, and he barely looked at him.

They ate in silence, only broken once by Gable, when he leaned back and pushed his plate further up the table. "That was a great meal, Flynn. I don't think food ever tasted this good."

Flynn nodded, silently acknowledging the compliment, and got up from the table to do the dishes. Bridget, as usual quite ladylike, sat next to him in the hope that some of the dinner scraps would make it to her, but this time Flynn didn't give her anything. "Go sit by Gable," he told her, after which she reluctantly drooped off.

Flynn didn't know what to do, and he was becoming increasingly worried about what the night would bring. He hated this tension, this walking on eggshells, never knowing whether he was showing Gable the care and love he needed or stifling him with it. He was going to have to talk to him, and hoped that Gable would cooperate.

After wiping down the table and the counters, Flynn joined Gable in the living room, where he was dozing in his easy chair. Maybe now wasn't the time to stir the pot and make Gable angry again. They were both tired and they hadn't decided where Gable was going to sleep yet, so Flynn pulled a chair closer and touched Gable's hand.

"Time for bed, love."

Gable slowly opened his eyes, and to Flynn's relief, he even smiled a little. "I wanted to say thank you for bringing me home and being there for me the whole time... in the hospital. And for taking care of the ranch."

Flynn shrugged. "It's nothing. It's just what you do when—"

"It's what *you* do, yes," Gable interrupted. He changed how their hands touched and squeezed Flynn's. "I know I'm not very good at...."

Flynn shook his head, more as a soothing gesture than to deny what Gable was about to say.

"Let's leave the heavy conversation for tomorrow, okay? It's been a tiring day."

Gable nodded. "I'd like to sleep upstairs. It'll take me a while to get there, though."

"I can—" Flynn wanted to say that he could help, but Gable gave him a look of warning so he closed his mouth and smiled apologetically. "I'll go up first and see that everything's ready there." He was rewarded by a smile from Gable.

It wasn't easy for Flynn to sit upstairs and wait for Gable to make it up the narrow staircase. Craig had taught Gable that as long as his arms weren't strong enough for short crutches, the easiest way was to do it sitting down and scooting up one step at a time, but Flynn felt he was taking forever. He'd already sneaked a peek at Gable's progress twice after he'd washed and changed into his pajamas. He had taken Gable's crutches up, so he could use them there as well, and Flynn sat looking at them, standing between the nightstand and the bed, when Gable appeared in the doorway, balancing on one foot.

"Those would be useful, if you don't mind?"

Flynn rushed to get them to Gable and then stepped back to let Gable pass. "Your PJs are nice and warm. I put them on the heater when I came up."

Gable just nodded, with an amused smile playing around his mouth, and Flynn was grateful he didn't lash out again, because when he thought about it, he knew he was being too much of a mother hen. It wasn't like he could help himself, so as soon as Gable was seated safely on the bed, he excused himself and left the room, just so he'd give Gable the space to get undressed by himself.

When he returned, Gable was under the covers.

"I thought you'd gone to bed?"

Flynn nodded silently. "I think I should sleep here, in case you need anything during the night."

Gable gave Flynn his warning look again, so Flynn continued. "Gable, please. I won't be able to sleep in the other room if I'm worrying about you all night. What if you fall and can't get up?"

"I'll shout for you."

"I might not hear you. Just indulge me this one bit, okay? I promise I'll let you do whatever you want to do."

Gable sighed, then conceded, so Flynn crawled into the large bed.

"I'll stay on my side, and you on yours," Flynn joked, drawing an imaginary line between them, which elicited a chuckle from Gable. Flynn lay on his side as Gable turned out the light. He knew they were both tired, but didn't think he'd be able to doze off until Gable's breathing had calmed down enough for Flynn to think he was asleep, so they both lay awake for some time. Then Flynn felt Gable's hand move closer until it wrapped around his own. He squeezed back and, content with Gable's contact, fell asleep.

Flynn woke up some time later when he sensed movement. He opened his eyes, and after a moment of adjustment, he heard Gable get up, hobble out of the room, and then return. "Everything okay?" he asked.

Gable nodded, then answered. "Needed to pee. Couldn't sleep."

Flynn waited for Gable to crawl under the covers again and then moved a little closer. "I can hold you like I used to in the hospital. If you want. It would always make you fall asleep, remember?"

After some hesitation, Gable nudged closer and Flynn held him until he became heavy in his arms. They both woke up a few times that night, and although it wasn't entirely restful, Flynn felt their first night at home was a success.

THE next morning they both came downstairs early and had a mostly silent breakfast, which wasn't all that different from before Gable's operation. Flynn went outside to take care of the horses, and despite the fact he thought it was good to leave Gable to fend for himself a bit, his mind wasn't on the work. There was too much left unsaid between them and that made Flynn feel antsy and insecure. The fact Gable hadn't wanted him in his bed last night was still causing him heartache. He understood that making love was out of the question for a while, at least until Gable regained some of his strength, but the fact it hadn't occurred to Gable that, even without sex, Flynn would want to share his bed was making him worry. Where did that leave him? What were Gable's feelings for him right now?

Walking back to the main house, Flynn resolved to attempt to broach the subject with Gable, although he had no idea where to start. When he walked inside the door, Gable was standing near the window and smiling broadly. "It's a long morning cooped up here alone."

Flynn closed the door. "I'm yours all afternoon if you want. Just have to get dinner going, but even that can wait until after lunch." He thought Gable looked like he was in a good mood. "Why don't you sit down and I'll make us a few sandwiches. I'd tempt you to the porch, but it's a bit cold to eat outside right now." He smiled, remembering the many weeks they'd spent that summer, silently devouring their lunch before going back to work.

When he returned, Flynn was not surprised he had to wake Gable up again. "Hey, sleepyhead," he said, touching Gable's hand.

Gable smiled at him and made Bridget move to the other side, so Flynn could sit down. He then took his plate from Flynn.

Flynn hoped that Gable's high spirits would make it easier to start a difficult conversation. "We need to talk, Gable."

"Okay," Gable answered, taking a large bite out of his sandwich. "This is good!"

How could he explain to Gable how he was feeling without hurting his feelings? He sighed deeply and then took an even deeper breath in. "I want to be honest with you, Gable."

Gable's smile disappeared and he looked down at his plate. "I know you want to leave, and it's okay."

Flynn didn't believe his ears. Did Gable actually *want* him to leave?

Before Flynn could formulate an answer, Gable put his plate aside and started getting up from the sofa. "Sorry, need to pee," he said by way of apology. Flynn stepped back and held out the crutches so Gable could focus on finding his one-legged balance. Then Gable yanked them out of Flynn's hands with such force it almost made him topple over. He managed to stay upright, though, and hastily made his way to the back of the house. Flynn heard him swear and hit things, but he didn't move closer until he saw a crutch fly into the hallway.

"Gable?"

No answer, just a loud bang, which sounded like a door being thrown shut. Bridget found her refuge underneath the guest bed.

Flynn tentatively walked closer to the downstairs bathroom, which was a long, narrow corridor with a toilet in the back and a wash basin near the entrance, and saw the door was still ajar. He slowly pushed it open some more.

"LEAVE! Just... GET OUT OF HERE!"

Flynn was surprised at the booming quality and commanding tone of Gable's usually very quiet and understated voice.

"Gable, I don't want to leave. I'm here for you." Flynn tried to keep his voice steady but he was only partially successful.

Suddenly the door was pulled entirely out of Flynn's hand and Gable appeared, leaning on one crutch and holding onto the door for balance. His eyes looked wild and he was red-faced and breathing heavily. "Why don't you just leave right now? I'm sure Calley will put you up for the night. It was never a problem for you to find somewhere to rest your head, right?"

"Gable, I—"

"You what?" Gable spat out, and then had to take the time to breathe. "You feeling guilty yet? I wasn't good enough for you with my bum foot, was I? Well, it's worse now. You and Calley finally got your way and now you have me where you want me. But I'm not going to be taken for a ride by the two of you. It's bad enough she has every man wrapped around her finger. I didn't think she'd get you to help her too."

Flynn couldn't quite follow Gable's train of thought; in fact, he didn't feel like his lover was making any sense at all. "Gable, please calm down."

"Just leave," Gable demanded. "Be a good boy and run upstairs for that beat-up backpack you came with and shut the door behind you when you leave. You can take the old truck, since it's not like I'll be doing any driving anyway." He tried to close the door, but had to back up and didn't quite succeed. "Fucking hell!" In his frustration, Gable knocked his fist into the wall, which happened to be adorned by a mirror, and the glass fell to the floor, shattering into a million pieces.

Flynn wanted to come inside to pull Gable away from the shards, but Gable shut the door with a bang, effectively shutting Flynn out.

"Gable, you'll hurt yourself."

"*Leave*. I never want to see you again."

Flynn felt the words sting. Even if he wanted to, he couldn't leave, he just couldn't. "Gable...."

"*Leave!*"

Flynn sank down to the floor, not daring to repeat Gable's name. He knew Gable was going to have to calm down and come to his senses eventually, but he could only hope that Gable wouldn't hurt himself before then.

—15—

FLYNN didn't know how long he sat on the floor outside the bathroom, listening to the sounds inside. He heard Gable curse and hit things and mutter and swear. Then the sounds died down, which made him even more worried.

Eventually, he knocked on the door.

When Gable didn't answer, Flynn slowly opened it and looked inside. It was half-dark, the room only illuminated by the light coming from the corridor, and he saw Gable look up at him from the other end of the room. The broken glass cracked under Flynn's shoes and he was grateful that, for once, he hadn't come into the house through the mudroom, where he would have taken his boots off.

"Can I come in?"

Gable looked dazed and confused and didn't answer.

When Flynn came closer, he saw blood on Gable's hand, and when he tried to turn on the light, he noticed the light bulb was shattered as well. Flynn quickly wet a washcloth and slowly walked toward Gable. When Gable didn't react, he sat down next to him, keeping a minimal distance without letting their bodies touch.

"Can I clean up your hand?" Flynn asked tentatively. "Will you let me check if it's okay?"

Gable didn't nod, but he held out his injured hand and let Flynn gently wipe off the dried blood. Besides a few superficial cuts, it didn't look too bad in Flynn's eyes, and he held onto Gable's hand. Gable's position was a little awkward. His bad leg was tucked under him and his side was leaning against the wall. Flynn wanted to try to coax him off the floor and into the living room, where it was also warmer.

"Are you feeling a bit better now?"

"Why are you still here?" Gable asked. Although the question sounded harsh, there was no longer any recrimination in Gable's voice, as if he simply wanted the answer to a less laden question.

"Because I couldn't leave you. Not when you were sick and certainly not now," Flynn replied truthfully. "I want us to be together, Gable, and I think you know we could make it work. Deep down, you know." Flynn wasn't as sure as he sounded, but he wanted to make sure that Gable understood that he'd made up his mind about this a long time ago.

"You should have let me die."

Flynn closed his eyes for a moment, trying not to be overcome by the emotions Gable's flatly spoken words caused him. "I couldn't do that." He rubbed his thumb over the fleshy part of Gable's palm. "I wouldn't have been able to live with myself."

"Well, I can't live with this."

Although Gable hadn't actually spoken the words, Flynn knew that for the very first time he'd acknowledged the amputation. "I know it's hard right now, but it will get better. Once you're stronger and you've learned to walk with the prosthesis, there's no reason why you wouldn't be able to ride horses and work around the ranch and take the truck into town for groceries and all that stuff. It'll take some hard work, but you've never been afraid of that, Gabe. See it as a challenge. Something else to overcome, when you've overcome so much already. It's just another hurdle."

Gable's face was still blank, but at least they were talking. Flynn softly put his hand on Gable's thigh and didn't get pushed away, which calmed him some more. "Let's get up off this cold floor and into the living room so I can clean this mess up, okay?"

It took some pulling and finagling, but eventually Flynn got Gable to the guest bed in the living room by letting Gable balance on one crutch and resting his other arm across Flynn's shoulder. Bridget came out of hiding and joined them next to the bed.

"What do you think, girl?" Flynn asked Bridget. Her ears peaked immediately. "Will you sit with Gable while I clean up the bathroom?

It didn't take Flynn long to return, and to his surprise, Gable was still awake, so he sat down next to him.

"You know, you're much more valuable to me alive than dead. Can I tell you a story?"

Gable nodded just a little.

"I told you I left home quite young, right? I worked some odd jobs on other ranches, but Dad found ways of telling my employers not to hire me, so I had to move farther away, and I ended up in the city. I got a job cooking in a greasy spoon and it was nice to be on my own and away from my family. That's where I met Lee. He was Chinese, from a very conservative Chinese family—"

"Clouds and rain," Gable interrupted.

Flynn nodded. "Yes, Lee told me about the clouds and rain."

"And showed you too?"

"Yes, he showed me too," Flynn admitted with a smile. "His parents wanted him to marry a nice Chinese girl, but we didn't care. We were happy together and that's all that mattered. We thought."

Flynn sank down next to Gable on the bed and tried to find a position where he was comfortable without crowding Gable too much. It wasn't easy on the single bed.

"So what happened? Did his parents find out?"

"Oh, they knew. Lee had told them that I was living with him."

"That's not quite the same, is it?"

Flynn turned a little so he could see Gable's expression. "No, it isn't. They were still setting him up with nice Chinese girls."

Gable put his hand on Flynn's hip and pulled him closer, so Flynn buried himself in Gable's warm embrace. "He got sick. Leukemia. It was all very sudden and there wasn't much time to talk. He knew he needed some major chemotherapy and that he'd need to stay in the hospital for a while and that's when his mother took over. She wouldn't let me visit him, and I let it happen. I thought we had time. That he'd come home when he was better and then we'd be together again, but he only got sicker." Flynn looked up at Gable. "I only found out he'd died when his father kicked me out of the apartment."

Gable pulled him into a tight embrace and rocked him.

"So you see, I had to stay with you, Gable. I couldn't go through that again. I had to fight for you, because I didn't fight for Lee."

Gable nuzzled him, and when Flynn looked up he felt Gable's lips gently touch his. Flynn wanted this so much, wanted to feel loved by Gable again. He kissed him back, at first soft and gentle, but soon enough their kiss became more passionate and Flynn's hands were all over Gable, until suddenly Gable pulled away.

"I can't, I'm sorry."

Flynn caressed Gable's jaw. "It's okay, I understand if it's all a bit soon. You still need to get your strength up."

Gable rolled to his back as much as he could on the narrow bed and covered his eyes with his hand. Flynn tried to stay patient, but Gable's silence was worrying him and he was afraid that Gable was going to crawl into his shell again.

"It's more than my strength," Gable eventually said.

"You don't want to do anything with me anymore?" Flynn asked, clearing his throat when the sounds came out a little croaky.

Gable took a deep breath. "I want nothing more than to make love to you, Flynn. I dream about it at night even, but… I suppose it doesn't matter much for a bottom…." Gable shrugged.

It was a relief that Gable still wanted him, but Gable's hesitance to tell him what was really wrong puzzled Flynn. Then again, talking about important things was never Gable's strong side.

Then it dawned on Flynn and he understood why it was a touchy subject. "You mean you can't…?" He wiggled his finger vaguely in the direction of Gable's groin.

"I can't," Gable answered calmly. "Doesn't work anymore."

"Gabe...." Flynn didn't know how to react. Gable looked sad, but not devastated, which was what Flynn knew he'd be if the shoe was on the other foot. "I don't know what to say."

Gable shrugged, but Flynn could tell he was trying to hide how much it hurt him.

"It doesn't matter to me, Gable."

"But it matters to me, Flynn," Gable replied softly. "If I didn't need you so much, I'd throw you out."

"As I recall, you did and I refused to leave," Flynn answered without thinking. It was true, of course, but as he heard himself say the words, he thought that reminding Gable of his breakdown wasn't his best idea. "Let me rephrase that." He tried lifting Gable's head so he could look at him, but Gable refused. "It does matter to me. Because I hate to see you miserable and, yes, I can't imagine myself living without sex for the rest of my life, but there's more to this, Gabe. You've been really sick. Your body needs time to heal and sex isn't exactly a priority right now."

Gable shrugged again and Flynn cringed at seeing him so defeated.

"Let's focus on you getting better first. Fight to get fit again and walking, and then we can go horseback riding again and you know that will make you feel better."

Gable nodded and Flynn pulled him closer again.

"I'll be here for you. You should know that by now," Flynn whispered, kissing Gable's temple.

"But what if it never...."

"We'll face that when it happens," Flynn answered resolutely. He had to admit to himself that it did scare him and he wasn't entirely sure he could live with a man and not share the intimacy of a relationship as well. "If there's one thing life has taught me, it's that you can't see the future and you never know what will happen. Let's just live in the now, okay?"

Gable conceded, but Flynn could tell it wasn't wholeheartedly. At least Gable wasn't pushing him away again.

"I just don't want to tie you down."

Flynn gave Gable a compassionate look. "I'm a grown man. I can leave when I want to."

Flynn knew Gable would be exhausted, so they laid together for a while until Gable fell asleep. It took some careful maneuvering but Flynn managed to move from the bed without waking Gable up, and after putting the throw over him to keep him warm, Flynn got everything ready for dinner before returning to the stables.

He mucked out T.C.'s stall, like he'd done for Brenner's that morning, and took the paint horse out for a ride around the perimeter to check the fences, something he knew he'd neglected to do in the last weeks. About three quarters of the way around, Flynn checked a part of the fence that looked like it had been recently mended and tried to recall whether this was something Gable had done before he got sick. He shrugged it away. The only thing he remembered was that he hadn't done it, but it looked pretty solid, so that was all that mattered. Near the end of his ride, he steered T.C. toward the shed where the horses sheltered themselves during storms, and there, too, he saw that a hole in the side was battened shut with a mismatched plank and some nails. It wasn't much to look at, but it clearly made the wall more solid and less penetrable by the wind, so it served its purpose. The last thing he spotted was a shiny new spring lock on a gate between Gable's ranch and Hunter's.

On the way back, Flynn considered exchanging his horse for the truck to make a quick grocery run and ask Calley whether she'd sent Bill out to help, but he decided that she'd probably deny it, even if it were true, so he went straight home again.

To Flynn's surprise, Gable was awake but still lying on the guest bed, staring into nothingness. He took his boots off and dropped them in the mudroom before sitting down next to Gable.

"Did you get a good rest?"

Gable nodded absentmindedly.

"I'll go get dinner started." Flynn patted Gable's thigh and got up from the bed.

"I'm not hungry."

Flynn turned around and sat back down. "You didn't eat lunch either and spent quite a bit of energy this afternoon. I'm making spaghetti, the way you like it, with lots of meat and fresh tomatoes from Calley's shop."

Gable nodded, but Flynn had the feeling he'd simply agreed so Flynn would leave him alone. There wasn't much he could do about it, though. He mentally picked himself up and went into the kitchen to make the spaghetti. That's all he could do, he felt; keep thinking positive thoughts and hope that it would all blow over soon. He hadn't forgotten the shouting, though, or the conviction with which Gable had told him he never wanted to see him again. Maybe he was living under the assumption that Gable loved him and maybe that wasn't the case. What if he'd just been a good fuck?

Flynn hissed as he cut himself and felt the tomato's acidity run into the wound. As he held his injured hand under the streaming water, he resolved not to make any major decisions right now. He liked working on the ranch and didn't mind the housework. Taking care of Gable made him feel needed enough to stay on, and right now that would have to be enough. Gable seemed a lot calmer, and if that meant Flynn wasn't going to be shouted at anymore, it was a good thing. Maybe somewhere in the future, the love he felt for Gable would be returned again, and if it wasn't, then he still had plenty of time to leave when Gable was better. At least then, time would have healed some of the emotional wounds.

When the sauce was simmering, Flynn went into the storage room at the back of the ranch house and took out the bed table that Calley had told him about. It needed a good scrub down, but could be useful, he supposed.

When Flynn arrived in the living room with two plates and the bed table, Gable was lying on his side on the guest bed. He was awake, but so deep in thought he didn't notice Flynn.

"I know you said you weren't hungry, but I'd like some company while I eat, okay?"

Gable sat up on the bed. "Okay."

Flynn was a little surprised when Gable didn't object to the bed table or the fact that Flynn placed a plate of food in front of him. Trying to keep his spirits up, Flynn sat down next to Gable with his back against the wall and proceeded to eat from his lap. It wasn't lost on him that Gable only picked at his food and ate very little, but he didn't want to push him now that they'd obviously reached a stalemate. When Flynn went for seconds, he actually caught Gable looking out for him when he returned from the kitchen and that made him happy. He was going to have to hold on to the little things for a while.

The next few days passed pretty much in the same way. Flynn left Gable alone for most of the morning and part of the afternoon to work on the ranch, and every time he returned he would find Gable staring at the wall. It worried him to see him so sad, but he knew Gable needed time to adjust. Gable did seem to get used to navigating around the house and was finding it easier to make his way up the stairs at night.

One afternoon, after Calley had left them their week's groceries, Flynn sat down next to Gable. "I know you think I'm too much of a mother hen, but I'll help you take a shower if you want."

"Are you telling me I smell?" Gable asked, his eyes lighting up with mischief more than sadness for the first time in weeks.

"No," Flynn answered. "I'm telling you that it might feel good to stand under a shower, but I know it will probably take a lot out of you, so if you need a helping hand…."

"I can manage," Gable replied. There was still a hint of a smile on Gable's face, and Flynn squeezed Gable's thigh before walking off to the kitchen with a much bigger smile on his own face.

A little while later, Flynn heard the bench being dragged along the concrete outside and then the spray of water hitting the floor. He quickly got a fresh bath towel out of the hall closet and put it in the slow cooker to heat it up quickly. When the shower was turned off, it took him just moments to take the warm towel outside.

When Gable spotted Flynn, he was sitting on the bench and looking like a drowned cat. He quickly covered himself up with the towel he'd brought out himself, including his injured leg.

Flynn threw the warm towel over Gable's shoulders and rubbed them dry. "Thought you might like this."

"Nice. Thanks," Gable replied quietly, sounding like he'd been caught doing something he shouldn't.

Flynn shivered in the cold evening air and could only imagine how cold Gable was. "I wouldn't have suggested the outside shower exactly...."

"Yeah, I know. I didn't realize it was this cold until I took my clothes off." Gable chuckled as he quickly looked at Flynn and then looked away again.

"Will you be okay getting back inside? Maybe you should come inside to dry off and get dressed, because it's freezing!"

Gable nodded and Flynn reluctantly left him outside. A few minutes later Flynn heard the familiar tick-tock-step sound of Gable's crutches and waited as long as he could in the kitchen before walking into the living room. By that time, Gable was half-dressed, and although he was discreet about it, Flynn couldn't help but notice how he tugged the leg of his trousers down over his stump as soon as he saw Flynn.

"You know, I don't mind seeing it. Your leg," Flynn elaborated as he sat down on the bed next to Gable.

"Well, I do," Gable replied curtly.

"I suppose I've had more time to get used to it," Flynn shrugged, trying to make light of the situation. "I saw it right after the operation and then when it was healing...."

Gable scooted further up the bed and away from Flynn, but Flynn put his hand on the cloth-covered stump. He purposely didn't look at Gable's face, knowing it could show anything from surprise to disgust, but when Gable didn't pull away, Flynn put his hand inside the trouser leg and did look Gable in the face. Feeling the stump was strange, but he hoped he could keep his face from displaying any emotions.

"It's a part of you, Gable."

Gable's eyes welled up and he looked away. "Well, I can't deal with that part of me right now."

"Don't you want to walk again? Be able to leave those cumbersome crutches behind?"

Gable didn't respond.

"We're going to have to call Craig soon, because the longer you wait, the harder it's going to be."

Gable nodded and Flynn could tell he was fighting his emotions.

"You don't have to do this alone, Gable. I'm right here for you." Flynn let go of Gable's leg and moved up the bed so he could put his arms around Gable. Although any other time it would have felt stifling, now Flynn reveled in feeling Gable cling to him.

—16—

GABLE pretended to be asleep the next morning. As usual, Flynn got up early to start work, and more often than not these days, Gable joined him for breakfast, but today Gable wasn't ready for the confrontation.

It had been an emotional evening and he really didn't want to think about what had happened, but he couldn't shake it out of his mind. Flynn's revelation that he was making up for a mistake of his youth by taking care of him now wasn't the easiest news to take, but Gable had to admit that Flynn's care was just about the only thing that had kept him from killing himself.

Flynn had stayed with him, holding him tightly against his chest, and Gable had slowly calmed down enough to talk. It was clear they'd avoided the really important subjects, talking about the ranch and how everything was going and how Flynn would need to start working more to keep the ranch going now that the winter was almost over. Later, after Flynn had helped him upstairs and they'd gone to bed, Flynn had again pulled him closer, this time with the objective of persuading him to call Craig, but Gable wasn't ready. He'd agreed with Flynn, just to get him off his back, but his leg still hurt too much to learn to walk again. He was fine getting around on his crutches. He'd done so for weeks after the accident and now that he was slowly feeling the strength return to his muscles, it was getting even easier.

The mornings were long, though, and sitting by the window trying to catch a glimpse of what Flynn was doing near the barn and the lower paddocks only kept him occupied for so long. He knew he'd be useless in the barn with his crutches, but he was longing to see Brenner and T.C. again and smell the horses. The snow had melted and he estimated he could make it there and then he could rest a bit before walking back. It was still reasonably cold outside, so Gable put on his oilskin duster and started making his way to the barn. Despite his initial courage, he had to stop halfway there to catch his breath. He wasn't about to be defeated though, especially not when it also started raining. Gable looked up at the dark sky and saw it split by lightning, so he took a deep breath and quickened his hobbling pace toward the warm and dry barn.

Gable didn't regret coming here. The smell of the horses, the hay stacked to the side, it all helped to make him feel at home again. After a particularly loud thunderclap, he heard Brenner whinny, so he made his way over to his horse's stable.

"Here, boy, everything's all right."

The horse came closer, obviously recognizing his owner, and nuzzled his hand. "Sorry, boy, didn't bring any carrots or apples," Gable apologized. He scratched the animal's nose. "Has Flynn been taking good care of you?" Brenner moved even closer by way of an answer. "Can't ride you right now, boy."

Suddenly, Gable looked toward the barn door as he heard a ruckus and saw a dripping wet figure on T.C.'s back storm into the barn. He wasn't wearing any rain gear and Gable could just make out the plaid pattern of Flynn's fleece work jacket.

As Flynn dismounted and shook the rain out of his long curls, he looked up and startled at seeing someone else in the barn.

Gable smiled at Flynn's seemingly excessive reaction. "Doing something we weren't supposed to do?"

Flynn's eyes were still closed from trying to calm his heartbeat down. "I just didn't expect anyone to be here," he answered as he looked at Gable sheepishly.

"Fair enough," Gable replied teasingly.

"I got caught out in the rain," Flynn continued, clearly trying to change the subject. "Didn't see that one coming."

"You should know by now that the weather can be a bit unpredictable here," Gable said, moving around until he could get to a bale of hay where he could sit down.

"Weather man said five percent chance of rain, and it was a clear blue sky when I left."

Gable chuckled. "I'd like to meet the weather man who can predict this weather."

Flynn sat down next to him and took off his soaking jacket. "So what are you doing out here?"

Gable shrugged. "Got tired of sitting inside and I figured I'd come visit the barn."

"Good," Flynn smiled back. "Want to go riding when the rain stops?"

Gable's face went sullen again and he shook his head.

"Brenner misses you," Flynn tried. "But maybe as a first ride, you should take T.C., since he's easier to handle?"

Gable shook his head again.

Flynn put his hand on Gable's knee. "You're an experienced rider. You don't need the stirrups. We can take them off or tie them up so they don't bother you? I'm sure you can manage."

"I still need to make it up on the horse, Flynn."

"Ah, I thought of that!" Flynn exclaimed as he got up from his seat and grabbed a handful of straw, which he wrapped into a tight ball. He walked over to T.C., who was fidgeting because he was still dripping from the rain, and started wiping the water off the paint's coat. "We get two bales of hay and stand on those and I give you a leg up."

Gable thought about it. "I don't know, Flynn."

"We don't have to do it today, but maybe tomorrow? I can take the side off the porch railing and bring T.C. to you, and you can get on from the house too," Flynn suggested. "I think the porch is about the right height."

"You really thought about this, didn't you?"

Flynn nodded. "I have a lot of time to think when I'm working. Besides, it'll give me the chance to ride Brenner some more. He needs the exercise just as much as T.C. does, but I find myself saddling up T.C. more because he's a much better workhorse. Brenner tends to get bored when we're checking fences, and then he get into all sorts of mischief." Flynn took the saddle off T.C.'s back and put it in its place near the side of the barn. He then continued rubbing T.C. dry.

Watching Flynn work gave Gable the time to think. He wanted nothing more than to go riding again, but could he? He knew he could ride without stirrups; he'd ridden T.C. bareback more than once before the accident and even after it, but he still had to get up on the horse, and he remembered how hard that was right after he'd injured his foot that first time. More importantly, could he fail in front of Flynn?

Flynn led the horse to his stable and closed the half door before coming back to where Gable was sitting, flopping down next to him with a deep sigh.

"Were you done with work?" Gable asked, moving a little bit closer to Flynn.

Flynn shook his head. "I should grease some of the leather. I broke a stirrup on one of the training saddles yesterday and I should fix that too. I fear I've been letting the maintenance slip a bit," he added softly.

"And all that after you brought it up to par again," Gable soothed, alluding to how run-down everything was before Flynn had arrived and how well he'd helped out after that. Gable raised his arm and put it across Flynn's shoulders. "I can do the saddle maintenance. It's one of those things you can do sitting down." Then he realized something. "I know this means you need to do all the leg work, but right now, that's my best offer."

Flynn nodded and even smiled slightly.

Gable was glad Flynn didn't bring up calling Craig or learning to walk again. He knew it was inevitable, but his inner procrastinator was holding him back for now.

"You're wet," Gable said, rustling Flynn's hair playfully.

Flynn snuggled closer into Gable's embrace. "So are you. Glad it's warm in here, because it's still raining cats and dogs out there."

Flynn turned his face in Gable's direction and Gable leaned forward to let their lips touch. He didn't dare press on, knowing how quickly these overtures always turned into something more, something he couldn't give Flynn right now. At first Flynn didn't deepen the kiss either, but Gable could feel him suddenly open his mouth and delve in.

Gable wanted it too, but pulled back anyway. To make the gesture less harsh, he squeezed Flynn into his arms.

"I'm sorry."

Flynn shrugged and licked his lips. "'S okay."

"Why are there two mares in the barn, Flynn?" Gable asked, hoping to break the tense situation. "These are outside kind of horses. They're used to bad weather. No need to mollycoddle them."

Flynn looked away. "I know."

"So why are they here? Are they lame? Sick? Do we have to call Bill to come and take a look at them?"

Flynn shook his head. "Bill's already seen them, and he suggested keeping them in as long as it was this cold."

Gable was getting a bit suspicious because he felt Flynn was avoiding answering the question. "There's more than fifty horses still outside. What makes these two different?"

"They're with foal."

"How did a stallion get in with the mares?" Gable was getting a little uncomfortable.

Flynn sighed. He moved away from Gable's embrace and leaned his elbows on his knees. "Listen, I know you said you didn't want to breed the horses, but Hunter wanted a foal from Brenner and I thought we could give it a try."

"Brenner sired these foals?"

Flynn nodded. "I know I should have asked."

"I explicitly said I didn't want to breed our horses," Gable interrupted. "This isn't your ranch, Flynn!"

Flynn got up and created some distance between them. "I know, but I was the only one making decisions here. And there was no money to buy new horses and I couldn't get the ones we had ready for auction on my own."

"But I know nothing about breeding horses, Flynn," Gable replied, exasperated. "And we have no money for the vet's bills as it is."

Flynn turned around. "But I do. I grew up on a stud farm."

"You weren't allowed to do any ranch work, you said!"

"Nothing could keep me away, Gabe. And my brothers didn't mind one bit if I did their chores. How do you think I got good at this? They preferred spending time with their girlfriends in the hayloft while I mucked out stalls. And Bill's doing this as a favor to you. It's only two horses, Gabe. It's an experiment."

Flynn sat down next to Gable again and Gable conceded. When Flynn took his hand, Gable sighed and leaned closer to Flynn. "I'm sorry. That wasn't fair."

"Yes, it was," Flynn replied softly. "You're right, you did tell me not to breed the horses and I just went ahead with my idea. I should have asked you first."

"I would have said no."

"I know," Flynn acknowledged. "And I really didn't want you to worry about the money."

"How bad is it?" Gable asked, although he really didn't want to hear the answer.

Flynn shrugged noncommittally and shook his head. "I think you better ask Calley about that."

"Flynn…." Gable cautioned him. "What have you been hiding from me?"

Flynn hesitated, then obviously decided it was no use. "Your hospital bills were pretty steep."

"Are you saying we're bankrupt?"

Flynn shook his head. "No, but we owe Calley and Bill a nice sum and Hunter already owns these foals."

"He took a big gamble."

Flynn nodded. "It took some persuading. I had to talk him into it, but if we ended up losing the ranch, I wanted to know I did everything to prevent it. Yes, this means that we're still working for money we've already spent, but the bank was threatening to make us sell off the horses and I couldn't let that happen. Some of those horses will fetch a good buck when we take them to auction next year and others will need more time, but if we sell them off now, they'll put them up in one big lot and we won't get half of what they're worth!"

Gable could tell Flynn was getting all worked up about it and it warmed his heart. He was talking about a future, about working toward next year and maybe even longer and he didn't even seem to contemplate leaving anymore. For the first time, Gable felt that Flynn wasn't just saying these things in an effort to take care of him; the passion with which Flynn defended his decisions made it clear that he was doing it for himself as well.

"You really like it here, don't you?" Gable asked quietly.

"Of course I do," Flynn answered without hesitation. "You have no idea what this means to me, Gabe. I love working here. I love the horses and the fact that most of the work is done outdoors—"

"In the pouring rain," Gable interrupted with a chuckle.

"I don't mind the rain. I like it better when I'm wearing something like you're wearing, but even when it's as cold as it is now and you saddle a horse and ride up to the paddock and see them all standing there, huddled together for warmth, it's just great."

"Yeah, I know," Gable agreed quietly.

Flynn leaned closer and moved until he could kiss Gable. Again, it was a chaste kiss, full of tenderness, and Gable let his hand caress Flynn from his shoulders until he could rest it in the small of his back. It felt good to feel Flynn close, to smell his slightly musky scent, although since he had come in from the rain, he also had some "wet dog" about him. For some reason that made Gable smile, and Flynn pulled back, looking a little puzzled.

"I was just thinking this felt good," Gable explained shyly.

Flynn smiled at him and Gable could see his eyes light up. "I'll do anything to make you smile," he whispered, nuzzling Gable.

"Don't," Gable replied. To take the insecurity from Flynn's face, he continued. "You're your own person. I don't want your happiness to depend on mine. I'm a morose SOB, Flynn."

"And I still love you," Flynn replied. "Go figure."

Gable sighed. "I'm sorry I blew up over the pregnant mares."

"I'm sorry I didn't consult you." Flynn suddenly shivered violently.

"You're cold." Gable opened his oilskin duster and enveloped Flynn in it, pulling him closer and enjoying the feeling of Flynn's arms snaking underneath it to wrap around him.

Flynn inhaled deeply. "I could get used to this, but I'm hungry. I think we should go inside."

The moment was too short. Flynn pulled away from Gable, leaving Gable to feel the cold, as they heard the sound of Bridget's nails on the barn floor and then her shaking her fur out.

"Hey, girl, did you come to fetch us?" Flynn asked her. He scratched her head. "You're practically dry. Has it stopped raining?" She cocked her head as if to say, "Sure it has. Would I come out here if it were wet outside?"

Flynn came closer again and quickly kissed Gable. "Mmmh, we should probably take advantage of the fact it's stopped raining and go back to the house. Not to mention I need to feed you." He poked Gable in the ribs. "You're still way too skinny."

After Flynn extricated himself again, Gable got up and was handed his crutches. Just as Flynn turned around to leave, Gable couldn't help but speak. "Flynn." He hesitated, especially when Flynn turned to face him, still smiling as he was stroking Bridget. "What is keeping you here?"

"Gable," Flynn said, as if the answer to that was obvious.

"I'm sorry, but I need to know."

"I'm staying because this is what I always wanted." Flynn took a step closer, but then stopped. "A ranch with horses, small enough to manage with just the two of us. We work hard, but in the end it's all worth it, right? Gable, I want to grow old here. If I live a long life and they bury me in this soil at the end of it, I'll have had a great life."

Gable looked down at the straw on the floor.

"But the one thing that's keeping me here is you, Gable. The fact that I can share this with you. And I know I'm presuming a lot. This is your ranch and it will always be yours, but I hope you'll let me run it with you."

"You do all the work." Gable still couldn't look at Flynn. He wasn't prepared to see that look in Flynn's eyes. The look that told him how much Flynn loved him. He couldn't look up because it made him feel guilty, because he knew all too well how little he gave back to Flynn.

"You know I don't mind. I know it won't be like this forever. One day you'll feel good enough to work with me again."

Gable swallowed to hold back the emotions, but Flynn was too close to him. He could smell him and feel the warmth radiating off him and then he felt Flynn's lips against his forehead.

Flynn shushed him and kissed him again. "Let's go inside before heaven's floodgates open again, 'kay?" Flynn pulled back and walked toward the barn door. "I love you, Gable. That's all that matters." And with that he disappeared around the corner, taking Bridget with him and leaving Gable alone in the barn.

Gable waited for a while and then spoke to the horses. "Did you hear that, guys? He loves me. He must be crazy, but hey, I take it as it comes."

—17—

FLYNN briskly walked back to the house with a much lighter heart. It felt good to know that Gable knew exactly where they stood. Flynn also knew that hearing himself say the words made him believe them even more. Yes, he loved Gable, with all of his heart. They'd been through hell and back and still had a lot of healing to do, but at least Gable hadn't pulled away or denied any of Flynn's feelings, and he hadn't been even half as mad as Flynn had predicted he'd be when he told him about his little horse-breeding experiment.

Bridget darted around him, clearly picking up on his happy mood. It was only now he realized how withdrawn the dog had been these past weeks. "You happy, girl?" The dog jumped up at him, and he took her head between his hands and rubbed behind her ears. "Think Gable's happy too?" She tried to lick him. "Yeah, I think he will be happy too, from now on."

They made their way inside the house and Flynn decided to take a quick shower before starting dinner. When he came downstairs again, dressed in clean, warm, and above all, dry clothes, Gable was sitting at the kitchen table, fixing Bridget's dinner. Flynn couldn't stop smiling, realizing what a difference he saw in Gable. Was it the trip to see the horses or his declaration of love that had brought about this change? In any case, Flynn was glad to see Gable take the initiative to do things other than sit on his daybed and stare into nothingness.

"You're going to get a five-star dinner, girl," Flynn told Bridget, who was sitting next to Gable, tongue dangling and an expectant look directed at her master. She barely looked away from the meat Gable was carving up for her to acknowledge Flynn's words, but then Flynn wasn't looking at her either. He was looking at Gable, who was smiling. Flynn couldn't resist the temptation to walk behind him and put his hand on Gable's shoulder.

"I'll start dinner, okay?" Flynn said more than asked Gable.

"Potatoes are peeled," Gable stated as if this was the most natural thing in the world.

"Thank you," Flynn answered quietly, unable to form a more eloquent answer. He walked toward the stove, where he found the pot with the potatoes, glad Gable was too preoccupied with Bridget's dinner to see the mix of emotions on his face. Flynn couldn't think what had brought about this change in his lover, but he was happy about it. It meant Gable was finally moving forward instead of dwelling on the past, and that was surely a good thing. Maybe the overture in the barn also meant that Flynn's stolen touches would be returned again. He hated to admit it to himself, but he needed more from Gable than Gable had recently given him, and sex was only a small part of it. He didn't dare bring it up, though, fearing Gable would retreat back into his shell again. He was going to have to coax it out of him in other ways.

As Flynn was standing over the hot pots, his nose started tingling and running, so he blew it in a paper towel.

"Getting a cold?" Gable asked, looking concerned.

"Nah," Flynn shrugged it away. "I'll be okay."

Gable smiled at him and Flynn knew that would make it all better, even though running around in wet clothes on a cold day was probably what had caused this.

Dinner passed quickly and they didn't talk about anything important, simply exchanged ideas about the ranch and talked about the money they owed, and Flynn reveled in the openness and positive attitude he felt now. After the dishes were done, Flynn returned to the barn to make sure all the horses were comfortable for the night.

On his way out, after he'd turned off the light in the barn, he tripped over a bucket he didn't remember leaving there and instantly felt uncomfortable. Having an unknown benefactor fix a gate and a lean-to was one thing. It could easily have been one of their neighbors who knew about Gable's illness and decided to lend a hand. But finding things out of place in the barn, so close to their golden mares and equally close to the house, didn't sit right with Flynn. For all he knew, this stranger had less than good intentions, and although no items had gone missing, Flynn wished there was a better way to secure the house and the animals. Then again, Gable's house didn't even have a key to lock the front door, so finding ways of locking up the barn was probably overkill.

Flynn put the bucket where it belonged and closed the barn door before walking back to the house.

"Anything wrong with the horses?" Gable asked from the daybed as Flynn entered the house.

"No, they're fine. Why?"

"You look worried."

Flynn sat down next to Gable and put a hand on his knee. "I hope nothing happens to them. Those foals are worth a lot of money."

"I'm sure they'll be fine," Gable replied, soothingly placing his arm around Flynn's shoulders.

Flynn turned into the embrace and hesitantly kissed Gable. To his surprise, the kiss was not only returned, but instantly deepened. Flynn gladly let Gable take the lead. It felt like a natural progression from what they'd done in the barn earlier, and Flynn had a hard time restraining himself from letting it go even further. After such a long time without feeling Gable's touch, Flynn's body was clamoring for more, and now Gable seemed to be picking that up. The heat was rising way too fast, so Flynn pulled back.

"Easy, Gabe."

Gable hugged him closer. "Why don't we go upstairs? Or is it too soon for bed?"

Flynn understood the double entendre, but decided to play it safe for now. "It's dark out, so I don't see why it's too soon."

Gable smiled and got up, taking a little longer than Flynn to make it to the stairs. Flynn waited for him, tidying the room some to not make it too obvious. Gable was getting quite adept at walking up the stairs with his crutches now, so it didn't take long.

The tension was still there, though, the same tension that was there every night they went to bed. It had eased some after the few times Gable had stopped Flynn from coming closer at night. They now each slept on their own side of the bed, rarely touching anymore, but Flynn hoped that was about to change again. He decided to flaunt it a bit, walking around the bedroom in only his boxer shorts as he put his clothes away. He didn't need to look at Gable to see that his lover's eyes were following him as Gable changed into the long-legged pajama bottoms he had taken to wearing after the operation.

Since Gable didn't seem to have any plans of making overtures, Flynn had no other choice than to crawl into his side of the bed. He was almost shaking with anticipation, though.

"Do you want to...?" Flynn asked hesitantly.

"Yes," Gable answered, so quickly and with such conviction that they launched themselves toward each other without much care for the power of their impact. Their kisses were passionate from the word go, open-mouthed and intense, and Flynn couldn't help his hands from wandering. When he cupped Gable's ass and pulled him closer, grinding their bodies together, Gable pulled away.

"I'm sorry. Got carried away," Flynn apologized, immediately loosening his grip.

Gable leaned his forehead against Flynn's. He was panting heavily. "Don't apologize. I want you to fuck me." Gable immediately kissed Flynn again, as if he wanted to stop Flynn from protesting, but now it was Flynn's turn to retreat.

"Gabe?" Flynn tried to look Gable in the eye, but Gable averted his gaze. It wasn't that he didn't want to make love to Gable; in fact, he was incredibly turned on and he knew his body showed all the signs of it. But Flynn didn't see the same reactions in Gable, making him wonder why Gable had asked him.

"Flynn, please. Don't make me beg for it. I need to feel you," Gable murmured before kissing Flynn again.

Flynn didn't need to be asked twice. He wanted to feel Gable too, wanted to recapture that one night they'd really connected physically. It had been in this bed and Flynn remembered it vividly, despite the fact it was months ago and surrounded by two less-fortunate bouts of lovemaking.

The abstinence made his power to resist Gable dwindle, and Gable's hands on him made the nagging feeling that Gable was only doing this to please him fade quickly.

"Okay," Flynn finally whispered, feeling the urgency of his body's needs.

Gable turned around, settling on his side with his back toward Flynn. It wasn't Flynn's favorite position, but it did mimic the way they'd made love here before, so Flynn took the lube out of the bedside drawer and molded himself against Gable's back. He kissed his neck and felt Gable lower his pajama bottoms.

"You know I don't need much prep. Just fuck me, please."

Gable's hand between their bodies was making it crystal clear to Flynn that he wanted this desperately, and Flynn was beyond protesting. He slicked up his erection with the lube and rubbed it over Gable's puckered opening.

"Yeah, like that," Gable moaned.

It was no surprise to Flynn that he easily slipped inside. He was desperately trying not to give in to his body, which demanded that he thrust deeper. Gable turned his torso toward Flynn and kissed him, making the heat rise even more. Flynn let his hand wander over Gable's chest to his belly, but was swatted away.

"No," Gable whispered, his voice somewhat strained, at the same time pushing his ass back to urge Flynn on.

Their position was a bit awkward but it did make it less objectionable for Flynn, who always missed kissing when he was spooning.

Gable hitched up his top leg. "Come on, Flynn, Show me what you got."

Flynn pushed in a few times. Gable groaned in response and Flynn stopped holding back. His body was demanding some sort of release, but as Gable swatted his hand away again, Flynn started feeling like he always did during a one-night stand. He listened to his body, but knew already that his orgasm wouldn't be a satisfying one. He was beyond stopping, though, and hoped he could still make it good for Gable. If only Gable would let him.

"Please tell me you're close too?" Flynn murmured when they came up for air in between kisses.

Gable didn't respond immediately, but Flynn could tell from his expression that the answer was "no." Still, Gable pulled him closer, and Flynn was already too far gone to stop himself from coming. As his hips reflexively thrust forward a few times, he felt the familiar tension build up in his groin and, despite feeling selfish again, he came.

Like Flynn predicted, it wasn't very satisfying. He was panting from the exertion, but in no way riding the blissful cloud he had been aiming for. Seeing the rather sad, defeated look on Gable's face completed the picture, and the air seemed to have been sucked out of the room all of a sudden. Flynn couldn't breathe. All he could do was pull back and run. Get out.

Flynn got out of bed and grabbed some clothes from the chair. He ran out of the room and down the stairs, then out the front door. It was cold out, and dark, but he didn't care. He needed air and he needed solitude.

"FLYNN, come inside. You already have a cold and I don't want you to get sick."

"Go back upstairs. I'm fine."

"I came all the way down here, I'm not about to crawl back up there without apologizing, but I want you to come inside first."

"Just give me a minute. I need some time to think." Flynn sneezed, making it all the more clear to him that Gable was the rational one and he should listen to him. He'd come down here to get away from Gable, thinking that Gable wouldn't struggle down those narrow stairs on his crutches, but he had been wrong. It was damn cold, though, and he was shivering, which wasn't surprising since he was wearing next to nothing.

The door behind him opened again.

"If I go back upstairs, will you come inside?"

Flynn turned toward Gable and nodded. "But stay here. We need to talk."

Gable looked concerned, and Flynn knew his words were only going to make that worse, but he had no choice. Too much had been left unsaid and this night was another prime example of that. He walked inside, Gable holding the door open as best he could, leaning on his crutches. As Flynn felt the warm air from inside, he shivered violently. He wanted to throw himself into Gable's arms, but besides not being very practical, it would also defeat the purpose. They were going to have to talk and that meant not sitting too close to each other.

It wasn't until he passed Gable that Flynn noticed Gable was carrying his oilskin coat. He threw Gable a short thankful look and took it from him before putting it on and going inside.

"I figured since yours was still drying...." Gable said, with clear hesitation in his voice. "We should really buy you one of these too. The rain flows right off them and they're very warm."

Flynn huddled into the coat and sat down in the single chair next to the daybed, slowly feeling the warmth seep into him. It didn't hurt that it smelled of Gable.

"It's expensive," Flynn replied, knowing he was just looking for something to say that was less laden than what he was supposed to talk to Gable about.

Gable shrugged as he sat down on the daybed, but Flynn could tell he was nervous and trying hard not to show it. Then Gable's expression changed.

"You've been crying."

Flynn shook his head and wiped his face with his hand. "It's bloody cold out," he replied, knowing he was lying and Gable was right.

"I'm sorry if I made you cry."

Now it was Flynn's turn to shrug. He couldn't look Gable in the eye, though, not even when Gable scooted a little closer. Flynn knew it would be hard for Gable to keep his balance, leaning toward him from the daybed to touch him, with only one leg to keep him from falling forward. Flynn allowed Gable to take his hand, but he didn't squeeze it.

"I'm sorry I made you do something you didn't want to do."

Flynn shook his head. "I wanted it so badly, Gable. I wanted to make love to you so badly, but I wanted it to be good for you too. Not like this. Not like it was." He vaguely gestured upstairs.

Gable pulled their joined hands toward him, and at first Flynn resisted, but he couldn't hold out for long. He wanted Gable to hold him and tell him everything would be okay, even if he knew it wasn't true. He allowed himself to be pulled to his feet and onto the narrow daybed next to Gable. He let Gable kiss him too, not the passionate hungry kisses that had led to the debacle upstairs, but slow, tender, and chaste kisses.

"I wish I could give you more, but I wanted it too. I wanted to feel you inside me, hoping it would wake something up down there, but it didn't. The doctors told me it could possibly recover, but they warned me that it might not."

When Flynn finally dared to look into Gable's eyes, he saw they were wet too. He ran his hand over Gable's cheeks, even though no tears had rolled down them.

"I meant what I said, Gabe. I'm not leaving."

"You deserve a real man," Gable protested.

"You are as real to me as I need," Flynn replied firmly. "We'll find a way to make this work."

"You deserve better."

"No, I don't." Flynn shook his head determinedly. "I can live without the sex, Gable, but I can't live without this. I need to be allowed to be close to you. I need to be allowed to hold you and touch you and kiss you without feeling that you can't wait to get away from me. And I need the little things too, the little gestures between lovers. I need you to touch me too. I need you to want to touch me and not get the feeling you're just doing it out of some sort of…. " Flynn couldn't immediately find the right words.

"I need this too, Flynn."

‌‌‌‌

‌‌‌‌‌‌‌‌‌‌

"I know," Flynn nodded and kissed Gable again. "Don't think I didn't notice all those times you took my hand in the middle of the night when you thought I was asleep."

It was a relief to just let himself enjoy the intimacy and not feel the tension caused by their mutual sexual frustration. Gable had snaked his arms underneath the heavy coat Flynn was still wearing and Flynn was caressing Gable's naked back underneath the T-shirt Gable had hastily put on before coming downstairs. This was what Flynn needed more than the sex. Still, he was surprised to feel himself grow hard again. He couldn't pull away, though. Not after he'd admitted to Gable that was the bit that hurt the most, so he stayed close, trying to ignore his body's demands.

Of course, Gable noticed.

They broke for air, stopping their kissing but not moving away from each other.

"Let me take care of that?" Gable whispered against Flynn's temple as he let his hand wander down between Flynn's legs.

"No, it's okay. It'll go away." Flynn gently pulled Gable's hand away.

"I want to, Flynn. Don't take this away from me too."

Flynn looked into Gable's eyes and saw no reason to believe Gable didn't mean what he said. His conflicting feelings returned, since he wanted to be able to give something back to Gable as well, but then he realized that maybe Gable felt the same. Maybe Gable wanted to selflessly give something to Flynn too?

As soon as Flynn stopped resisting, Gable broke eye contact, pulled Flynn's T-shirt up, and started kissing his way down Flynn's chest. By the time Gable had licked Flynn's nipples until they'd pebbled and then moved down to his belly button and his hip bones, Flynn was rock hard and having a hard time not leading Gable's head toward his leaking cock. He had tried to simply lie back and enjoy the feeling of Gable worshipping him, but he couldn't stop looking at what Gable was doing to his body as Gable pulled Flynn's boxers down. Flynn was happy to see Gable smile just before he took his cock in his mouth and couldn't stifle a groan when Gable sucked on the fleshy column. Gable's clear enjoyment of what he was doing only added to Flynn's pleasure, slowly pushing away the feeling he was being selfish for allowing Gable to satisfy him in this way. Gable clearly knew what he was doing and Flynn was certain he wouldn't last long. Flynn instinctively spread his legs a bit and Gable responded by cupping his balls, then slowly massaging the sensitive skin behind Flynn's sac. Flynn dug his fingers into the mattress, his knuckles white from the force he was exerting. He knew he was making a lot of noise, but he didn't care. This felt so good, he had no intention of holding it all in. When Gable's finger slipped into his entrance, Flynn roared and reared up, unable to resist pushing into Gable's mouth and coming violently.

The next thing Flynn remembered was feeling the heaviness of Gable's body against his and a blanket being pulled around him. When he moved instinctively into the warm embrace, his mouth was captured by Gable's and he could taste his own release in Gable's mouth.

"Don't think I ever made a lover pass out on me before."

Flynn opened his eyes slightly and looked straight into Gable's self-assured smirk.

"I didn't pass out," Flynn defended himself. "It was just... pretty intense."

Gable pulled Flynn closer and Flynn felt the warmth of Gable's love spread inside him. He wanted to stay just like this for all eternity.

"Thank you," he murmured.

"For what? Don't think for a minute that I didn't enjoy that too."

Although Flynn wasn't so sure he could believe Gable, he was tired and it was the middle of the night, so he snuggled closer into Gable's warm embrace and allowed himself to fall asleep.

—18—

"YOU should stay in, Flynn," Gable commented after Flynn sneezed for the fourth time since he sat down in the kitchen to have breakfast.

"No, I'm okay," Flynn answered, his nose sounding really stuffed up. "It's just a cold. The horses need me."

Gable raised his eyebrow, but didn't say any more. He knew he couldn't win when Flynn had his mind set on something. If Flynn was really as sick as his red eyes suggested, he'd be back inside as soon as the most necessary maintenance was done and he'd reassured himself that the horses in the paddock were doing fine. And why wouldn't they? They weren't pampered riding horses, but sturdy outdoor working horses. "At least wear my oilskin then? It's a lot warmer than your coat, and since it's raining again...." Gable didn't finish his sentence.

"Okay," Flynn conceded.

Gable smiled. Getting Flynn out of the house did have its benefits. He was trying to build up his strength a bit before calling Craig, because he knew the physiotherapist would give him one hell of a lecture about waiting so long to call. He finally felt ready to move on, but he knew he couldn't do it alone. He just didn't want Flynn to get his hopes up too much. At least not yet.

"I'll do the dishes," Gable offered after Flynn finished most of his plate.

"You sure?" Flynn asked skeptically.

"Sure," Gable shrugged, trying to sound matter-of-fact. "You know I'm getting around quite well on these crutches now. If I can walk to the barn, I can putter around the kitchen."

Flynn still looked like he wasn't entirely convinced, but he got up anyway, putting on Gable's oilskin duster before venturing outside. Gable got up as soon as Flynn closed the door behind him and watched him until he disappeared into the barn. Then he positioned himself between the kitchen table and the sink and started on the dishes.

It took him longer than it used to before the operation, since Flynn had moved certain items, like the dishwashing liquid and the fresh towels, but still, Gable didn't take too long. After one more quick look outside to assure himself Flynn was nowhere near the house, Gable got down on the daybed and started doing crunches and sit-ups. He'd started doing them a few days ago and it was getting easier every day. Gable also did push-ups to strengthen his back and his arms and was slowly finding his balance doing them again, with only one foot to support himself. He was sure Craig would be able to give him pointers when he called him later.

The first day he'd started exercising, Bridget had stared at him as if she were mystified by his strange actions, but by now she only looked up when he got started and then put her head down on her front paws again.

Now he'd finally made the decision to get on with life, it couldn't happen fast enough for Gable. He wanted to work outside again, ride a horse and spend time in the pastures riding with the herd. He also wanted to help Flynn train the horses. He knew it would take time for him to regain all his abilities, to be able to mount a skittish, nervous young horse and simply by his own physical self-control and inner calmness, make that horse tolerate him on his back. Until he could do that again, he wanted to be out there with Flynn, helping him with everything else that needed to be done. Gable hoped Flynn would allow him to give him pointers. He was older, after all, and he'd been training horses since he was old enough to ride, which, in sheer years, was much longer than Flynn.

Gable's sudden impatience hadn't been rewarded, though. When he called Craig, the therapist had laughed at him and joked it was about time he came to his senses, insisting that Gable had to come into town for his temporary prosthesis to be fitted before he could begin his rehabilitation. There was no way Craig could do it at the ranch. The problem was that Gable didn't want to tell Flynn yet.

Gable was going to have to find a way to get Flynn away from the ranch so he could ask Calley to drive him into town. He didn't like having to ask someone to help him, but for now, he'd have to swallow his pride.

GABLE had already made preparations for dinner when Flynn finally arrived back at the ranch house. Gable saw him jogging over from the barn, water streaming down from his hat and off the bottom of his coat, and went to meet him at the entrance to the mudroom. When Gable opened the door, he saw Flynn shiver.

"Come inside. The fire's on, but you better jump in a hot shower or you'll get even sicker than you already are," Gable cautioned him.

Flynn sneezed before he could answer, so Gable shook his head and left him to take off his wet things and come inside.

"Smells good in here," Flynn remarked after joining Gable in the kitchen.

"I can peel potatoes and boil them. Same with the veggies. I can broil a steak, but you'll need to add the fancy trimmings, I'm afraid," Gable said, smiling. He quickly accepted Flynn's kiss. "Now go upstairs and warm up because you're cold to the bone."

When Flynn returned ten minutes later, he was wearing dry clothes and his wet curls were all over the place. He also looked slightly flushed. Gable wasn't sure whether that had anything to do with him standing under a hot shower, or whether Flynn had used his shower time to take care of a little urge. Although Gable was tempted to joke about it, he didn't. He quietly hoped that the weather would soon turn warmer so Flynn would take his showers downstairs and he'd get to watch. Then again, maybe a better bet was for him to get more mobile so he could follow Flynn upstairs as soon as he heard the shower being turned on.

Flynn came up behind Gable and hugged him close. "Add some salt and pepper," he suggested, looking over Gable's shoulder at the kale he was searing in the pan. "Let me get a little lemon juice."

"No, stay," Gable asked playfully, grabbing Flynn's hands around his waist to keep them there.

At first, Flynn complied, even squeezing Gable a little tighter, but then he let go anyway. "I'll be back. I like your style of cooking."

Flynn grabbed a lemon out of the fridge and cut it in half with the studied casualness of someone who used to do this for a living. He then squeezed it over the kale, his hand underneath it to catch any pits that might fall from the fruit. The pan sizzled and steamed, but the aroma was amazing. Flynn also took out a clove of garlic and started carving it up.

"You know, before you came along, I didn't have all that fancy stuff in my kitchen," Gable remarked.

Flynn chuckled. "I remember what your kitchen looked like the day I arrived." He shuddered theatrically. "It was not the sort of place I wanted to prepare food in. I'm still surprised you managed not to poison yourself."

"Well, that's not the only thing you turned around in my life," Gable said, turning toward Flynn.

Flynn looked him in the eye and moved into Gable's personal space. Gable thought he was going to get a kiss, but Flynn sort of hovered. "I'll make a good wife out of you yet."

Gable raised an eyebrow and pulled back without stepping away. "Meaning?"

Flynn smiled, unable to hold his serious face. "You're cooking already. Pretty soon you can do the cleaning too, and the laundry."

"I've always done the laundry," Gable defended himself.

"Okay, I'll give you that," Flynn conceded. "So just the cleaning?" he teased.

Gable growled at him and let go of one of his crutches to grab the back of Flynn's head and kiss him.

"Mmmh, I love to get you all riled up," Flynn admitted with a groan after Gable let go of him. "Is this the sort of thing it takes to get you to top?"

For a moment, Gable was taken aback, given their fiasco of the night before, but Flynn didn't even blink, so he straightened his face. "Who needs to top when they have you?" he quipped.

Flynn molded himself against Gable. "Sometimes, I don't mind turning the tables."

"I'll have to remember that," Gable replied, leaning toward Flynn to kiss him again.

Suddenly Flynn broke the kiss. He pushed Gable aside and almost made him topple over.

"Damn, we ruined the kale. I knew this was going to happen." He laughed and took the burned pan off the fire, throwing it in the sink and opening the faucet to cool it off.

"We can always open a can of beans," Gable suggested.

"We're hopeless, aren't we?" Flynn said.

Gable moved closer and was happy to see a broad smile on his face. "Maybe we are, but at least we're hopeless together?"

Flynn nodded. "Yeah, at least we're together."

BECAUSE of their little mishap in the kitchen, dinner was decidedly more bachelorlike than usual, but neither seemed to mind.

"I was talking to Hunter," Gable said casually, biting into a nice piece of steak. "He's a wrangler short to muster a large group of horses. I suppose he wants to sell some and I suggested asking you. Unless you're too sick, of course."

"I'm not too sick," Flynn was quick to answer. "This cold will be gone in a day or two. I can work. When does he need me?"

Gable was glad Flynn seemed so eager. He tried hard not to look too happy, though. "Day after tomorrow. He'll need you most of the day. He suggested sending one of his ranch hands over to help here, but I said we could manage. Nothing much going on here anyway. Besides, we'll probably need his ranch hands at a later date anyway. He's going to pay you for your work, of course." Gable looked at Flynn sideways to gauge his lover's reaction, but Flynn seemed oblivious. Of course he'd called Hunter and asked him whether he could do him a favor. He knew Hunter, with his big ranch, was always short of able hands, and with the winter almost over, as they were moving herds to higher paddocks, they were stretched pretty thin. It was a little white lie, but Gable wanted to keep his secret a little while longer.

TWO days later, Gable called Calley as soon as Flynn had left. It was the one day she had help in the store and could leave for a few hours.

"Glad you're back in the land of the living," Calley remarked as they were driving into town. "At least you look good. Flynn is taking good care of you."

"I can take care of myself, thank you," Gable was quick to answer. Then he realized it sounded a bit harsh. "We're good," he reassured Calley. "He does take good care of me, but now it's time I started taking care of myself again."

Calley raised an eyebrow and looked at Gable sideways, but soon turned her eyes to the road again. They settled into their usual silence, with Gable staring out to the side of the road. The drive took some time but neither felt the need to fill that time with small talk.

"I can manage," Gable stated as Calley dropped him off at the entrance of the hospital. "I'm sure you'd much rather go shopping or something instead of waiting for me in here." That might be true for a lot of women, but Gable knew Calley wasn't one of them; still, he knew she wouldn't argue with him. "Pick me up in about two hours?"

She gave him an annoyed look, but nodded and then drove off. Gable knew he'd have to make it up to her somehow, but she wouldn't hold it against him. They went back too far for that.

As soon as Calley's car was out of sight, Gable turned around and made his way inside the hospital. It was quite a big place and he soon had to stop to catch his breath and let the pain in his leg die down. He cursed under his breath like he did every time he was confronted with the limitations of his body, and when he realized he'd taken a wrong turn somewhere in the vast labyrinth, he conceded and sat down for a moment in one of the waiting areas. He was already late for his appointment with Craig, but he really needed a few moments to recuperate. From the other side of the room, a gaunt, bald child in a wheelchair smiled at him and his mood lifted. Why was he feeling down? He'd lost a foot, would have to learn to walk again, but he was pretty healthy otherwise. This kid was probably dying of some really bad disease and might never see the outside of the hospital again, yet she was smiling and seeking contact with a stranger. Gable smiled back and the girl's eyes lit up. He waved, and she shook her mother's arm to tell her about this strange man across the room waving at her.

Gable got up again and winked at her. He hobbled to the reception counter and asked for directions to the physical rehabilitation department, and found it was just around the corner.

CRAIG was happy to see him, but as Gable had predicted, he gave him a lecture on why he should have come by earlier.

"Muscles are wasting away, man," Craig cautioned him. "Hasn't that boyfriend of yours commented on it yet? I bet you no longer have a nice, symmetrical ass."

Gable narrowed his eyes but didn't react. Craig had always been a bit brash, but he was a good therapist and knew how to get him just mad enough that he would want to prove him wrong. Also, Gable was standing upright between two bars and Craig was behind him, squeezing him in all sorts of appropriate and maybe not so appropriate places.

"You've been working out, though?" Craig asked as he came into Gable's field of vision. He was wiggling his eyebrows, which made Gable roll his eyes.

"Yes," Gable answered, unable to hide the fact he was quite pleased Craig had noticed. Although he was fully dressed, Craig's unashamed staring at his body made Gable feel very self-conscious. It also made him feel strangely aware of the physiotherapist. He shook his head. This guy wasn't even his type. In his wilder years, when he used to drive into the city to cruise and get laid, he might have taken a guy like Craig up on it. But right now, even if his body had been in full working order, he wasn't going to.

"You'll need to work harder," Craig deadpanned, bringing Gable right back down to the ground. "Let's take the casting so we can make you a temporary prosthesis, and then we'll agree on a schedule for your exercises."

Gable nodded. He wasn't looking forward to this, but he wasn't the type to run away from the hard realities of life. At least not when he'd finally decided he was going to give it his all.

GABLE didn't return home until later that afternoon. He'd taken Calley out to lunch to smooth their friendship over a bit and to get his mind off that morning. Having the casting made had been a major confrontation. Craig had examined the stump carefully and had made Gable look at it with him, instructing him what to look out for once he was wearing the prosthesis. He'd cautioned him to not overdo it and check for small wounds around the amputation site to make sure he kept his leg in full working order. Although Craig was happy with the way everything had healed, for Gable it was hard to look at what was left of his lower leg. He'd long since forgiven Flynn and Calley for agreeing to the operation, but that didn't mean it was any easier to be confronted with the result.

Once he was home, he realized just how worn out he was. He knew he had to start on dinner, because Flynn would be coming home pretty tired as well, but right now he didn't have the energy, so he laid himself down on the daybed and soon dozed off.

When some noise woke him up, it was getting dark outside, and he was wiping the sleep out of his eyes when Flynn walked in from the mudroom. He didn't look like he was in a good mood.

"Everything okay?" Gable asked cautiously.

"Yeah, fine," Flynn answered flatly. "What's for dinner?" He didn't wait for an answer as he ran upstairs. Gable figured he was going to take a shower, so he got up from the daybed and hobbled to the kitchen on his crutches.

When Flynn came back downstairs, yesterday's leftover potatoes were frying in the pan and Gable was adding some vegetables and getting ready to throw a couple of eggs over it. "Omelets okay with you?" he asked Flynn, who nodded. "You better add the seasoning then," Gable added, trying to be more lighthearted than Flynn looked.

Flynn still didn't smile, but stood next to Gable at the stove. Gable looked at him while he was adding salt and pepper and a bit of cayenne, but Flynn was either ignoring him or his thoughts were miles away.

"So how was it at Hunter's?"

Flynn threw him a stern look.

"Must have been nice to work on a big ranch again?" Gable asked, trying to get Flynn to loosen up.

Flynn sighed and then turned toward Gable. "Why did you send me there?"

Gable shook his head as if he had no idea what Flynn was getting at. Deep down, he was worried that Flynn was on to something, though.

"They looked like they were surprised to see me. They had a hard time finding stuff for me to do, as if I was just some day laborer Hunter had picked up at a stoplight. We moved some horses, and I fixed a few bridles and mucked out some stalls. Happy?"

Gable couldn't help feeling the anger in Flynn's words. Damn Hunter! Then again, he couldn't blame Hunter for this. He was going to have to make amends with Flynn.

"I'm sorry, I—"

"Why did you need me to be away from the ranch, Gable?" Flynn interrupted him. "I'm your partner, Gabe. At least I thought I was, after everything we've been through. What's going on? Are you taking Grant back?"

Gable was flabbergasted. "Wh-what are you talking about? What does Grant have to do with this?"

"Grant's working Hunter's ranch," Flynn spat out. Gable could tell Flynn was slowly losing his cool, so he moved a little closer. "He's working this place too, although I haven't caught him in the act yet. Well, I had plenty of time to think while I was mucking out Hunter's stables and I figured that was why you wanted me gone. Grant's been here, hasn't he?"

"Flynn?" Gable called after him, but Flynn had run outside by the time he reacted.

"I haven't seen Grant since he left me, Flynn," Gable said, standing in the doorway and looking at Flynn standing on the porch. Flynn's hair was still wet from his shower and it was cold outside. "Come inside to talk before you get sick again."

Flynn didn't budge.

"I know he came to the hospital because you told me, but I don't remember. I swear I haven't seen him since then."

Flynn swallowed, but seemed calmer already. Gable hoped he would come inside soon.

"Why wasn't I allowed to be around the ranch today?"

Flynn's voice was calm, but he was still looking sternly toward the barn.

Gable knew he would have to tell Flynn the truth and expose his little white lie. "I went to the hospital today."

"Why?" Flynn asked, turning around to face Gable. Suddenly Flynn's face was full of concern. "Is everything okay?" Flynn moved closer and gave Gable the once-over.

"Everything's fine. I just needed to see Craig for some physiotherapy."

Flynn's face lit up and a soft smile appeared. "And he's going to make you a prosthesis for your foot? So you can walk again?"

Gable nodded.

"Why didn't you tell me? I could have driven you there and...." Flynn's smile disappeared. "I'm your partner, Gabe. Why couldn't you tell me?"

Gable had to admit he didn't know. Flynn was right. He should have shared it with him. "I don't know," he admitted softly. "You had every right to know. I just...."

"What?" Flynn asked when Gable hesitated a bit too long.

Gable looked away. "I wanted to surprise you."

"Hearing you say you were going back to the hospital for this would have been enough of a surprise, Gabe. I'm glad you're moving forward. I just wish you'd include me in your plans from time to time. I wanted to share this with you, Gabe. That's what partners do."

By now, Flynn was standing very close to Gable and it came as no real surprise when Flynn's lips gently covered Gable's.

"Let's go back inside, okay?" Flynn gently nudged Gable.

When they entered the house, a burnt smell accosted them.

"That's it," Flynn sighed, throwing the blackened omelet in the trash. "I'm not eating beans again. I'm driving us into town for Chinese food."

—19—

WAKING up so close to Gable was always a treat. There was something so manly about his smell, which, in combination with the fine hairs that covered large parts of his body and the sinewy muscles of a man who was used to working with his hands, never failed to make Flynn grow hard, if he wasn't already. For months, Flynn had almost been ashamed of his physical reaction, afraid it would mock Gable's inadequacies on that front. Flynn had grown accustomed to releasing his tension under the shower, the one place where he felt he had enough privacy, but that didn't mean he could go without feeling Gable's touch.

Slowly they'd discovered each other again. The last few days they had taken to sleeping close together, something they hadn't even done at the beginning of their relationship. Still, it had taken some time for Gable to persuade Flynn that he needed sex too, the intimacy, the tenderness, even though he couldn't grow hard and he couldn't climax. Flynn dreaded seeing the frustration in Gable's eyes sometimes, so he tried to compensate with lots of kisses and caresses; seeing Gable relax and become comfortable in his embrace was enough of a reward for now. Flynn still let Gable instigate most of their intimate moments, but he stopped feeling guilty about his own arousal and started enjoying the blow jobs he got from his lover, knowing Gable enjoyed them as well.

In return, Flynn tried to find Gable's sensitive spots. His nipples and the insides of his thighs were obvious. The dimples just above his ass and a certain spot between his shoulder blades were less straightforward, but Flynn's favorite spot was Gable's neck. He loved lying behind him, holding Gable close and kissing and licking the place where Gable's shoulder muscles merged with the ones around the top of his spine, right where the hairline stopped. Flynn loved the smell of him there, and adored the way Gable tried to get even closer to him when he did that.

Last night, Flynn had come like that, his aching cock receiving the necessary friction between Gable's ass cheeks as Gable pushed back while Flynn was kissing him and playing with his nipples. Gable was moaning and clearly fully aware of what he was doing to Flynn. For a moment, Flynn thought Gable was playing it up because he knew it would turn him on, but then his climax hit so hard, any coherent thought had left his brain to seek out areas with more action. They had fallen asleep like that, close together, Flynn floating on sated bliss and Gable with a proud smile on his face.

Now, Flynn was slowly letting the early morning light drift into his consciousness. Gable was lying still in his arms, his back against Flynn's chest, breathing evenly. Flynn wanted this moment to last forever, but as soon as he stirred, Gable woke up as well.

"Mmmh," Gable mumbled, hand moving back to touch Flynn's naked skin. "Time to get up?"

"Just give it a moment or two." Flynn snuggled closer, fully aware that his morning erection was prodding Gable's ass.

"Fuck me."

"What?" Flynn asked, now fully awake.

"Fuck me, make love to me," Gable answered, his eyes still closed as he leaned back. "You're rock hard. Don't let it go to waste." He reached to pull Flynn closer so he could kiss him.

"That didn't go so well last time, remember?" Flynn reminded him.

Gable turned his shoulders so he could put his arm around Flynn. It was only then that he opened his eyes. "I know it wasn't good for you, but I liked it, Flynn. It felt good to have you inside me again. And last night, when we made love and you came, rubbing up to me like that, all I could think of was that I wanted you to come inside me."

"But… it must be so frustrating for you," Flynn answered quietly.

Gable kissed him again. "I don't have the same expectations now as I did then. It may never come back, Flynn, and I don't want to stop making love to you. Unless you do, of course."

The uncertainty that returned to Gable's demeanor made Flynn cave. "I want nothing more than to make love to you, but I always feel like I'm taking advantage of you. Even last night…."

"Sssh," Gable interrupted. "Let me be the judge of that?"

"But I know you… love me," Flynn said hesitantly. "And that means you'd be willing to endure it because it gives me… pleasure."

Gable turned around completely so he was facing Flynn. "I don't love you *that* much."

The harshness of Gable's words made Flynn finally seek eye contact and he realized Gable's face didn't match his words. His look was soft and loving, albeit slightly mocking.

"It's scary, Flynn," Gable continued. "Why would you stay with me if I couldn't…?" Gable didn't finish his sentence. They both knew what he meant and speaking the words made them too real right now. "But I wouldn't ask you to fuck me if I didn't want it. I know you… masturbate in the shower." Gable cocked his head and looked away from Flynn. "But I'd much rather you jack off in front of me."

"Gable!"

"I do," Gable confessed. "Why hide it? It's what I fantasize about sometimes, so why wouldn't you?"

"Because it's embarrassing!" Flynn chuckled.

"Masturbation?"

"Yes," Flynn admitted.

Gable tried to make Flynn look at him again. "Just because I can't, doesn't mean that it can't turn me on. Seeing you pleasure yourself would be a lot less frustrating than knowing you couldn't wait to jump in the shower, just so you could."

Gable reached for his nightstand and took the lube out of the drawer. He flipped the lid open and offered to squirt some on Flynn's hand.

Flynn hesitated before holding it out. It was a strange idea, to masturbate in front of a lover. Sex was one thing, but pleasuring himself? This felt like high school all over again. Flynn fervently remembered spending lazy summer afternoons, after all his chores were done, up in the hayloft with Davy, his best friend. They would jack off and hold contests how fast they could come and how far they could shoot. Even then, he wanted to hold Davy's cock and longed for Davy to touch his, but he never did. They never even kissed. The last thing he'd heard of his friend was that he was married and had a whole litter of kids. It was just that. Kid's stuff. Not something you did with a lover.

Gable gave him an encouraging nod. "Go on, give it a try. If you don't like it, we won't do it again."

Flynn accepted the clear lube and rubbed his fingers together to warm it up. Then he enveloped his half-hard cock with his hand and rubbed it gently. He had to admit it felt good, and although he'd gotten quite used to his own hand, having Gable's eyes on him gave it a strange twist. Just when he started overthinking it again, Gable leaned closer and kissed him tenderly, teasing him.

"You look good, touching yourself like that," Gable murmured against Flynn's lips, urging him on. "Take it slow. Show me what you like."

"You know what I like," Flynn replied.

"Mmmh," Gable agreed. "But it's always different to see it demonstrated."

Flynn closed his eyes and tried to enjoy what he was doing without being constantly confronted by Gable's gaze. That was too much of a distraction right now, although he constantly felt Gable's mouth close to his and his breath ghost over his skin. Then Flynn heard the lid pop off the lube. When he finally dared to open his eyes, he saw that Gable's hand was behind him.

"Are you opening yourself up for me?" Flynn asked hesitantly.

"I told you I wanted you to fuck me. Just because I can't... you know, doesn't mean I can't be turned on, and seeing you touch yourself turns me on so much."

Flynn's breathing sped up. Hell yes, of course he wanted to fuck Gable! That was a given. Always. He'd held off after their last disaster, but now that Gable was coming on to him strong, his resistance was crumbling fast. He continued fisting his cock while he pushed Gable to lie back.

Gable immediately changed the position of his hand and spread his knees, opening the way for Flynn to lie between them. "Just do it. Just come inside me. I'm ready for you."

Flynn tried to ignore Gable's flaccid cock and decided instead to focus on his lover's rapid breathing and encouraging words.

"Want you inside me. I'm open for you, Flynn. Please?"

Hearing Gable beg broke down the last of Flynn's resistance. He positioned his cock at Gable's entrance and easily pushed into the tight heat.

"Nnnguh," Gable grunted. "Fuck, yeah, feels... so good!"

Flynn nodded and dove in to kiss Gable as he slowly started rocking back and forth. It felt good to be so close together, in each other's arms, facing each other and kissing while they were making love. He felt cradled and safe and Gable's rhythmical moaning and encouraging words eased the feeling of blindly taking advantage of him.

"Feels so good," Gable murmured. "So close. Don't stop."

Hearing those words made Flynn stop anyway. "What?" He raised himself up and looked between their bodies.

Gable grabbed the back of his neck and pulled him down. "Fucking don't stop. Fuck me harder. Make me come. Please."

Gable kissed him almost violently, and Flynn could do nothing else but comply. Hearing Gable beg like that made the lust rise so fast, he simply had to obey his body and started pistoning in and out like a mad man. He had no idea how long he would last, but it felt good to abandon the last of his control. Suddenly Gable's face contorted and his back arched off the bed with amazing force. Flynn felt the warm stickiness of Gable's release between their bellies and couldn't resist looking.

"You came?"

Gable was panting too hard to answer, but he nodded.

"You're not even hard."

Gable slowly shook his head. "Felt pretty amazing, though."

As Flynn gently pulled out, Gable's breath hitched and his groin still twitched. "You didn't come yet?"

Flynn shook his head with a teasing smile and took some more lube in his hand, crawling higher up Gable's body until he straddled him. "You kind of took me by surprise and then I thought, you asked me to jack off for you. Would you still like me to?"

"Hell yeah," Gable answered with obvious pleasure in his voice.

Flynn slowly started fisting his rock-hard erection. It wasn't usually his style to put himself on display like this, but the way Gable bit his lip while looking at what Flynn was doing and not hiding the clear pleasure it gave him all became part of "giving something back," and Flynn was even tempted to ham it up a bit. It was getting harder and harder to take it slow, though. He was rolling his hips, effectively fucking his fist, and when Gable took hold of his buttocks and started kneading them in time with Flynn's movements, Flynn felt his control slipping. He desperately wanted to come, so when he felt the tingling at the bottom of his spine, he upped the tempo a bit and tightened the muscles in his abdomen until the wave hit him and he collapsed in Gable's arms.

Flynn didn't know how long they laid like that, Flynn panting and Gable soothing and cradling him. He was vaguely aware of Gable wiping them off, but Flynn felt so safe and warm he eventually fell asleep. When he woke again, bright sunlight was creeping around the drapes and he was looking into Gable's sparkling blue eyes.

"Hey, sleepyhead."

"I'm sorry," Flynn apologized.

"What for? We had the most amazing experience, then you fell asleep, and so did I, and now we're awake again."

"What time is it?" Flynn asked, dreading the answer, although it didn't really matter. They needed to get up either way and he didn't want to leave their safe cocoon just yet.

"Oh, elevenish?" Gable answered casually.

"What?" Flynn called out, suddenly wide awake. He jumped out of bed and started sorting out his clothes. "Bloody hell, we need to get up and work!"

Gable didn't budge. He sat in bed with a big smirk on his face, watching Flynn get all worked up. "Come back to bed, Flynn."

"There're horses that need taking care of and stables to muck out and leather to oil and fences to mend and... and...."

Gable chuckled. "Horses can't tell time, honey. They don't care when you show up. And as long as they have water and juicy grass, they don't even care *if* you show up." He leaned out of the bed and grabbed Flynn's hand to pull him closer. "Now I, on the other hand...."

Flynn reluctantly let himself be pulled into bed again. Gable's merciless kiss made his resistance break.

"I unleashed something in you, didn't I?" Flynn asked as soon as they broke for air.

"Oh, I don't know," Gable replied innocently. "I hoped that after your little rest you'd be good to go again?"

Flynn rolled his eyes and smiled before tossing aside the T-shirt he'd hastily grabbed and crawling under the covers again.

—20—

"IF I'D known it was this easy, I would have called you weeks ago," Gable chuckled as he stood on the porch, low crutches in both hands, looking down at Craig.

"Don't boast yet. You're barely putting any weight on your prosthesis," the therapist answered from his crouched position, aligning Gable's feet.

"I... Fucking hell!"

"Told ya." Craig could barely contain a chuckle. "You're going to have to take it easy. Now, bend your knee slightly."

"How am I supposed to do that?" Gable asked gruffly.

"You tell your leg to relax and then you slightly pull up your knee."

Gable wobbled a bit and had a tough time keeping his balance.

"Come on, Gable," Craig urged him on. "Concentrate. You've been getting around on crutches for months now. This can't be that much harder."

At that moment Gable looked up, hearing a noise, and saw Flynn running toward the house.

"Everything... okay?"

Flynn whizzed by him, entering the house. Just moments later he exited, carrying Gable's shotgun.

Before either of the porch dwellers could react, Flynn was running back toward the barn.

"What the hell?" Gable murmured before setting out after him, hobbling along on his new crutches.

"Hey!" Craig yelled. "Be careful with that leg!" He soon became the third person to hastily make his way across the driveway.

"Flynn?" Gable called out as soon as he arrived, panting, in the barn. "Flynn?"

"Back here," Flynn said in a subdued voice.

Gable trotted behind the last stall, where the ladder to the hayloft was situated, and found Flynn pointing his gun at two rather familiar men, who were standing, western-movie style, with their hands raised.

"Hunter," Gable nodded. "Grant," he said in a slightly different tone of voice. "Mind if I ask what you're doing here?"

"Can you get him to lower that gun first?" Hunter asked, pointing at Flynn but speaking to Gable.

"You're trespassing," Gable replied, still sounding decidedly calm.

"Listen, I can explain, just get him to—"

"I can't command him to do anything," Gable interrupted with a certain amusement in his voice.

"He's your stable boy, of course you can," Grant intervened.

"Oh, he's a lot more than my stable boy, Grant. You of all people should understand that."

Gable could see Grant starting to fume, but he realized that it no longer fazed him.

"Listen," Hunter said, taking charge again by giving Grant a curt nod. "Flynn, we're unarmed, so please stop pointing that thing at us. Then I'll try to explain."

Flynn briefly looked at Gable, then uncocked the rifle and lowered it. He still didn't look relaxed, though.

Hunter and Grant lowered their hands. Gable continued to have a hard time not laughing at the situation, doing his best to stay serious.

"So explain," Gable said, trying to sound stern.

"We're just here to protect our investment. Hunter's investment," Grant corrected himself.

"Why don't you send your stable boy to your car or whatever else you're hiding for transportation, Hunter?" Gable admonished. From the corner of his eye he saw Grant frown. It gave him a perverse sort of pleasure.

"Grant's not my...." Hunter stopped midsentence, then changed the subject. "We... I wanted to make sure that the mares and their unborn foals were doing okay."

"Come on, Hunter," Gable said, trying to smooth things over. "You could have just called at the house and asked to see them. Although I appreciate your investment, for now, they're still my mares and they're still on my property and in my stable and eating my grass and my hay and my oats. I believe the only thing you and Flynn agreed upon was that the foals would be yours? After they're born."

Hunter nodded.

"So for now, let us take care of them and I promise I'll give you a call as soon as one of them starts to announce his imminent arrival."

Hunter tipped his hat at Gable and gestured to Grant to follow him out of the stable.

For the first time that afternoon, a smile broke on Flynn's face. He and Gable exchanged a look, but Flynn was clearly not ready to explain anything as long as Craig was still present.

"I think I'd better get on with my exercises," Gable suggested.

"Yeah, I have work to do as well," Flynn agreed, a clear look of mischief still all over his face. "Can you take the gun?"

Gable lifted his crutches and threw Flynn an apologetic look. "Craig?"

"Oh no," the therapist answered, waving his hands. "I'm a city boy. I'm not touching that."

Flynn chuckled and held the rifle over his shoulders in a decidedly James Dean stance. "Yeah, I grew up shooting rabbits. Two butch boys wouldn't have thrown me off too much."

Gable chuckled quietly and shook his head. "Let's go, Craig, before Dirty Harry here gets any more ideas."

As they walked out of the barn, Craig's professional demeanor returned quickly enough. "Put some weight on your leg, Gabe."

Gable tentatively put his foot down and it hit the ground hard, making him pull it up again. "It's hard to tell where my foot is. I'm afraid I'll stumble over it."

Craig put a soothing hand on Gable's shoulder. "That'll come in time. It takes some getting used to, Gabe. You'll have to learn to feel it all over again. Right now, because you haven't put any weight on that leg for so long, it feels like all the nerve endings are wired wrong, but that'll change eventually."

Gable wasn't too sure, but he didn't want to argue. Instead he set a good pace back to the house, trying, like Craig asked, to at least put his foot on the ground. It still felt alien, like it wasn't his leg, but then again, it wasn't.

Later that night, after they'd gone to bed, Flynn fell asleep almost immediately. Gable was still lying awake, though. For once he wasn't fretting over something; tonight his muscles were sore. His butt cheek felt overworked, and rubbing it didn't help. Maybe Craig was right and he'd waited too long. The therapist had been adamant that he would recuperate. It would just take longer than with the average amputee. He'd have to rebuild his muscles all over again.

Gable turned onto his side, careful not to wake Flynn. That felt better on his back and his ass, but it made his bad leg twinge. He contorted his face, trying not to succumb to the uncontrollable need to shake it, to get rid of the itch at the sole of his foot—a foot he could no longer scratch.

"Anything wrong, love?" Flynn asked.

Gable shrugged. "Didn't mean to wake you. You worked hard. You're tired."

Flynn snuggled closer. "I don't mind." He wrapped his arms around Gable and Gable gratefully accepted. "Does your leg hurt?"

Gable shrugged.

"Is it so hard to admit?"

Gable shrugged again. Of course it was hard to admit.

"Does Craig push you too hard?"

Gable shook his head. "If anything, he tries to hold me back. Tells me I have to do it gradually."

"Yeah, but gradually isn't in your book, is it?" Flynn wiped the hair away from Gable's face. "Nothing gradual about the way you seduced me either." He chuckled.

"I don't deserve you." Gable couldn't look straight at Flynn. He couldn't even face how much he needed his lover right now.

"Let's not go there again. I think we've established by now that we totally deserve each other."

Gable let himself roll onto his back again and stared up at the ceiling. To his surprise, Flynn threw back the covers and turned on the light.

"Let me look at your leg?"

Gable displayed a pained expression and shook his head.

"Gable," Flynn cautioned, his face very much like one of the schoolteachers Gable remembered from his childhood. He'd feared for his life every time she looked at him that way, and although he knew he had nothing to fear from Flynn, he also knew better than to protest.

Flynn sat up in bed and let his hand travel down Gable's bad leg to the stump. When he took the sock off, it looked red and there was a small abrasion on the side near the surgical scar. "That does it," Flynn declared. He got out of bed and retrieved the first aid kit from the bathroom, then sat down and started cleaning the small wound with antiseptic.

Gable lay back passively, not even hissing when Flynn swabbed the abrasion with the cold liquid or looking up at Flynn when he returned from the bathroom after putting the first aid kit away, carrying a bottle of hand cream he'd found at the back of the closet.

Flynn didn't let on he noticed. He simply warmed the cream in his hands and started rubbing it over Gable's knee and around the stump, carefully staying away from the small wound. Gradually, Gable started to relax. Flynn didn't talk. He moved his ministrations higher, massaging Gable's thigh and dipping under Gable's boxers to rub his buttock. When he was done, he put the elastic sock back over Gable's stump and crawled into bed, wrapping the blankets around them, before turning off the light and taking Gable back into his arms.

"You're as stubborn as a mule. You do know that, don't you?" Flynn asked.

Gable didn't answer.

"You don't have to say thank you. I'm your lover, it's implied," Flynn teased.

"Thank you," Gable murmured, barely audibly. "How did you know?"

"I broke my ankle shortly after I left my dad's ranch. Couldn't walk on it for a while, and when I finally could again, I remember the first day my ass hurt really badly. Plus, I've been sleeping next to you for months, Gabe. I know your aches and pains, even when you pretend you're fine."

"I'm not good at…."

"Yeah, I know," Flynn said, rubbing Gable's back. "You think you can sleep now?"

"Tell me about this afternoon?" Gable asked instead of answering Flynn's question.

"This afternoon? Oh, you mean me catching Hunter and Grant coming down from the hayloft?"

"Coming down…?" Gable extricated himself from Flynn's arms and sat up. "What were they doing up there?"

Flynn chuckled. "Beats me, but they were flustered and very bothered and I don't think it had a lot to do with me pointing a gun at them."

"What do you mean?" Gable asked as Flynn pulled him down to the bed again.

"I mean, I think they were doing more than 'checking up on their investment'." Flynn paused for effect. "I think they were doing what two people do in a hayloft, and it isn't stacking bales."

"That's ridiculous," Gable said, dismissing Flynn's idea. "Grant doesn't like to admit he sleeps with men and Hunter isn't gay."

"I wouldn't be so sure."

"Flynn, Hunter may be the only man around a ranch full of women, with his mother and three sisters still living there, but that just means he's got too many women nagging him to find himself a wife. It doesn't mean he's gay."

Flynn looked at his lover, his eyes adjusted to the darkness well enough to see his face by now. "Why do I half-expect you to tell me you know this firsthand?"

"I just know."

"Yeah, right," Flynn replied. "So tell me this. Grant has a big enough mouth to speak for Hunter, and Hunter, being his boss, rarely calls him on it. They communicate silently, with looks and gestures. We can do that, Gabe, but I don't see a ranch owner and one of his ranch hands doing that if they barely know each other."

"When you round up horses or cattle, you gesture to each other. You get to know each other pretty well working together. How did you think Grant and I… you know…? With Grant refusing to admit he likes to fuck guys, it wasn't like he was the one putting the moves on me, at least not directly. But tell me, why would they come here to…?"

Flynn waited for Gable to finish, but the fact that Grant was involved clearly didn't make that easy. "I don't know. They like the idea they could get caught?"

"They'd probably have a better chance of that at Hunter's ranch, and then it would be the boss and one of his employees fucking," Gable suggested. "Not to mention the women there have eyes in the back of their heads."

"I rest my case," Flynn giggled.

—21—

GABLE'S walking steadily improved to the point where he could make his way to the barn every day with just one crutch to support himself. Although he started taking on more work, from cleaning and mending saddles and bridles to mucking out stalls and sweeping floors, he still hadn't ridden a horse yet.

From time to time Flynn would suggest giving it a try, but Gable always found an excuse not to. As the summer slowly came to an end, the weather was getting worse, and Flynn knew it would be better to move the horses to the lower paddocks, where it would be warmer. He just couldn't do it alone. Although their herd wasn't anywhere near as big as Hunter's or any of their other neighbors', two people was the minimum if you wanted to move more than a few horses.

"So do I need to ask Hunter for a horse wrangler to help me out or can you?" Flynn asked over breakfast one morning.

"It's too early," Gable answered. "We don't have enough hay to add to their feed and the higher paddocks still have good grass."

Flynn knew it was just another excuse, but he didn't argue. He'd learned the hard way that he could only push Gable so far before he stopped talking to him, and since they had a good thing going, he stopped just short of Gable's breaking point.

The following morning, Flynn woke up alone, and he instantly sensed something unusual was going on. He rushed to get dressed and ran down the stairs. The kitchen table was empty and there were no dishes in the sink, so he figured wherever Gable was, he hadn't had breakfast. The house was eerily quiet. A quick look out the window assured Flynn that the truck was still parked out front. So Gable hadn't left the ranch. He wasn't anywhere inside, so Flynn quickly put together a few sandwiches and made his way to the barn.

The saddles were all in place, but T.C.'s tack was missing and so was T.C. A few bales of hay were stacked to the side, and just in front of them he spotted Gable's prosthesis. Flynn couldn't help but chuckle at the sight of the orphaned limb. He smiled as he saddled Brenner, put the sandwiches in the saddlebag, and strapped the prosthesis to the back before rushing outside.

It was still early and already fairly cold for the time of year, with a low mist hanging over the paddock. All Flynn could see were legless horses' backs sticking up out of the gray blanket of fog. Here and there, a head would pop up, only to lower again, but one of the horses had a rider. Flynn slowly walked Brenner over to where he could make out Gable on the back of the paint horse. The image reminded him of the moment he fell in love with Gable, as the man slowly made his way among the herd, the horses flocking to him as if they were welcoming a long-lost son. Gable greeted each of them with a gentle pat on the back, a stroke up their flank, and a click of his tongue. Some of the horses came to nuzzle Gable as if they needed to reacquaint themselves with him, and Flynn stayed back to watch the scene and give them time to do just that.

Suddenly Gable spotted Flynn and he smiled. Flynn felt all warm inside. *He's back in the saddle, literally and figuratively*, he thought.

"So are you checking whether you're up to helping me move the horses?" Flynn asked.

"I told you we still had time. They have more grass up here than we have down there," Gable answered. "Give it a few more days."

Flynn knew Gable wasn't asking for a few more days until the weather got colder; he wanted a few more days to get used to riding again, but Flynn simply agreed as he directed Brenner to stand beside T.C. He put his hand on the small of Gable's back. "Must feel good to be back in the saddle, so to speak?" He grinned, since Gable was riding T.C. bareback.

Gable simply nodded, his gaze directed over the fields. "It's a little strange, but I'm sure I'll get used to it again." He looked down at his hands holding the reins and then at Flynn, and Flynn used his knees to make Brenner move a little closer so he could lean toward Gable to kiss him. Gable reciprocated, but just as their lips touched, Brenner became skittish and propelled Flynn forward.

"Bastard," Flynn yelled at Brenner, making him buck even more.

Gable chuckled. "Hey, that's my horse you're talking to. He's got very delicate feelings!"

"He's a jealous bastard, that's what I think," Flynn answered only half-jokingly, steering Brenner alongside T.C. again.

"Well, if you were a bit nicer to him, he might be a bit nicer to you too," Gable teased. This time both horses remained calm and the men managed to kiss good morning.

"Why did you bring that?" Gable asked when he spotted the artificial leg strapped to the back of Flynn's saddle.

"I thought it could come in handy. I also brought breakfast."

"Mmmh." Gable cocked his head. "When I woke up this morning, I got the sudden urge to come and take a look at the horses. I guess if my stomach had protested, I would have realized I hadn't had any food yet, but it wasn't even light then."

Flynn shook his head but smiled nevertheless. He was actually quite happy about Gable's sudden urges.

The fog was slowly lifting and the horses were starting to graze.

"So is your stomach still not protesting?"

Gable pulled a face as if he was reaching down into his gut and checking, just to be sure. "I could probably do with a sandwich."

They found a spot near the fence where the land sloped up a bit and there were some trees to sit against. Flynn dismounted and let Brenner free to roam then took T.C.'s bridle to keep him steady so Gable could dismount as well. Not that it was necessary. As Flynn had predicted a long time ago, T.C. was well aware that he had a less-able rider on board and he was extremely calm and patient, even looking back as Gable jumped down to make sure he was okay. Gable landed on his good leg and held onto T.C. for a moment to get his balance, then hopped over to where Flynn was standing.

"I'm not wearing that, unless you want to go for a stroll?" Gable said, pointing at the prosthesis, which Flynn was untying.

"Maybe later," Flynn replied, picking up on Gable's unease.

They sat down on the damp ground, silently sharing breakfast.

"It still doesn't feel like mine," Gable remarked eventually.

"It will, in time," Flynn answered, making clear that he knew what Gable was referring to. "Once you can walk on it without thinking about it, it will be like you never lived without it."

Gable threw Flynn a questioning look, but bit into his sandwich and didn't say anything. He spoke again after a long pause. "It really doesn't bother you?"

"Nope," Flynn said resolutely. "It's a part of you, Gabe. Like that beat-up ankle was in the beginning, only then I worried that you weren't taking care of yourself."

"Guess I still need you to do it for me," Gable replied, referring to the times when Flynn would take care of his sore stump in the evening, when he'd far extended the time Craig had told him to walk on it.

"I don't mind," Flynn shrugged.

"So you like me all needy and stuff?"

Flynn looked at him sideways. "No, but I like to be needed and wanted. There's a difference."

Gable squared his jaw. "Yeah, I suppose there is." He leaned back and placed his hat over his eyes, stretching his arms up so he could rest his head on his hands.

"Hey," Flynn protested. "You're making me feel very unwanted!" His last bites of sandwich discarded, he moved so he could straddle Gable's thighs and worm his hands underneath Gable's warm coat. As he wiggled them, he could feel Gable's stomach muscles tense and then saw the hat move as Gable tried not to laugh.

Eventually Gable lifted his hat to show his broad smile. "It worked, didn't it?" Gable didn't let Flynn answer. Instead he pulled him down and kissed him passionately. When they came up for air, there was wonderment in Flynn's face as he ground his growing bulge against Gable's groin.

"You're hard, Gable. I can feel it."

Gable nodded almost imperceptibly. "I woke up hard this morning."

"And you didn't wake me?"

"It was 4 o'clock, Flynn."

"Hell, for that you can wake me up any time! Literally."

Gable seemed to shy away. "I had no idea how long it would last. If it *would* last."

Flynn kissed him again. "I don't care. I'm not letting it go to waste."

"Flynn, we're out in the open, in a field."

Flynn giggled. "We can barely see far enough to spot our horses. Even if someone came by on Hunter's side of the fence, we'd have to make a hell of a lot of noise to get noticed."

Gable conceded, as if he needed to. Flynn wasn't about to let anyone or anything stop him as he unbuttoned Gable's fly and uncovered his clearly excited cock. "Let's give the bird some air, hey?"

Before Gable could protest, Flynn took him in his mouth, licking and sucking as if it was the only source of water in a desert. Gable could do nothing but let it happen. The nagging doubt in the back of his mind—that it wouldn't last and he'd probably go slack again before he came—prevented him from fully enjoying it, but then again, the feeling of a heavy cock was something he barely remembered, so he closed his eyes and tried to think happy thoughts. Flynn's hot mouth did feel good, and what if he did lose his erection again? He'd come quite frequently these past weeks without an erection at all.

Suddenly the ministrations stopped and Gable felt the cold. When he opened his eyes, Flynn was standing up, hastily getting rid of his jeans. He stepped out of them, along with his boots, before straddling Gable again.

"Please just let me? Just this once?" Flynn asked, panting hard.

Gable didn't immediately register what Flynn meant until he saw Flynn spit on his fingers and reach between his legs to sink over Gable's distended cock with a deep sigh. Flynn felt incredibly tight, which was no surprise, and the slightly pained expression on his face made Gable very worried. He soon discarded the feeling when Flynn started riding him and his face turned from stressed to blissful. Gable held on to Flynn's hips to steady him and felt Flynn's heavy cock flop down on his belly every time he hit rock bottom, only to rise again when Flynn did. Flynn's movements became more fluid and Gable dared to release one hand, instead using it to touch Flynn's cock.

"Oh, God, yeah," Flynn sighed. "Been so long."

Although it felt great to be ridden like that, Flynn's tight passage milking his cock with every movement, it still felt strange to have their positions reversed. Gable never imagined topping Flynn—even from the position he was in now—and he certainly hadn't imagined that Flynn would like it so much. Then again, Gable liked that very position too, so it wasn't a total surprise.

"Oh, fuck, you're going to make me come, Gabe," Flynn panted, moving between Gable's cock and his hand.

Gable started thrusting up and Flynn stilled his movements, swatting Gable's hand away so he could fist his own cock.

"Need to come. Feels so good."

Flynn threw his head back as he thrust into his hand and the small shiny beads that had been collecting at the tip turned into thick strands, shooting out all over Gable's oilskin duster. Gable felt Flynn's channel spasm around him and then Flynn collapsed on top of him. He was panting hard, and all Gable could do was wrap his arms around him to keep him warm.

It seemed to take forever before Flynn looked down at him again. He was sporting a smile and biting his lower lip. "You're still hard, stud."

Gable chuckled. "And your ass is getting cold."

Flynn didn't move, though. If anything, he snuggled even closer. Then something seemed to dawn on him. "You didn't come yet, did you?"

Gable calmly shook his head. He rarely came from fucking, which is why he was seldom the top in a relationship, or even in a one-night stand.

"We'll have to do something about that," Flynn said as he slowly got up and let Gable slip from his body.

Although Gable could see Flynn was still half hard, he didn't think he'd be ready to fuck him again so soon.

Flynn had other ideas, though. "Come on, drop 'em," he said with a wink, gesturing toward Gable's jeans.

Gable unbuckled his belt and lifted his ass off the ground as Flynn pulled his jeans down.

Licking his fingers, Flynn smiled at Gable and inserted them between Gable's legs, making him jump just a little. "You? Sensitive when I come close to your favorite body part? What have I done to you?"

Gable sighed and pulled Flynn down so he could kiss him. "Don't stop," he whispered against Flynn's mouth. He sucked in air as Flynn's fingers breached him. "Fuck me?" he begged.

Flynn smiled, their lips still only a fraction of an inch apart. "I hate to admit it, but I can't yet. Doesn't mean I'm not going to try, though." He twisted his fingers and made Gable gasp again. "Right there? That the spot you like?" Gable could only nod as he repeated the action. "Of course I know exactly where your spot is." Gable's breathing sped up along with Flynn's ministrations until all the muscles in his body tensed up and he came all over the bottom of his hitched-up coat.

"I LOVE you," Gable said as they were slowly making their way down to the house, both of them sitting on T.C.'s back with Brenner trailing behind them, Gable's prosthesis still firmly strapped to Brenner's saddle.

"I know," Flynn answered, squeezing Gable's chest and pulling him even closer. "I love you too," he whispered. "Wanna go upstairs and...."

"Make out?" Gable answered, chuckling.

Flynn rolled his eyes. "You're such a kid sometimes."

—22—

"YOU are like a kid again and you make me feel old," Flynn pouted, although he clearly didn't mean it.

Gable pulled him closer and kissed him again, like they had been doing all afternoon. They'd gone riding that morning, picking out the horses that were ready for training and separating them from the herd, but after lunch they'd ended up in their bedroom for some strange reason. Flynn suspected that Gable had planned it all along, but he wasn't complaining. They were, after all, making up for lost time.

"So, are you enjoying our anniversary?"

"Anniversary?" Flynn asked, truly perplexed. He searched his mind, first to remember what day it was, then to try and figure out what made it so special.

"Exactly a year ago you walked into my barn and asked for a job."

"Doesn't seem like that long. Seems...."

"Longer?"

Flynn chuckled. "Seems like only yesterday I first met you. I don't think I saw you smile once that first week."

Gable smiled now, though. "I was so used to being on my own, and frankly, after Grant, I thought I'd live out my life that way."

"You seem okay around Grant now?"

Gable shrugged. "I suppose I forgave him. And Hunter's a good friend. If you're right about him, I'll have to deal with Grant a lot more from now on. Too bad I never knew about Hunter before. I wouldn't mind...."

Flynn thumped him in the chest. Hard. "That's not why I told you!"

Gable collapsed back to the bed in a fit of giggles. Every time he looked at Flynn's serious face, he laughed harder, until Flynn couldn't hold back either.

"You just want to get back into Grant's pants," Flynn teased.

That made Gable turn serious again. "No, I don't. Grant is ancient history. If he and Hunter are happy together, then I can live with that, but I don't trust him enough to want him back."

"Good," Flynn answered, snuggling closer. He left his hand drift down Gable's chest, trying to gauge whether his lover was ready for another round, and smiled when he discovered that he was. "If I had known all that abstinence would yield these results...." He didn't finish, but instead kissed Gable passionately. His body reacted accordingly and within no time, he was hard again and raring to go.

Gable was already moaning under Flynn's ministrations when they heard the front door slam shut.

Flynn immediately looked up. "Did we leave that open?"

"Bridget would be barking if we had trespassers," Gable said, equally worried.

"She doesn't bark if it's Calley," Flynn commented.

"Damn!" Gable cursed. "She can't catch us in bed in the middle of the day. We'll never hear the end of it!" He jumped out of bed, then realized he was one leg short and sat down again to put on his prosthesis. After pulling up his jeans, he found he had a difficult time tucking himself inside them.

Flynn chuckled, having just as much difficulty, but his jeans were a much snugger fit than Gable's, who still wasn't back to his weight from before the surgery.

Gable was quite good at making his way down the stairs quickly, pushing himself up on the handrails and letting himself slide down, rather than run. Flynn wasn't far behind. They found Calley in the kitchen with Bridget next to her. The dog was wagging her tail so enthusiastically her hind legs could barely keep to the floor.

"Hi, Calley. Ooh, lovely fresh vegetables!" Gable greeted Calley with a quick kiss on the cheek and then dove straight into her box of supplies, missing her curious and rather amused look.

Flynn didn't miss it, though. "We were upstairs moving furniture."

"Hanging curtains," Gable said at almost exactly the same time.

"Well, I wish Bill would hang more curtains for me. You two should explain to him how you do that one day," Calley replied, helping Gable put things away just to prevent herself from laughing. "He never hangs my curtains," she added, just to show how silly the men were for trying to fool her.

Flynn looked at Gable and Gable had to look away. He was blushing.

"So how is Bill?" Gable asked semiseriously. "We hardly see him these days."

"In the spring it's lambs and calves, the summer it's foals. It just never stops. The stork still doesn't have our address, though. That or I pissed him off too much." She seemed serious and not her usual lively self all of a sudden.

Gable took her hand and squeezed it and that seemed to bring her smile back. "Oh, well," she sighed. "We know it wasn't meant to be. Time to go, my darlings." She gave Flynn a quick peck on the cheek and then turned to Gable. She tried to do the same to him, but he wouldn't have it. Instead he pulled her into a tight hug and held her for a while. She let him, holding onto him. When she eventually pulled away, there were tears in her eyes, but she was still smiling. "I better leave before I turn into a puddle and can't stop. I'll be okay, Gabe. Thanks." She squeezed his hand and then took her empty box outside to her car.

Gable and Flynn came out to the porch to wave her off and make sure Bridget didn't follow her too far up the driveway.

"I don't mean to pry and it's probably none of my business, but...." Flynn waited and hoped Gable would anticipate his question. Instead, Gable pulled Flynn into a hug and held him like he'd held Calley.

"It's okay, I'm not jealous of Calley," Flynn said as Gable loosened his grasp.

"I know," Gable answered quietly.

Flynn could see Gable was fighting his emotions too and didn't push him to say anything more, but that didn't mean he wasn't curious. Ever since that first time he'd met Calley, he had a feeling there was more to their friendship, especially after he found out there was also some sense of betrayal, the depth of which he still didn't know. Just like at the hospital, today didn't seem like the right opportunity to ask.

Gable remained broody all through dinner. After the dishes were done, they sat outside on the porch for the first time that fall. Flynn noticed Gable still put his foot up on the foot rest, but the solitary chair was now replaced with the wooden bench that Gable had spend most of the summer fixing up. This way Flynn could sit next to Gable, and they sat close together, watching the sun set.

"Calley and Bill have been trying for kids for at least ten years now," Gable said out of the blue. "It's a long story."

"I have time," Flynn tried. He snuggled closer, putting his feet up on the side of the bench, while resting his back against Gable.

"It's a really long story. Maybe one day I'll tell it to you."

"If it's such a deep, dark secret, maybe I don't wanna know," Flynn answered, looking sideways at Gable.

"Yeah, maybe that's best," Gable replied, much to Flynn's disappointment.

Flynn wasn't happy with the way Calley's visit had changed Gable's good mood to something very much resembling his attitude before the surgery: gruff, difficult, and moody. Only this time, the pain he seemed to be feeling was more of the emotional kind. Maybe there were some deeply hidden feelings there. Why was Gable so reluctant to tell him about them? He felt left out, and even if it wasn't his business—or especially if it wasn't his business—he couldn't dismiss the pang of jealousy. Pushing Gable any further was useless, but knowing that didn't make the feeling go away. He could only hope that, in time, Gable would explain a few things to him.

IN THE next few days Gable's spirits seemed to lift some, as they started training the older horses again. Gable's riding had steadily improved over the last weeks, to the point where he was riding with a saddle again and he was keeping his leg on. He'd also take Brenner out on some occasions, and that was a horse that needed a lot of leg control, so Flynn was silently proud of his lover.

Most of the horses they'd chosen were already broken, either by Gable before his surgery or afterward by Flynn, and simply needed to get used to regular handling. That meant they needed to take them out to ride regularly, so they would become good working horses that didn't give their riders too much trouble. It kept them very busy for a few weeks, returning every hour or two to change horses and continue riding them along the fences and lean-tos scattered around the ranch.

Occasionally they'd meet one of Hunter's ranch hands along their shared fence. At one time they spotted Hunter and Grant riding together, seemingly checking fences just like they were doing, but they didn't stop, simply tipped their hats at each other and went about their business. Flynn couldn't help giving Gable a "told you so" look, but Gable just shook his head. He was smiling, though, and Flynn pretty much knew Gable didn't completely dismiss Flynn's feelings about the two men.

One night, as the evenings were becoming colder, Flynn went to check on the barn one more time before closing it up for the night. He knew the mares were both close to giving birth to their foals and wanted to make sure they were okay. He hoped Hunter would be happy with the new horses. Even though they were only going to stay on their ranch until they were weaned from their mothers, Flynn was already looking forward to the little ones. He'd grown up around them on his father's ranch, and although his father always scolded him, he could never stay away from them. He'd helped hand-rear a few of them, and also helped his brothers in getting the foals used to being touched by people. He couldn't wait.

Tonight it became clear he wasn't going to have to wait much longer.

"Gable!" he shouted. "Call Bill! One of the mares is in labor!"

—23—

B<small>ILL</small> looked tired when he arrived.

Flynn knew he was one of the most experienced vets in the county and therefore on the payroll of most of the large horse ranches in the area. Occasionally he also helped out at the smaller cattle ranches. Flynn could imagine that Calley pretty much had the store all to herself. And her house too, he supposed.

"So what makes you think she's about ready to foal?" Bill gruffly asked Flynn.

"She's waxing," Flynn answered, clearly proud of himself. "Since she's a first-time mom, I've been washing her teats with warm water to get her used to having them touched and they've been filling up these past days. Then when I came to check on her this evening, she was restless and tense."

"So you've been playing with her nipples?" Bill asked amusedly. "You don't seem the sort."

Flynn ignored the taunt. "I've been around enough pregnant mares to know."

"Then you should also know that most mares give birth without intervention."

Flynn nodded. "But these are first-time mothers and the foals are precious. We don't know how they'll deliver yet and we can't afford to lose either of them."

Bill conceded. "I suppose you're right." He sighed deeply and walked inside the box to take a closer look at the mare.

At that moment Flynn's attention was drawn to the barn door that was swung open by strong hands. Gable entered first, then Hunter, and eventually the owner of the hands: Grant. Instantly the tension rose.

"Foal here yet?" Hunter asked nervously.

"You sound like it's your very first one, Hunter." Gable smiled. "And I know for a fact that your very first foal was born more than twenty years ago, right by your outer fence, because I helped you deliver him."

Flynn thought if there was more light in the barn, he'd see Hunter blush, but now he could only hear the big guy chuckle shyly.

"You know I prefer to be in control," Hunter replied.

Gable looked at Grant briefly and then at Flynn, but he averted his look almost immediately, stifling a laugh.

"Looks like the lad is right," Bill intervened. "She's showing signs of being in labor so let's give her some privacy." He directed the men back to the entrance of the barn. "Since I'm here anyway, I'll keep an eye on her in case she can't manage herself."

"No way," Hunter was quick to reply. "That's my foal and I want to see it be born."

"And it's my mare, sired by my stallion, so you're not keeping me away either," Gable said, siding with Hunter.

Grant kept himself suspiciously quiet. He exchanged looks with Hunter, but didn't speak and stayed in the background, while Hunter and Gable leaned on the side of the box stall to peer at the restless mare.

Flynn knew what needed to be done and he figured three curious men was more than enough for the young mother. He'd cranked up the heater in the back of the barn so they had some warm water and he'd taken out the foaling box he'd put together as soon as he knew the mares were expecting. He had some antiseptic in there and fishing wire he'd use if the birth was too quick and the umbilical cord ruptured before its time. He had a sharp knife to cut the birthing sac if they needed to grab the front legs to help the birth along and a piece of soft, clean cloth to help them grip the slippery foal. With any luck, they wouldn't need any of it.

Flynn managed to keep away from the mare until he heard Hunter say the horse was settling down and he could see her water break. Just when he got ready to squeeze in between all the broad-shouldered men, the barn door opened again and Calley walked in carrying a large thermos of coffee.

"How's it going, boys?" She threw a quick look into the stall and then stood to the side, where Bill was leaning against the wall.

"Not long now. She's doing well," Bill updated her.

"Thought you could all use come coffee, but we'll leave that for the celebration afterward, okay?" Calley suggested.

At that moment a well-developed hoof popped out of the back end of the mare.

"Damn," Bill cursed. "It's a breech. Not something we need for a first time."

Hunter became nervous and Flynn managed to spot the very fleeting but still calming touch Grant bestowed on Hunter. He didn't miss Hunter's thankful look either.

Flynn put his arm around Gable's waist and let his hand rest possessively on Gable's hip, in full view of Grant. "They'll be okay," Flynn assured the others, but he had to admit he was happy that Bill was there in case something didn't go exactly according to plan. He'd seen breech births before, both natural ones and the kind that needed a helping hand, and knew that a calm mare was a godsend. For now, this little lady was doing a superb job.

"We can't see properly," Hunter said. "Can we move to the other side?"

"No way," Bill waved him off. "We can't choose how she gets down and we're *not* moving her. Give her some space, guys. You can't crowd a lady, but then I can't blame you all for not knowing that."

Gable chuckled, but neither Hunter nor Grant did. The tension in the barn was thick enough to cut with a knife and nobody spoke. The mare grunted from time to time, but remained fairly calm, lying down on the fresh straw that Flynn had put in her stable.

"It's taking too long," Bill suddenly said, walking outside to get his bag out of his car. He returned almost immediately, moving to the back to wash his hands and then walking into the stall, shutting the half-door behind him and thereby effectively barring entry to the rest of them.

"Can I help?" Flynn dared to ask.

"Not now," Bill barked. "You'll just get in the way."

Flynn fidgeted, but didn't give in to his urge to step in and "get in the way."

They watched how Bill carefully cut the sac further and wet his hand with some of the amniotic fluid before sliding it into the horse to extract the other hoof. "Cloth?" he asked curtly, and Calley was quickest to hand it to him. He wrapped it around the hooves to get a better grasp and pulled gently. The foal didn't move. Bill muttered something that sounded like "damn" and then tugged again.

This time, Flynn didn't ask for permission. He opened the stable door and entered, crouching down next to Bill to use his own cloth to grab one of the legs.

"We'll need to change the angle a bit. Mind if you pull while I feel around for what's keeping this thing stuck?" Bill asked.

Flynn simply nodded and kept the tension on the foal's hind legs while Bill adjusted his angle and felt around inside the mare. Suddenly, something seemed to give way and Flynn fell back into the straw as the tension eased. The mare whinnied and the foal became partially dislodged. Bill waited for a moment to see if the rest of the birth would happen naturally, but eventually helped it along a bit until the foal was all the way out, before pulling away the rest of the birthing sac.

Neither horse moved and everyone seemed to hold their breath. Flynn bunched up some straw and started gently rubbing it over the wet foal.

"Easy, be gentle," Bill cautioned in a much softer voice than before. "Give them time." He stepped back and stood there watching the new mother and her completely still foal intently before leaning on the half door.

"It's a big boy," Bill told Gable.

"Come on, boy, breathe," Flynn said in a soothing voice. "Show us what you're made of."

After a few tense minutes, the foal suddenly shivered and then raised its head.

"Fucking hell!" Hunter called out. "I thought he was never going to catch that first breath."

Grant was smiling too now, and Flynn couldn't help but move a little closer to Gable as the mare got up and the afterbirth slipped out of her. All of them knew they had to give the mare some space to bond with her foal.

"One down, one to go," Flynn told Gable. "The other one's showing no signs, though, so it may take as long as a few more weeks."

Gable pulled Flynn into a hug across the low stable door and kissed him on the forehead. "We're not paying the vet anyway," he said with a chuckle.

"Don't remind me," Bill intervened. "Calley," he called out as he exited the stable. "Get me some coffee."

"You're standing right next to it," Grant pointed out. Those were the first words he'd said all evening.

Bill shot him a mean look. "When you find yourself a wife, maybe you'll understand what it means to be well taken care of." A smile broke on Bill's face when his gaze turned to Hunter. Flynn could tell Bill was dying to say something else bordering on caustic, but he was happy when Bill held his tongue.

"Let's just all get a cup, hey?" Flynn cut in.

When Grant spoke again, Flynn knew things were getting out of hand. "That's no way to speak about Calley, Bill. She doesn't deserve to be ordered around."

Before any of the other men could react, Bill planted his fist in the much taller and broader horse wrangler's face. Grant wavered but didn't fall and was caught by Hunter, then quickly regained his footing and repaid the favor.

It took a stern and surprisingly strong "STOP IT!" from Calley to halt the men in their tracks. "That's it," she concluded. "Are you done? Then stick your peckers back into your pants and back off." After which she briskly walked out, shortly followed by Bill, who was rubbing his sore jaw.

"What was that all about?" Flynn asked Gable, but Gable simply dismissed him with a curt shake of his head, making sure Flynn understood he wasn't going to tell him anything right then.

Grant was sitting on one of the bales of hay, swatting Hunter's hand away as Hunter checked that Grant's split lip was just that and nothing else was hurt.

Gable walked over to them. "Pretty tense evening."

Hunter straightened his back as if he'd been caught doing something he shouldn't and faced Gable. "Yeah, it was. Listen, we better go. Thanks for calling and we'll be around to visit from time to time, if that's okay with you. And of course, it would be mighty nice if you called again for the second mare." He gazed into the other box and his face lit up. "I think you won't need to call us again!"

Instantly they all hit the stable door, scrambling for the best view.

"Shall I get Bill back?" Gable asked slowly, as if he was watching a car wreck in slow motion.

"No," Hunter answered. "Girl's doing fine."

The mare was making pretty much the same noises as the first one, but she was more restless and kept looking up. This one had gotten down with her hindquarters facing the four men, so they had front-row seats to the second miracle of the day. This time there was none of the nervous tension and none of the pulling and stress of the first birth.

First one tiny hoof and then a second popped out, still covered in the silvery birthing sac. A few moments later a nose appeared as well, which slipped back for a moment and then the mare grunted and Flynn could actually see her push the rest of the foal out. It seemed so natural he almost forgot how difficult the birth of the little colt in the next stable had been.

Flynn took one step inside, just enough to pull the amniotic sac away from the foal's face so it could take its first breath. It took both horses some time to recuperate, but pretty soon the new mom was standing up to investigate her child and the foal was quick to get up as well, wobbly as hell for a few minutes, but already searching for mother's milk.

When Gable put his arms around Flynn and pulled him close so he could nuzzle his neck, Flynn looked sideways and saw Grant do pretty much the same to Hunter. Their hug had something so manly about it, so butch, yet Grant also displayed a certain tenderness he'd never seen or even expected in the big guy. It was so obviously an unguarded moment for the other couple and something they never did in front of others. Just when Flynn discreetly wanted to alert Gable to what they were witnessing, Grant remembered they were not alone and immediately let go of Hunter.

"Hey, no need to hide from us, guys," Gable drawled. "We've been on to the two of you for a while now."

Grant and Hunter looked at each other, but didn't resume their intimate moment, making it slightly awkward. Just to stress his point to the other men, Gable pulled Flynn even tighter to his chest.

—24—

"TIRED?" Flynn asked as they were walking back to the house. He'd noticed that Gable's limp was more pronounced, so he'd guided Gable's arm around his shoulders and let him lean a bit as they walked under the starlit sky.

Gable nodded. "Glad you're a romantic," he joked. "But it was a long day."

They'd waited until the two colts were suckling well and they were content that their mothers were taking good care of them before saying their good-byes to Grant and Hunter and closing the barn door.

"They look like good little horses," Gable continued as they navigated their way up the porch steps without letting go of each other. "The second colt looks just like Brenner when he was little."

"Too bad we have to give them to Hunter."

"Hunter will take good care of them, no doubt," Gable replied as he made his way upstairs with more difficulty than usual.

Once upstairs, Flynn retrieved the first aid kit and the hand cream from the bathroom. By the time he walked into the bedroom, Gable was flat on his back on the bed, still fully clothed.

"Come here," Flynn teased, pulling off Gable's boot and unbuckling his belt.

"I'm too tired for that, Flynn," Gable sighed.

"Not too tired for a little TLC, I hope?"

Gable looked up and smiled at Flynn. "Maybe a little."

Flynn knew Gable was dead tired, because he usually protested letting him look at his stump.

ZAHRA OWENS

"Your leg looks good. I expected it would be chafed, but it's just a bit red."

Gable grunted a reply and let Flynn massage some of the cream into his skin. "Feels good, love."

Flynn just smiled, enjoying the fact that Gable was getting quite casual about his leg now. He finished up and got ready for bed as well, leaving his clothes in the dirty linen hamper near the bedroom door.

"So can you tell me what's going on now?" Flynn asked as he snuggled into Gable's arms.

"Nothing's going on," Gable dismissed him.

"Why did Bill whack Grant?"

Gable inhaled and then sighed deeply. "It's a really long story and we need to get up early to take care of the foals."

"So give me the short version then," Flynn insisted.

Gable grumbled, but then scooted up so he could sit leaning against the headboard. "Bill and Grant just don't get along."

"Does it have something to do with what he did to you?"

Gable shook his head. "No, it has to do with Calley."

"Oh?"

"I told you it was a long story."

Flynn sat up too. "I still want to know. Was it juicy?"

Gable chuckled. "Not really." He squared his jaw and sighed again before continuing. "Calley and Bill have been trying to have a baby for as long as they've been married."

"Hence Calley's tears the other day, after the stork comment?"

Gable nodded. "They've been seeing doctors and trying to figure out why they can't conceive, but other than that Bill's sperm apparently isn't grade-A quality, there doesn't appear to be a cause. At least that's what Calley said. So one day about four years ago, she asked me if I would consider 'donating a sperm sample'."

Flynn nodded, careful not to interrupt Gable's train of thought now that he'd finally got him to talk. It answered a few of Flynn's question, notably why he always had the feeling there was history between Gable and Calley.

"I declined, trying to be really nice about it," Gable admitted. "It's not that I never considered being a father or that I thought Calley wouldn't do a good job as a mom, but I have to admit that if I ever help conceive a child, I want to be its dad, not just the 'donor'."

"I get that," Flynn nodded.

"I wanted to help her and would have done anything to make her a mom, but not that."

Flynn snuggled into Gable's arms again. "I'm sure she understood?"

"She did. But then Grant came along. I always knew he slept with women too. He'd go to town on Saturday evenings, to the dances or into the city to the clubs, and I knew he wasn't faithful to me then."

There was still some hurt in Gable's voice, but not nearly as much as when he used to talk about Grant, which soothed Flynn.

"What I never expected is that he hooked up with Calley."

That surprised Flynn too. "Grant and Calley?"

Gable nodded. "My hayloft. At the time, Calley and Bill were practically living apart. Calley told me the stress of visiting all those fertility doctors and the hormones she had to take were getting to them and Bill had moved to his practice in town."

"Were they in love? Calley and Grant?"

"Oh no," Gable answered. "Calley was lonely and she figured a pleasant side effect might be that she could possibly get pregnant. Grant was harder to read. I think he still carries a torch for her."

"And all this happened right in front of your eyes?"

"Not exactly," Gable said. "I'm sure it did, and maybe I didn't want to see it, but they were pretty discreet around me. I think especially Calley felt very guilty. I know she avoided me for a while."

"But even Grant couldn't get her pregnant?"

Gable chuckled, but not out of amusement. "As a matter of fact, he did."

"But Calley doesn't ...."

"Calley went into labor early and the baby was stillborn. That's when she confessed everything to me. She apparently told Bill too, but much later."

"Oh, wow, poor Calley."

"So you see why she still has a pretty good rapport with Grant and why Grant ticks Bill off. I can imagine it can't be easy for Bill to know his wife's ex-lover is still hanging around here."

Flynn agreed. "And we can assume he's going to be around for a long time. He really seems to hit it off with Hunter."

"Oh yes," Gable sighed.

"Are you jealous?" Flynn asked half-seriously.

"Jealous? Me?" Gable was quick to protest. "No. Grant and I weren't good for each other. Besides, I have you now."

Flynn poked him. "You better believe it."

"I'm still surprised about Hunter, though."

"I can't believe you didn't know that Hunter was gay," Flynn giggled.

"Come on, Flynn. It's not written on his forehead," Gable replied. "I know he's never really had a steady girlfriend, but I thought he was just too busy on the ranch. Plus, I can imagine that with three sisters and a mother in the house, you wouldn't want to bring a poor, unsuspecting girl into that."

"Or a guy."

"Certainly not a guy," Gable agreed. "I seriously doubt that Hunter's mom and sisters know about Grant. They're great girls, but I think they'd be pretty devastated."

"Would they throw him out?" Flynn asked, feeling sorry for Hunter.

Gable smiled. "He's still the man around the house. They all work around the ranch, but he runs it, and despite the fact he never finished school, he's got a really good head for figures. He runs that ranch even better than his father did."

"You know him quite well, don't you?"

Gable nodded. "We've always been neighbors. My father and his father forged a pact that he wouldn't buy my father out like he'd bought out all the other small ranchers around here. Hunter's a bit younger than me, of course, but I watched him grow up. And then his dad died when he was fourteen and he had to take over."

"Couldn't have been easy for him," Flynn mused.

"No, certainly not. Our fathers died in the same year. Of course I was older and was running this place pretty much on my own anyway, but Hunter was just a kid. He spent more than a few nights in my barn, bawling his eyes out because he couldn't take the responsibility."

"So you were like a big brother to him?"

"I suppose," Gable answered softly.

"Is that why you still have a hard time believing he's gay?"

Gable shrugged.

"Or did you make a move toward him and he turned you down?"

"No way! He was a friend, and besides, he was way too young!"

Flynn chuckled at the way Gable vigorously defended himself. "But you did?"

"What?"

"Have a weak spot for Hunter?"

Gable smiled shyly. "You know I do."

"Even when he was fourteen?"

"Sixteen," Gable admitted. "Still way too young to put the moves on him, and besides, he never showed any interest in me and I wasn't that forward then."

"So you never...?"

"Flynn!" Gable cautioned.

Flynn snuggled back into Gable's arms. "I'll shut up now."

"Go to sleep."

"Yes, Daddy."

"Stop that," Gable replied, unable to stop himself chuckling. "I'm not your daddy and I never will be."

"I wouldn't have minded if Hunter knew about your hayloft from you instead of from Grant."

"I know," Gable said softly. "That would have made it a lot weirder, though. With Hunter and Grant now being together."

"I wonder what his mother and sisters will say," Flynn said sleepily.

"I doubt he'll tell them any time soon, but then again, they did look pretty serious together, so it's only a matter of time before those ladies are going to see it with their own eyes. I don't know if it's better for him to come out to them before that happens or not."

"Did you ever come out to your parents?" Flynn asked, more alert again.

"No," Gable answered softly. "Dad was the only one to see me grow up, and he died before I could say anything. Don't know if I would have, but I think he knew I wasn't really into girls much. It wasn't the sort of thing we talked about, though. I know he was a little disappointed that Bill got to Calley before I did, but other than that…. Let's get some sleep, okay?"

Flynn turned and wrapped Gable's arms around him so they were spooning. They both drifted off within minutes.

—25—

IT WAS a crisp, late spring morning when Calley called Gable.

"Darling, can I drop by around lunch to talk? In private?"

Gable shrugged. "Sure, it's your day to bring in groceries, right?"

"Yes," she answered a little hesitantly. "But I want to talk to you alone. I know this sounds awkward, but I think it's better Flynn not hear this."

Gable squared his jaw. He had no idea what Calley wanted to talk about, but he trusted her. He just had to find a way to gently break it to Flynn that he was going to have to make himself scarce for an hour or so.

"I'll figure something out," he assured her. "You staying for lunch?"

"Sure," she answered.

Gable put down the phone and stared at it.

"Trouble?" Flynn asked, walking into the kitchen and straight to the fridge to get something cool to drink.

Gable pondered for a moment and then decided to just tell Flynn the truth. "Calley's coming around for lunch and she wants to talk to me alone."

Flynn raised an eyebrow. "I hope she's okay?"

Gable shrugged. "I suppose she'll tell me. You okay with leaving us to talk alone?"

Flynn smiled. "Of course. She's not likely to tell you she's leaving Bill for you, now is she?"

Gable chuckled. "If she is, she needs a shrink."

BY THE time both men returned to the house, Calley was inside, making sandwiches.

"Hey, you're our guest, you don't need to make lunch!" Flynn scolded her with a broad smile. He bumped her away from the sink with his hip so he could wash his hands. "I can fix us all sandwiches."

Calley kissed him on the cheek. "I was early and you two were still finishing up, so I figured I'd get started. I don't have a lot of time, and I couldn't very well just sit here and wait."

When she turned around, she ended up right in Gable's arms.

"Easy, girl," Gable chuckled, hugging her tightly before letting her go.

"In any case," Flynn said, leaning over the lunch plate Calley had made, "I'll take two of these and take Bridget out under the tree. Then you two can talk."

He didn't give them a chance to reply, simply picked up two overstuffed sandwiches, wrapped them in a piece of paper towel and whistled for Bridget, who came bounding over only to follow Flynn outside almost immediately.

"You told him I didn't want him here?" Calley asked.

"Not in those words, but yes. I told him you wanted to talk to me alone."

Calley nodded, taking two plates out of the cupboard and putting them on the table.

"He didn't seem to take it the wrong way?"

Gable laughed. "No, why would he? He knows we go way back and, frankly, you're no threat."

Although she nodded in understanding, Gable could see she was still tight-lipped, and his curiosity had been piqued when she called him earlier. Now he almost couldn't hold back asking her. He knew she was a cut-to-the-chase sort of girl, though, so he was pretty sure he'd find out in no time.

"Coffee?" he offered.

After ten minutes of eating and talking about what was happening in town and with their neighbors' farms, Calley still hadn't said a word about why she was there.

Gable was about to burst. He poured her another cup. "So are you about ready to tell me why we banished Flynn to eat under the tree?"

"We didn't…!" Calley sighed. "I'm sorry, but this isn't easy."

Gable nodded patiently.

"Remember when I asked you a few years ago if you wanted to donate… sperm."

Gable chuckled. "Funny you should mention that, because I told Flynn about that just the other night."

"You did?" Her eyes went wide and she smiled. "How did he take it?"

Gable waved his hand at her. "Don't you change the subject. Just tell me!"

Calley bit her lip. "I know you said no, but I was wondering if you would reconsider."

Gable didn't immediately say no this time. Part of him still wanted to, but he could see the expectancy in Calley's eyes and he didn't have the heart. He wasn't going to say yes right off the bat either, though.

"Are you and Bill going to try again?"

"I am, yes," she answered.

Gable narrowed his eyebrows. "You and Bill splitting up?"

She smiled vaguely. "No, we're not. It's been rocky, but I still love him and I'm pretty sure he still loves me. We've just been dealt another blow and told we'll never have kids together."

Gable moved closer to Calley and took her hand. "I'm sorry to hear that."

"The doctors have figured out it's a genetic thing, so my only chance would be with donor sperm. I've had some really difficult talks with Bill, and that's why I'm here. Bill doesn't want some stranger to be our baby's father, but on the other hand he doesn't want to know who the father is. He wants to put the details in an envelope in case we need them for some reason, if the baby gets sick or needs a kidney or something."

"So you'll know who to blame?" Gable chuckled to hide his unease.

"That sounds bad, Gabe. No, but if the kid asks me who her father is when she's grown up, I don't want to have to tell her we got a sample from some doctor and have no idea who her father is."

"Instead you want to tell her that I am her father?"

Calley sighed. "Since Bill doesn't want to know who it is, I need more options, so I also asked Hunter and Grant; and since Flynn already knows, maybe we can ask him as well? That way there are four options?"

Gable chuckled and shook his head. "You and Bill are both blond, meaning if you choose any of your other three options, you'll end up with children that have dark hair. I'm your only option for fair-haired kids, Calley. At least if I remember my biology lessons from school. It's been a while; I might have it all wrong."

Calley nodded. "We'd like to leave it to chance. And if we get a dark, curly-haired kid, we'll still love it to bits."

Gable put his arm around Calley's shoulder. "Let me talk to Flynn about this, okay?"

Calley nodded. "Bill agreed that all of you should know the baby from the word go. That way if she wants to know, she'll know you well enough to just come over to talk to you."

Gable pinched her playfully. "You just want free babysitters."

Calley smiled. "I'm sure Bill thought about that one too, yes."

"In any case, if it's my sperm, you'll end up with all boys. No women in my family."

"Your mother was a woman!" Calley teased.

"Yes, she was. But she was the only girl, with six brothers, and Dad also had four brothers and no sister. So forget about that girl."

Calley got up and hugged Gable tightly. "Thank you," she whispered in his ear. "I'll call you later."

They walked outside together, Calley toward her car and Gable toward the tree where Bridget greeted him.

"So where was the fire?" Flynn asked, petting Bridget so Gable could sit down next to him.

"She and Bill can't have kids together. Apparently they're not genetically compatible."

"And she wants you to be a donor?"

Gable looked at Flynn intently. "How did you know?"

"You told me she'd asked you before."

"And I said no then. I told you that as well."

Flynn nodded. "Did you say yes now?"

"I told her I had to talk to you first."

Flynn hugged Bridget tightly and she let him for a moment, then she rolled on her back and begged for Flynn to rub her tummy. "I think you should. If you want. She's your best friend, Gabe. You love her to bits."

"I do," Gable had no problem admitting. "She asked me to ask you as well."

"You just did."

"Ask you to be a donor too," Gable elaborated. "She wants to leave it to chance. Also Bill doesn't want to know who fathered his children, so she now has four options."

"Four?"

Gable nodded. "She asked Hunter and Grant as well."

"Bill's gonna know anyway. Unless it's a kid with curly black hair, then it can be either Grant's or mine, but if it's got fair hair, it's yours, and straight brown hair will be Hunter's. Come to think of it… if it's a tall, curly-haired kid, it'll be Grant's, and if he's shorter, it'll be mine."

"I know," Gable shrugged. "That's exactly what I told Calley."

"I don't mind," Flynn mused. "It's not like I'm going to have kids any other way, and this way there'll be some piece of me still walking around when I'm gone."

"Even if you can't be its dad?"

Flynn shrugged. "Bill'll do a good job."

Gable rustled Flynn's hair. "Why am I not convinced?"

"You're projecting, Gabe," Flynn answered. "I'm not the one having parenting issues."

"Are you thinking you haven't had any decent role models and that's why you'd make a lousy dad?"

Flynn swallowed. "Maybe."

Gable could barely hear Flynn answer and it made him pull his lover tighter to his chest. "For the record, I think you'd make an awesome dad."

To prove the point, Bridget put her head on Flynn's thigh, begging for more petting.

"Don't worry, honey," Flynn soothed her, scratching her ears. "You'll always be my baby."

—26—

A FEW weeks later they met up with Hunter and Grant at a clinic about an hour's drive away from their respective ranches. Gable could tell both Hunter and Grant were nervous, although he figured they were nervous for different reasons. Gable knew Hunter didn't like hospitals. He'd seen his father waste away in one in a matter of days and really preferred to stay out of them altogether. The reason Grant was nervous was probably the same reason he himself wasn't totally at ease.

Unable to sit still, Grant got up. "I'm hunting for coffee," he announced. "I'll come with you," Hunter was quick to answer, leaving Gable and Flynn alone in the waiting room.

Gable watched them leave. He and Grant hadn't spent any time together in the same room since they'd split up, if you didn't count the night in the barn when the two colts were born. It was clear that Grant had been avoiding him, and Gable didn't mind. Now they probably wouldn't be able to continue giving each other the cold shoulder. Again, Gable felt he was okay with that. He was going to have to talk to him one day. Grant and Hunter looked like a pretty solid item, and he didn't want to lose Hunter as a friend. Besides, being nice to Grant was a way to show Flynn that he was over him, and hopefully Flynn would understand that he was the reason for these new feelings. Gable didn't think he could have survived the past year without Flynn, but besides telling him, Gable had no way to show his lover that. Maybe if Flynn saw that he could be congenial with Grant, Flynn would see it for what it was worth: a testament to the love and caring they shared.

"What's so funny?" Flynn asked, shaking Gable out of his thoughts.

Gable realized he was smiling broadly. "I was just thinking about spending time with Hunter and Grant. Should we all go out to dinner together afterward?"

Flynn snorted. "Only if Calley's paying!"

"I think it would be a good idea. Gives us a chance to smooth things out between the four of us. We're neighbors, after all, and Hunter has been more than a help in the past years. I can't blame him for falling for Grant."

Flynn gave him a questioning look. "Are you jealous?"

Gable chuckled. "No way. I told you before Hunter was welcome to have Grant. I just think we could be civil to each other. Grant's not a bad guy. We could even be friends." Flynn's forehead wrinkled even more. "Maybe," Gable added to put his lover at ease. Gable looked around the empty waiting room and then pulled Flynn closer to him, kissing his soft, curly hair. "I love you with all my heart. Trust me, I have nothing but honorable intentions with Grant."

Although Flynn pulled away, he was smiling again, and that was all Gable wanted. As he looked up, he realized why Flynn had pulled away from him. Hunter and Grant were walking toward them, both of them carrying two cups of steaming coffee.

"Didn't know whether you wanted cream in your coffee," Hunter said, handing one cup to Gable and another to Flynn before taking his own cup from Grant.

"I did manage to score us plenty of sugar," Grant added, dipping his hand into his jacket and unearthing a nice handful of sugar packets, which he dropped on the table in front of them.

Gable smiled at Grant. "You know the way to a man's heart. Flynn's got a real sweet tooth." He took three packets and Flynn held out his cup so Gable could empty the packets into the black liquid.

"Tastes foul without it," Flynn agreed, tasting it and holding it back out so Gable could add more.

Grant smiled and shook his head and Gable started feeling more relaxed. He could do this. It wasn't even that hard.

"Mr. Jarreau? Mr. Tomlinson?" a nurse called out.

Grant got up and Gable couldn't help noticing the little hand-squeeze between Hunter and Grant as the curly-haired man left his companion behind to follow the nurse. Gable had seen their little gestures of affection before, but only now realized they made him feel good too. He was happy for Hunter and, if he let himself admit it, he was happy for Grant too. When he looked over at Flynn, he saw a smirk on Flynn's face.

"You were eyeing Grant," Flynn said teasingly as he, too, got up from his seat.

Gable shrugged and gave Flynn a "so what if I was?" look. To his surprise, Flynn smiled widely, making butterflies flutter in Gable's stomach. He watched his lover leave the waiting area behind Grant.

"So, you think we're next?" Hunter asked, moving seats to sit next to Gable.

"You make us sound like lambs to the slaughter," Gable snorted.

"Well, it's not that bad, but the idea of jacking off in a cup seems sort of...." Hunter didn't finish his sentence.

"Just think of the bigger purpose. We're doing this for Calley. And in a roundabout sort of way, I suppose we're also doing it for Bill."

Hunter pursed his lips. "I suppose we are."

"And it's what? Five minutes of your time?"

"Hey!" Hunter nudged him with his shoulder. "Speak for yourself!"

"And you're young," Gable added. "If you go home and Grant has fresh ideas with you, you'll still be able to get it up. I, on the other hand...."

Hunter gave Gable a worried look, but the teasing smile on Gable's face made it disappear almost as quickly as it appeared.

"Flynn keeps me young," Gable admitted, a fair bit more quietly than before.

"Good," Hunter replied. "I'm glad. I know what it's like to love someone. Before I just thought I did, but now I know." He gazed off in the direction Grant had gone.

Gable looked at him sideways. "Then I'm glad too." He patted Hunter's knee but withdrew his hand fairly quickly, not wanting to draw attention to himself. "So Flynn and I were talking when you went for coffee and decided we should all go out to dinner together after we're done here."

"Are you sure? I mean…."

"You mean me and Grant in the same room, trying to exchange polite dinner conversation?"

Hunter nodded.

"I think I can manage. If Grant's okay with it, so am I."

Hunter scrutinized Gable, clearly trying to gauge whether Gable was simply putting on a brave face. "I'm sure Grant won't mind. I'll have to square it with him, of course, but I think he'd be more worried about your reaction than his own. Why the change of heart?"

Gable chuckled. "I'm like you. I used to think I knew what it was like to be in love with someone. Now I'm sure."

Hunter patted Gable on the shoulder. "So where should we go?"

Gable didn't get to answer, since Flynn walked back into the waiting room with a triumphant look on his face.

"Am I the first one?"

"Yup," Gable answered. "Grant's not back yet. I always thought you had more stamina than this." He winked at Flynn.

"I do when it counts," Flynn answered smugly. "Now the end goal was to produce… something, and I always think of the end product!"

Grant followed soon and close behind came the nurse. "Mr. Sutton? Mr. Krause."

"Our turn," Hunter said as he got up.

Gable followed them into a sterile-looking hallway with a counter, where they were asked to sign a form and then given a plastic cup and a room number. Gable eyed the cup suspiciously and entered the small room. It had a comfortable-looking chair and a window with colorful curtains. There was a TV on top of a low dresser and one of the drawers was open. He peered inside and realized it was full of porn, both DVDs and magazines. He shrugged when he saw all the bare boobs, but as he rummaged through it, he was surprised to find a DVD clearly meant for gay men. He decided against putting it in the player and figured he'd be able to conjure up enough images to get himself off. He cocked his head when he thought he probably wouldn't be able to beat Flynn's record time, though.

On the table next to the easy chair was a box of tissues, and Gable put the plastic container next to it before turning around to wash his hands like the nurse had very efficiently instructed them to do.

Gable looked at himself in the mirror over the washbasin. He had a few more lines around his eyes than he used to and he was still on the thin side, despite Flynn's excellent cooking, but what struck him most was that his hair, which used to be dirty blond, was now copiously streaked with gray. He shook his head while he dried his hands on a paper towel. He had no idea why a vibrant young man like Flynn would choose an old cowboy like him, but he didn't question it too much anymore these days. For that, Flynn's love simply felt too good.

Unzipping his pants, Gable plopped down in the chair and took out his limp cock. He realized it still made him nervous. Months of impotence after his near-brush with death had left traces after all. He was pretty much healed up now, although his injured leg and prosthesis still didn't completely feel like his own. He started touching himself, trying to bring Flynn's image to mind. Flynn always found ways to distract him and make him feel good. It was his infinite patience and caring that had restored Gable's faith in his own abilities and had eventually brought them a rather prolific sex life. He no longer doubted whether Flynn enjoyed it too. He just had to conjure up the image of Flynn leaning over him, driving into him; the determination and ecstasy in his face as he thrust hard and accurate, and Gable felt his cock swell. Yes, that was it.

The image easily turned to Gable riding Flynn. Gable liked being in control. He liked it a bit too much, but he'd learned to leave some of the initiative to Flynn as well, and since then Flynn often let him do the work. He'd lie there, smiling up at him, running his hands over Gable's lean thighs. Flynn would urge him on and not start thrusting up until

Gable was so desperate to come he was practically begging. Fuck, that man turned him on.

Gable was nowhere near to coming, though. He stopped his ministrations and sighed deeply. He wasn't even completely hard yet. This wasn't working. For a moment Gable contemplated putting the gay porn on, but he figured it would set him back even more, timewise.

At that moment the door was yanked open and Gable's immediate reaction was to cover himself and get up from the chair. It took him a moment to register who had entered.

"Looks like you could use a... hand?" Flynn said teasingly.

Gable let himself drop to the chair again.

"Hunter's been done for ages!"

Gable chuckled. "Amateurs."

Flynn moved in and straddled Gable's thighs, running his hand through Gable's long hair. "I'm serious. The nurse said it was okay for me to help you out if you needed it."

"The nurse said... what?"

Flynn laughed. "Your face is priceless. I didn't tell her, love. I snuck in here when she wasn't looking."

"How did you know where I was?"

"It's the only door still marked 'occupied'."

Gable didn't dare think what would have happened if there'd been two. He pulled Flynn's head closer to kiss him and felt the familiar surge of lust. "Guess you're right. You always know what I need."

Flynn pulled back and bit his lip. "I thought of you when I was in here. I thought of your tight little ass and that beautiful cock of yours and of how tight you feel when I'm inside you." He looked at Gable's groin and Gable immediately felt his blood run south. Gable took his cock in hand and started rubbing it up and down slowly.

Flynn eyed it seductively. "Maybe you should take off your jeans and your boxers and then I could fuck your ass with my fingers. Would you like that?"

"Fuck," Gable sighed. "Yeah, of course I'd like that." He could almost see himself grow.

"Problem is I wouldn't have a hand left to hold the cup, and you're too far gone when you have something up there to remember to aim." He chuckled amusedly as he took the cup and unscrewed the top. "So you'll have to do it all yourself, and then, when you bring me your bounty, I'll catch it. How does that sound?"

Gable nodded, his breathing heavier now that he was picking up some speed.

"Just think of the gift you'll be giving Calley," Flynn continued drawling.

Gable stopped what he was doing. "You sure know how to kill a mood."

"What?" Flynn asked innocently.

"Like it's always been my life's ambition to knock up a beautiful blonde."

Flynn chuckled and leaned over Gable to kiss him. "Sorry. You never liked blondes?"

Gable knew when he was being teased. "No, I prefer my men dark. With curly hair."

"Shall I go get Grant for you then?"

Gable pulled Flynn to him and kissed him violently. "I only want you," he said, panting after releasing Flynn.

Flynn looked down at the now almost purple cock Gable was fisting rapidly. "Guess I'll just have to fuck you long and hard when we get home." Flynn only just managed to position the plastic container when Gable's cock spasmed and ribbons of come shot out of the slit. "Good boy," he said, as if he was talking to one of the horses. Flynn put the cup on the side table and kissed Gable passionately as he came down off the high of his orgasm.

"I invited Hunter and Grant out to dinner with us," Gable eventually managed.

"So I'll have to wait?"

Gable nodded lazily.

Flynn snuggled closer to him. "What if you're the one to get Calley her baby?"

Gable shrugged, enjoying how Flynn was caressing his still-covered chest. "I don't see the problem."

"You said that if you became a father, you wanted to be more than just the donor."

"We'll just have to see how Calley handles it, but I don't think I'll be doing a lot of fathering. I don't think Bill will let me, for one. Besides, it's going to be their kid. We agreed on that when we said yes."

Gable looked at Flynn, trying to gauge the reason for Flynn's questions. Did Flynn want a child too? He didn't dare question it, although he was sure it would come up one day. He only had to think back at how protective Flynn was of the mares and the foals and see how well he took care of Bridget and how much of a mother hen he was when he was sick to know Flynn would make an excellent father.

Suddenly Flynn extracted himself from Gable's embrace and got up from the chair. "We'd better bring this little sample out to the nurse and get back to Hunter and Grant, or they'll think we left the building through the back door!"

"If that nurse sees us come out of this room together, she'll think we had full-blown sex in here," Gable replied matter-of-factly, tucking himself back into his jeans after cleaning himself up with a tissue.

"Would that be a problem?" Flynn asked cockily.

"No," Gable laughed. "Now let's go and get some food."

—27—

TO SAY the dinner started out a little tense was the understatement of the century. Hunter had picked out a typical mom-and-pop family diner with sturdy wooden furniture, red-and-white checked tablecloths, and steaks that barely fit on the already oversized plates. The tables were close together and most people had brought their broods with them, so there were kids running around all the time.

Flynn eyed them with some unease, since he wasn't really used to kids, and he found himself exchanging meaningful glances with Gable. There was no need for them to talk. Flynn could read Gable like a book.

"You sure you want to actually father any children you sire?" Flynn asked silently, with eyebrows raised as a small boy raced past them, wielding his fork as a weapon while chasing his taller sister.

"No way, José," was clearly behind Gable's smile and shaking head as they settled around the table. Flynn tried to keep as much distance between Gable and Grant as he could, but since they had a round table, this meant that at first Grant was sitting right opposite Gable, and the tension rose the moment they realized they were going to be staring at each other all through dinner.

"Let's switch," Flynn suggested to Gable. "More space for your foot," he explained as casually as possible. Luckily, Gable understood and immediately got up. It did put Grant next to Gable but it made it easier for Gable to ignore Grant as he now sat opposite Hunter and next to Flynn.

It wasn't until they were scrutinizing the menu that Flynn realized that Grant and even Hunter were quite comfortable with the rampant children. One overworked and tired-looking mother shouted "Jackson!"

across the restaurant as a mischievous-looking boy of about seven darted past their table. Hunter was quick to catch him in his sturdy arm, halting his progress. He picked him up and deposited him in front of Grant, who had put down his menu.

"You Jackson?" Grant asked with a broad smile that matched the little boy's mischievousness.

The kid nodded.

Grant mussed his hair. "Don't you think you should listen to your mother when she calls for you?"

"She's always shouting at me, sir," the kid answered.

"Maybe because you don't listen?" Hunter replied, exchanging a knowing look with Grant.

"Go on, go to her and tell her you're sorry for running away. Maybe if you're nice she'll let you come pony-riding at Blue River Ranch?"

"I'm big enough for a horse!" Jackson exclaimed.

"We have mighty big horses over at our ranch, you know," Hunter added to Grant's invitation.

"Thank, guys," the mother said as she reached them. "But don't put ideas into his head. He's horse-crazy enough as it is."

Hunter got up and shook the woman's hand. "Well, my partner here is right. We have pony-riding every Saturday morning and we show kids his age what it takes to take care of a horse. In other words, they learn how to muck out stalls as well as ride. And we take good care of them. You can come along if you like."

She eyed him up and down and briefly looked at the rest of the table's occupants, but her gaze was more of wonder than suspicion.

Hunter retrieved something from his pocket. "Here's our card. My baby sister is a gem with kids and she's the riding coach. Why don't you give her a call?"

"Can we, Mom?" Jackson asked impatiently.

"We'll see, Jack," his mother answered. "Thanks again. He's a handful," she said, turning back to Hunter.

Flynn watched the interaction and then looked at Gable. He was happy to see his lover look less tense, but he was more surprised at seeing Grant so loose and casual. He'd never expected Grant to be such a natural with kids.

"So you have pony rides at your ranch?" Gable asked after the waitress took their orders.

Hunter nodded. "Bernie's teaching the kids to ride, and she figured she could make a little extra money teaching the kids from town to ride as well. You know, classmates of Danny. She wants to try her hand at three-day eventing, but needs some extra money. We bought her a good horse, but the equipment and travel expenses are pretty steep."

"So that's why you've been buying the smaller horses," Gable said as if it had only now dawned on him.

"Yeah," Hunter said flatly. Flynn didn't miss the look he gave Grant and he couldn't shake the feeling they were hiding something. Then again, he didn't feel comfortable enough to ask, so he was pretty sure he was just going to have to live with his lingering questions.

"So, is the ranch doing well?" Gable asked.

"Pretty good," Hunter replied. "We lost a few foals over the summer. Still haven't figured out if it's horse thieves or a cougar, but one or the other is bound to get caught in time."

"Thanks for the warning," Gable said. "I'll keep the little ones close to the house."

The waitress brought their steaks and they ate almost silently. From time to time Hunter and Gable would talk ranch business and Flynn was glad that Grant was staying out of the conversation, since Gable seemed to be fairly relaxed now. It also gave Flynn time to observe his dinner companions. Grant was a handsome man, he had to admit. Not his type, but he had the feeling that if it hadn't been for the history between Gable and him, they could be friends. Hunter, too, was a looker. Flynn had noticed that the first time he'd laid eyes on him, when Hunter had come by the ranch to buy horses. The man's intense, piercing eyes were probably his biggest asset, but Flynn also liked his smile. It was warm and caring and not just directed at Grant, but at anyone who crossed his path, from the busboy who cleared their plates to the waitress who offered them the dessert menu, and yes, Hunter directed that flirtatious smile at Gable too. For just a moment Flynn felt a little jealous. Hunter and Gable obviously went way back and Gable had admitted that he'd had the hots for the younger Hunter, but would he ever be competition now Gable was sure Hunter was gay?

Flynn was brought back to the here and now with the feeling of Gable's warm hand on his thigh. "Be right back," Gable said before getting up and walking in the direction of the restrooms.

"Yeah, I could use a leak too," Grant said, following in the same direction.

Hunter must have caught Flynn's panicked expression. "They'll be fine," Hunter assured him, but Flynn could tell he wasn't all that confident either. "Grant's calmed down a lot. I think he just wants to talk to Gable alone for a moment."

"Well, I hope so," Flynn said, peeling his gaze away from the restroom doors and directing it at the laminated card in his hands. He couldn't read what was on offer. He was too worried about what was being said or done at the other side of the restaurant. He knew he couldn't go to Gable's rescue. He had to leave his lover with some dignity and not give the impression he was an overbearing or jealous lover. His heart rate didn't drop until Gable returned to the table, though.

Gable's smile made Flynn relax. "Are you getting anything?"

Flynn shrugged. "Probably not."

"I'm getting ice cream," Hunter said, obviously not totally reassured yet.

"Yeah, me too," Gable agreed. "Any idea what Grant wants? Because I see the waitress coming our way. He's the nuts and caramel type," Gable said so casually both Flynn and Hunter ended up staring at Gable, who didn't let on he noticed.

Hunter ordered for both Grant and himself and Gable only ordered his own desert after Flynn declined again.

"What did you get me?" Grant asked as he returned to the table.

"Vanilla ice cream with caramel fudge and crushed nuts," Hunter said.

"Oh goody," Grant replied, rubbing his hands together and smiling at Gable.

"So Grant told me you two are thinking about building another house?" Gable asked casually.

"Yeah," Hunter answered, fleetingly looking at Grant before redirecting his gaze at Gable. "We figured it would be easier to have our own place since the main house is rather... full."

Gable chuckled, while Flynn watched the interaction with some amazement.

"We were going to ask you and Flynn if you could lend a hand from time to time."

Gable gave Grant that curious look again, then turned to Flynn before answering. "Guess we can, after all the chores are done at the ranch, of course. It's the least we could do for all the help we've had from the two of you."

Flynn nodded almost automatically, but he didn't know how to read the suddenly easy interaction between Gable and Grant. He didn't get the chance to ask Gable anything until they were back in the truck and on their way home. He wasn't totally at ease asking Gable loaded questions while he was driving, because this was still something relatively new to him since the amputation, so he bit his tongue.

"You're awfully quiet," Gable eventually said. They were already on the last stretch before the ranch.

"It was just strange to see you tense one moment and then so relaxed another. After you came back from the restroom... When I saw Grant follow you in there, I thought... Even Hunter looked worried, Gable," Flynn stammered, trying to put all his feelings into words, but didn't feel like he'd succeeded.

"Everything's fine, Flynn," Gable reassured Flynn. "I admit I didn't know what to do when I saw him follow me in, but he just wanted to talk."

Flynn rolled his eyes at Gable because he felt the tears sting and he didn't want to cry. He hoped he could keep his emotions in check until they got home, so he wasn't happy when Gable stopped the car by the side of the darkened road and turned off the engine.

"We're obstructing traffic, Gabe."

Gable laughed. "This is our road. Nobody comes here." He took Flynn's hand. "He apologized, Flynn. He said he didn't know what had happened to me. He also apologized for all the lies and the denial. He admitted he was gay," Gable said with a chuckle. "I guess Hunter really is Mr. Right for him."

"Yeah, they are good together." Flynn said, squeezing Gable's hand in return and feeling a little bit calmer.

"So are we."

Flynn smiled and felt himself relax completely at Gable's loving words. "Does this mean Grant's forgiven?"

"No reason to carry a grudge. It's a waste of energy. I'd rather spend that energy on something else. Someone else."

Gable extricated his hand and put it on the back of Flynn's head, gently pulling him into a kiss. When they pulled apart, Gable reached for his keys to start the truck again, but Flynn stopped him.

"Can we just stay here for a little while?"

"Sure," Gable replied, putting his arm around Flynn's shoulders and letting him snuggle closer.

"Who's Danny?"

"Danny? Oh, Danny's Hugh's son. Hugh is Hunter's foreman and he's married to Lisa, who is Hunter's oldest sister, so I suppose Danny is Hunter's nephew. Oh, and his godson too, I believe."

"Does Danny have brothers or sisters?"

"Don't think so." Gable threw Flynn a questioning look. "Why?"

"When Hunter was talking about Bernie teaching 'the kids' to ride horses, he was definitely talking plural. Kids. More than one. Hunter has more nephews?"

Gable shook his head. "Not that I know of. He has three sisters, but only Lisa has a son. Bernie's the baby. She's barely out of high school. Middle sister's Izzie, who works the ranch. Sweet girls, although Izzie's a bit of a tomboy. Don't ever take her up on a challenge to arm wrestle. I've never met a guy who didn't walk away with a sore arm and a bruised ego."

"Including you?"

Gable bit his lip. "She almost tore my bicep muscle, and she was only twelve at the time."

"Wuss," Flynn said, poking Gable in the ribs. "So who do you think the other kids are?"

Gable shrugged. "Probably classmates of Danny's. Kids from town. Plenty there who've barely seen a horse up close."

Flynn wasn't sure Gable was right. He was sure Hunter had misspoken and then had tried to hide it by adding the comment about Danny's school friends. Eventually he shook his head and decided it wasn't worth mulling over.

When Flynn shivered, Gable withdrew his arm and started the car. "Let's go home. I believe you promised me something?"

"Promised?" Flynn parroted.

"Something about finishing what we started in the jack-off room at the hospital?"

"Aaah," Flynn said with a wicked smile. "Now there's an irresistible offer."

—28—

THE dinner with Hunter and Grant was more than just a good start. At least once a week Hunter seemed to find an excuse to visit the neighboring ranch, and Grant was usually with him. It started out with the two of them visiting the growing colts, but they'd invariably end up talking business, and eventually it went so far that Hunter included Gable in his mass purchases of extra hay and oats so that Gable could benefit from the better prices Hunter could negotiate because of the sheer quantity he bought.

For Gable it was nice to have a friend again. It wasn't until Hunter and Grant ended up staying for dinner one night that he realized how much he'd missed just spending time with friends.

"This was fun," Flynn said while they were clearing up the living room after the other two guys had left. "You're okay with Grant now, aren't you?"

Gable smiled pensively. "You know, I think I like him better now than when he still lived here. Back then we sort of tolerated each other, but now—"

"There's no need to apologize, Gabe. I can see it's just friendship."

Gable raised an eyebrow. "I'm not apologizing. I just now realized I actually like Grant, but he's not the same Grant I used to know."

"He's changed that much?" Flynn sat on the couch and pulled Gable down next to him, which forced Gable to put down the last plate he wanted to take to the kitchen.

"I lusted after him, but I didn't love him."

"You told me that before."

"I didn't even like him, Flynn."

"But you needed him then?"

Gable nodded regretfully. "I'm afraid so."

"We all did things for the wrong reasons, I'm sure," Flynn said philosophically. "I didn't fall in love with you at first glance either, you know."

"You didn't?" Gable quipped. "You mean my irresistible charm didn't win you over within the first week?"

Flynn smiled lopsidedly. "No, the fact you were a challenge was a much stronger attraction. I guess it's true, I like the chase."

Gable put his arm around Flynn's shoulders and pulled him until their lips were close enough together to kiss. He lingered, though, not bridging the final half-inch. "I'm glad you were persistent enough, because if it were up to me, I'd have let you go after six weeks and then we wouldn't have had this."

"You like this then?" Flynn asked teasingly as he let his lips ghost over Gable's.

Gable rested his forehead against Flynn's. "I can't imagine life without you anymore."

"Good, because I have no intention of living without you either."

Flynn snuggled closer and pulled his knees up so he could rest his legs over Gable's.

"You think Hunter and Grant have this?" Gable asked.

"You mean the cuddling and the lovey-dovey stuff?" Flynn chuckled.

"Grant doesn't seem the type."

"Neither does Hunter, if you ask me," Flynn agreed.

"Maybe that's changed about Grant too?"

"I'm sure they have a lot of crazy monkey sex," Flynn said matter-of-factly.

Gable almost choked. "Crazy monkey…?"

"You know. Fucking. Hard and frantic. In and out. Quick and dirty. They like exotic places too, like your hayloft."

"That's out of necessity, I'm sure. I bet they have this too," Gable said, caressing the sparse hair growth on Flynn's chin before tenderly kissing his lover.

"Mmmh, I bet they do. In the privacy of their own room. I bet it's hard to have crazy monkey sex with a bunch of sisters in the room next door and a mother down the hall."

"I bet it is," Gable agreed, kissing Flynn some more. By then he had his hand underneath Flynn's sweater and was caressing Flynn's tight stomach.

"They deserve a house of their own. I bet Hunter's a real screamer when he's being thoroughly fucked and you can only really let it out when there's nobody listening."

Gable pulled back to look Flynn in the eye. "You have some wild imagination, kid."

"Don't tell me you've never wondered about what those two would look like together?"

"I try not to think about that," Gable admitted.

"I do. Ever since I caught them in your hayloft."

"Our loft," Gable amended.

Flynn just smiled. "So we're going to help them build their house?"

"It's the least we can do," Gable agreed. "Thanks to Hunter I didn't go bankrupt, and he does seem to have a good influence on Grant."

"Admit you like Grant."

Gable eyed Flynn suspiciously.

"You know I don't mind."

Letting out a big sigh, Gable opened his mouth to speak, but then thought better of it and bit his lip.

"Gabe, he's your ex. This may sound pretty conceited of me, but I don't think I have anything to fear. You barely have a happy memory that features Grant, and although the tension when the two of you are in a room together has dissipated since that first dinner, I'm still pretty sure he has no idea your eyes are blue."

"Meaning?" Gable asked, eyeing Flynn suspiciously.

"Grant is just as afraid to look you in the eye as you are, Gabe."

Gable couldn't help but smile. All this time he'd been preoccupied with his feelings toward Grant and Flynn's feelings toward Grant and not once had he wondered how Grant felt about him. Not once had he asked himself why Grant had always seemed angry and uncomfortable around him. Maybe it was just Grant's way of acting because he didn't know how to deal with the situation.

"I don't hate him anymore," Gable eventually said. "I used to. I used to feel hurt and rejected, I suppose, but he didn't know I'd had an accident when he left."

Flynn hugged Gable tighter and put his chin on Gable's shoulder. "I know."

"I suppose it's a good thing that Grant and I are learning to spend time together without all this awkwardness if we're going to help them build their house."

"I suppose so."

"Grant took the first step in the restaurant restroom, I guess it's my turn to show him there really are no hard feelings."

Gable rested his head against Flynn's. He counted his lucky stars he had someone as forgiving and patient as Flynn. His current relationship with Grant was the best proof that he was no good at communicating about feelings and the fact he and Flynn had what they had could all be brought back to the effort Flynn put into the relationship they shared.

Flynn yawned and snuggled even closer.

"I think I better put you to bed."

"First one up the stairs gets to bottom," Flynn quipped, jumping up from the couch.

Gable pulled him back down. "Hey, that's not fair. I'm a cripple."

"You are?" Flynn asked. "I hadn't noticed." He pulled Gable to his feet and dragged him toward the stairs. "Okay, let's change it to: the first one up the stairs gets to choose who bottoms."

Gable smiled because he knew he'd get exactly what he wanted.

SEVERAL months later, while Flynn was in the stables, Calley came by to bring their groceries. As soon as Gable saw her crawling from the truck, he hurried to help her.

"I hope you have help around the store, Calley, because you're struggling," Gable said compassionately.

"Tell me about it," Calley sighed. "I'm done freaking out every time the doctor shows me there's two of them in there and I do see the upside of getting it over with in one go, but I already feel like a beached whale and I still have three months to go."

"Is Bill helping you out?" Gable asked as he took the box full of produce out of the back.

Calley snorted. "It's coming up to lambing season. I'm lucky if he sleeps next to me at night."

Gable looked at her empathetically, but she ignored him, so they walked toward the house. "You need to get help at the store, Calley. Not just for when you've had the babies, but right now, so you can put your feet up." Gable saw sadness creep into her face as he put the crate down on the kitchen table. He pulled up a chair and made Calley sit down while he unloaded everything she'd brought in.

"I didn't lose the last one because I worked too hard, Gabe."

Gable put his hand on her shoulder and squeezed it. "I know, but I'm just saying… You need to take care of yourself. These babies are precious and not just because I had a hand in conceiving them. You're precious too, you know that."

Calley put her hand over Gable's and pulled at it so he had to sit down next to her. She placed his hand on her belly and pulled him into a hug that brought his head close to hers. "They're fine, Gable." As if by command, the babies started kicking and Gable pulled his hand away, but she grabbed it back. "They like the attention."

"But it's Bill's touch they should feel, not mine." Gable didn't pull his hand away again, though.

"Bill is still having a hard time with all this."

Gable hurt for Calley. He knew how hard it was on Bill that he couldn't give his wife the kids she wanted so much and he knew their marriage was a struggle partly because of that, but he'd hoped those issues had all been resolved before the pregnancy. Obviously it hadn't been that easy.

"Bill loves you, Calley," Gable said, kissing her temple. "I'm sure once he lays eyes on these kids and everyone is patting his back for a job well done, he'll toot a different tune."

They sat together for a while, heads close together and their hands touching on Calley's belly. From time to time one of the babies would kick and Gable would smile. He'd shared a lot of highs and lows with Calley and considered himself a true friend, and he'd held her close because she needed it, but he was surprised about his own feeling toward the babies. He'd never let himself crave offspring because he knew early on that he'd never marry a woman and have a family. He'd always poured his paternal feelings into his dogs and his horses, but now he realized that he wanted to see these children grow up. Up until now he'd rationalized that he was just helping Calley and that he trusted her to take good care of his children, but that they wouldn't really be his, since nobody but the six of them involved would ever know Bill wasn't the father. So what had changed?

Gable didn't have the chance to think about it, because his little intimate moment with Calley and her babies was broken by the front door swinging open and Flynn walking in. Gable saw the spring in Flynn's step as he walked into the kitchen and then the change in his expression as he noticed his lover's closeness to Calley.

It was only then that Gable thought again of pulling his hand away from Calley.

—29—

FLYNN felt like he'd walked into something he wasn't supposed to have been privy to. He saw Gable pull his hand away from Calley's belly and Calley's stunned face, and before he could even think of asking for an explanation from Gable, his feet had carried him outside again, into the bright spring sunshine and the cold morning air.

Bridget came toward him, her tail wagging. "Let's go, girl. Back to the barn."

All he could think of when he was saddling T.C. was that his first impression had been right. There was something between Gable and Calley that Gable had neglected to tell him. All he could see was his lover sitting close to Calley, holding her, his head close to hers as if they'd just kissed and his hand on her belly, protecting the children growing inside. His children; Gable's children. The children Gable had always pretended not to want. The children Gable had always said he wouldn't help conceive because he wouldn't be allowed to play dad to them, and then he'd changed his mind.

God! He would have given an arm and a leg for those children to have been his. He'd always told himself that it was better that they weren't, because he'd want to raise them himself and he would probably muck that up as easily as he'd mucked up everything else.

Climbing into T.C.'s saddle, he knew he had to get away, put a little distance between himself and the ranch, although he couldn't in good conscience leave it right now. He knew he'd have to do the sensible thing. He had to return and talk to Gable about it, but right now, he couldn't. He would wind up saying things he'd regret later.

After letting T.C. run at full gallop for a few moments, he slowed down, knowing Bridget would be trying to follow. He was trotting when she caught up with them, panting, so he dismounted near a drinking trough and called her to him. Thaw had settled in and there was only a very thin layer of ice left on the water, so he broke it and let Bridget and the horse drink. He then found himself a spot in the high grass near the fence where most of the snow had already cleared and sat down.

Bridget settled half on his lap.

"You always know when I'm feeling a bit worse for wear, don't you, girl?"

Bridget looked up at him and then settled her head on his thigh. He stroked her head and flank and slowly felt himself relax. Even if Gable was keeping a secret from him, they were going to have to have a grown-up conversation about it, because that's what you did in a relationship. At least that's what he figured. It wasn't like he'd ever witnessed a grown-up relationship before. It was just hard to realize that there would always be uncertainties; that he'd never be able to be a hundred percent sure about what he shared with Gable. These last months they'd grown so close, and yet he'd never seen this coming.

Flynn's thoughts were interrupted by the sound of hoofs. He knew it was Brenner; he could distinguish the nervous trampling of the big stallion without fail every time. By the time Gable had approached, he'd slowed the horse down and seemed calm as he dismounted a few steps away.

"You okay?"

"Sure," Flynn answered, trying to sound casual.

"You didn't even say hello to Calley."

Flynn shrugged. "I didn't want to interrupt."

"You weren't," Gable said curtly. "She was dropping off the groceries. I had to help her because she's really growing uncomfortable."

"Oh, you were helping her all right," Flynn said, tapping Bridget's side so she moved and he could get up.

Gable stayed near Brenner and Flynn thought that was enough of a sign that something wasn't quite right. He walked to T.C. and took his reins, but Gable stopped him.

"What's wrong, Flynn?"

"You need to ask?" Flynn said, turning away from Gable. This time, Gable put his hand on Flynn's shoulder to stop him. "You and Calley? I knew there was stuff you hadn't told me. Now I wish you had."

"I told you everything you needed to know," Gable said hesitantly.

"Then you don't give me enough credit." Flynn tried to mount again and this time Gable didn't stop him. As soon as he felt the saddle underneath him and T.C. started dancing from one leg to the other, ready to run, he saw Gable's defeated look and stepped down again.

Gable didn't say anything.

"What exactly is your relationship with Calley?" Flynn spat out.

"I told you. We're friends. We've shared a lot over the past years. A lot of it bad."

"A bed?" Flynn said, still feeling the anger boil inside him.

"No, never that," Gable said calmly. "You know I don't sleep with women, Flynn."

"You were all over her." As soon as he'd said the words, Flynn realized he sounded like he was still in high school.

"I was comforting her. Bill is never around and she's hormonal. She's feeling lonely and uncomfortable and insecure and she's tired and worn out. I've never been more than a friend to her, Flynn. I'll admit I try to be a good friend to her, but there's no way I can ever repay her for all the things she's done for me over the years."

"You gave her your children. That should be enough." By now Flynn felt tears stinging the back of his throat. He tried swallowing them away, but his throat was thick and dry.

"They're not my children," Gable repeated for the hundredth time. "They're hers and Bill's. The only people who know they're mine are Hunter and Grant, you and I and Bill and Calley, obviously."

"But they are yours," Flynn said, barely louder than a whisper as he turned around, pretending to fix something on T.C.'s saddle. "I want them to be yours."

Flynn closed his eyes as he felt Gable's hand on his shoulder again and realized it felt comforting.

"I'm sorry you couldn't be the donor, Flynn. You know that, don't you? If it had been possible, then I would have let you father those children."

Flynn couldn't stop the tears. He turned around and flung himself into Gable's arms, hiding his face in the crook of his neck. Gable wrapped his arms around him and squeezed, slowly rocking him from side to side.

"I wish through some freak of nature I would have been able to give you those kids, Gabe," Flynn said once he thought he was able to speak again.

"I never wanted them, Flynn. I've never missed having kids." Then something seemed to dawn on him. "But you do, don't you?"

Flynn lifted his head but didn't dare look Gable in the eye. "Ironic then that you could probably get Calley pregnant sitting next to her, but I'm shooting blanks."

Gable wiped the hair away from Flynn's face, but Flynn looked over Gable's shoulder into the distance. He wasn't ready for what he would be able to read in Gable's eyes.

"I never thought you'd take the test results so badly, Flynn," Gable said softly. "I'm sorry I didn't realize it was so important to you. I thought you were like me, that you'd automatically concluded that since you'd never marry a woman, kids wouldn't be possible either."

"I guess I never gave up hoping that I'd find a way," Flynn confessed. "Don't ask me how I was going to manage that, but when that doctor told me I was infertile, my world fell apart." Gable squeezed him tightly and Flynn had to admit it felt good. "The only up side was when you agreed to be the donor. At least I'd get to watch *your* kids grow up, even if it was just from afar."

"I can ask Calley to share it with you, Flynn. I think if I explain it to her, she'd be more than willing."

Flynn shook his head.

"Frankly, I think she needs someone to share these feelings with. She's so afraid to be happy, so afraid that things will go wrong again, and Bill's not feeling like a dad yet, so he's ignoring them too," Gable continued. "It's so strange to feel the babies move inside her. They're so real. I think I felt a foot when one of them kicked, a tiny little foot, like you can sometimes feel a hoof through a mare's belly when the foal is about to be born. I know you've felt that, Flynn. I saw you patting the mares more than once just before they foaled."

Flynn nodded this time, both acknowledging what Gable had said and conceding that Gable was right. He wanted to share Calley's baby joy. His sadness was slowly dissipating as he realized that Gable understood him. There was one thing he wanted to clarify, though.

"I'm not jealous that you're their biological father, Gabe." His arm hooked underneath Gable's, they turned to the side and started walking, a horse at either side.

"Oh?"

"I'd probably mess that up too. Didn't exactly have the best role model where fathering is concerned."

"I have no doubt you would make one hell of a father, Flynn."

Flynn looked at Gable suspiciously and then returned his gaze to the path they were walking. "I just hope we'll get more than a casual glance of them growing up. I'll settle for watching to see if I recognize certain things about you in them." At that moment Bridget squeezed herself between them.

"Go on home, girl," Gable said, patting her behind. "Stop coming between my man and me," he added with a laugh.

Bridget ran ahead, but not much. She made sure she was always watching them.

"She's your baby, isn't she?"

Gable nodded. "And her mother before her."

"Ever thought of letting her have puppies?"

Gable smiled. "Tried. Didn't work. She and the male dog didn't exactly get along and although he had his way with her a few times, no puppies for Bridget. She's a bit old now."

"She's happy, though."

"She's got two dads. She should be," Gable concluded. "You feeling a bit better now?"

Flynn nodded. "Thanks."

THE next Saturday, they drove to Hunter's ranch after morning chores and found the outline of the new house already staked out. As they got out of the truck, Hunter darted over to them like a young puppy.

"They delivered quite a bit of the lumber on Thursday and we put the flags up when everything was still covered in snow," Hunter said eagerly. "What do you think? Does it look good?"

Gable looked over at the short spikes sticking out of ground and the red and white ribbon between them. He raised his eyebrows when he realized the new house was bigger than his own ranch house.

"Are you sure the four of us can manage building this?"

Hunter smiled. "Tim and Hugh are going to help, as well as some of the ranch hands who are eager for some extra money. And there's no real rush. We have a roof over our heads."

"Speak for yourself, Cowboy," Grant interrupted, knocking Hunter's hat off his head. "I can't wait for us to get our own place."

Hunter swatted at Grant, trying to grab back his hat, and would have tackled him if Grant hadn't been so steady on his feet. With Hunter still hanging half around his neck, Grant looked at Gable and smiled. "Thanks for helping us out."

Gable tipped his hat. "You're welcome." He watched how Hunter turned and started tickling Grant.

"There's coffee and lemonade and sandwiches under the tarp there," Hunter said while he and Grant walked to greet another group of helpers approaching.

"Thanks," Gable replied.

"Told you he'd be fine," Flynn said after the others were out of earshot.

Flynn hugged Gable from behind, and although Gable's instant reaction was to freeze up, he tried to ignore it. Yes, they were in public, but he knew the people here and he figured most of them knew about him and about the relationship he shared with Flynn. After all, Grant and Hunter didn't seem very shy around each other either.

"Relax," Flynn whispered.

Gable nodded as they started walking toward the tent that was leaning against the wood shed. There were kids and dogs darting around.

"Should have brought Bridget," Flynn remarked.

"Naah, leave the old girl at home. The kids would drive her crazy."

Flynn poured Gable some coffee and handed him the cup. "She might have to get used to kids around the house from time to time."

Gable saw the hope in Flynn's eyes and didn't have the heart to squash it. They had to face reality, though. "They're Bill and Calley's babies, Flynn."

"I know," Flynn said softly. "But you heard what Calley said. She knows we want to be a part of their lives and she says Bill seems okay with that."

Gable nodded, but didn't say anything. The day had started out happy and he didn't want to put a damper on things. They'd had this conversation a number of times, but he didn't see the two of them raising a child, let alone children they'd fathered themselves, and with Calley's children they'd be lucky if they got to babysit. Flynn was just going to have to be a father to all the foals he was going to breed.

"Let's get to work, okay?" Gable said instead. Flynn nodded, reluctantly.

Although it was still fairly cold for early spring, by noon they'd worked themselves into a sweat. Gable always enjoyed a good hard day's work, and by the time they'd had a quick wash from the rain barrel and were sitting down for lunch, he noticed his leg hadn't bothered him all morning. They'd lugged around quite a bit of lumber and had started digging a foundation, which made his back ache, but his leg felt better than it had in the past year.

While they were eating sandwiches and drinking coffee, Izzie came from the house with her new baby, and within no time, Flynn had the newborn on his arm.

"Come on, Izzie, don't give him the baby. He'll never give it back," Gable said, only half joking. Flynn threw him a disgruntled stare, but the smile returned to his face as soon as the baby girl started cooing.

Izzie sat down next to Flynn and kissed his hair. "That's okay. I know he'll take good care of her." She then turned to Gable. "Calley's coming this afternoon with more food. That is, if she makes it. She looks like she's about ready to burst. Doc says she won't make it to full-term."

Gable nodded, feeling worry creep up on him. "She's okay, though?"

"Oh yes," Izzie nodded. "She has help at the store now and it's only open in the mornings anyway. There's a woman who comes in to help out and she brings her son with her to lug some of the crates, so most of the heavy lifting is done by the time school starts and he needs to leave again. She'll probably keep the store open when Calley's recuperating from the delivery too."

"Good," Gable replied, still not feeling entirely comfortable. He knew he'd feel better once he saw Calley.

Hugh joined them, smacking Gable on the back. "Enough lazing around. Let's get this show back on the road, guys."

Gable turned to Hunter. "Who does he think he is around here? The foreman?" Both of them laughed as they got up and walked back to where they were digging the foundation. Most of the heavy digging was done with a machine, but there were always edges to settle and extra soil to be carted off to the side.

Just as they all took a break to have a drink of water, Gable spotted Calley's truck in the driveway, so he walked over to where she'd parked.

"You look like you could use some help there, mama," Gable said, holding out his hand as soon as she'd opened the door. She took it with grace and gratefulness and managed to get up out of the truck. It was only then that Gable noticed she wasn't alone.

"Ryan? Can you put the food under the tarp there, please?"

A boy who looked about ten years old got out of the passenger seat and walked to the back of the truck. Gable was torn between helping the kid and making sure Calley made it to a chair in one piece. He decided to stay with Calley.

"Flynn, can you lend a hand?"

Flynn ran up to them. "What? She can't walk anymore?" Flynn winked at Calley to tell her he was kidding her.

Gable pointed at the truck. "Help the kid with the food, will you? Those crates look heavy and I wouldn't want him to get hurt."

"Oh, he's fine," Calley said loudly so Flynn could hear. "I know it's child labor, but I pay him well and he lugs even heavier stuff at the shop." Then she turned to Gable and said conspiratorially, "His mom needed me to take him off her hands for an afternoon. I don't know why. Around the shop, he's an angel. You barely hear him and he works hard. He's very strong for thirteen."

"He's thirteen? He looks about ten," Gable said, looking over his shoulder at how Flynn was trying to get the kid to relax as they hauled the food to the dining area.

Gable had to smile at the contrast between Flynn's happy demeanor and the kid who looked as if someone had stolen his dinner. Suddenly Gable saw a soft smile break on the kid's face.

"Don't think I've ever seen that before," Calley commented in a low voice. "Your man doesn't just have a way with animals, does he?"

Gable smiled and said nothing.

—30—

THE only Saturday Gable and Flynn didn't spend working on Hunter and Grant's house early that summer was spent in the maternity ward of the hospital, or rather, in the waiting room outside of it.

Flynn had spotted Gable's mild worry that Calley had called them before calling Bill when her water broke four weeks before she was due to deliver. Everyone knew that she had a better chance to make it to the hospital if they drove her than if she had to wait for Bill to show up, but Flynn knew it unsettled Gable that even now, Calley couldn't really count on Bill to be there when she needed him. They both hoped Bill would mend his ways once he saw his children, but they weren't holding their breath.

To their considerable surprise, Bill almost beat them to arriving at the emergency room and Gable graciously stepped back to give Bill his moment of glory.

After two anxious hours, Bill stepped out into the waiting room looking as if he'd given birth to the babies himself.

"A boy and a girl, lads," Bill announced gleefully, patting both men on the back as they got up to ask him if everything was okay. "Every man's dream. They're doing beautifully."

"And Calley?" Gable asked dryly.

"Oh, she's good. That girl can survive anything."

Gable looked at Flynn, and Flynn returned a raised eyebrow. They didn't need to say anything to know what the other one was thinking. Gable had never been Bill's biggest fan, but Bill was an extremely competent vet and he'd more than once rendered his services free of charge when they were in dire straits; still, Flynn knew that Gable just didn't like him much as a man and only tolerated him socially because of Calley. Hearing how unfeeling he was toward her now, Flynn saw the anger boiling up in Gable and he knew Gable was trying hard to keep his temper in check around Bill.

"Can we see her?" Gable asked, looking calm, but only on the surface.

"She's resting, buddy," Bill said, slapping Gable's arm. "Thanks for bringing her. Wasn't a moment too soon."

Bill walked past them toward the exit.

"Where are you going?" Gable asked Bill.

"Got work to do. She called me when I was about to do a C-section on a cow. Guess another C-section took precedence."

Bill's mocking smile made Gable see red. "I'd think your wife could still use you more than that cow, Bill."

"Naaah," Bill answered with the same smile on his face. "She's tired; she doesn't want me around."

Gable pushed Bill against the wall and Flynn could only just stop him from slugging the larger man. Flynn put his hand on Gable's shoulder, which seemed to help Gable keep his temper, though Flynn felt Gable tense again when Bill made to leave, still smiling.

"I'll be back later, guys."

Gable stepped back and they watched Bill walk out.

"I can't believe that bastard!" Gable shouted, turning around and slumping against the wall

"Gable," Flynn warned him. He put his hand on Gable's arm, but Gable pulled away from him.

"After everything they went through to get these kids, he just walks out to go to work?"

Although Gable rarely lost his temper, Flynn knew he had to be the calm one; otherwise Gable would lose himself in his anger. "Sit down for a minute."

Reluctantly, Gable complied.

"How well do you know Bill?" Flynn asked, hoping that talking would help Gable settle.

"I've known him for ages," Gable admitted. "He's always been the regular vet around here, but he's not the only vet. I have no doubt that the ranchers would understand if he took a few days off when his wife just had twins, Flynn."

Flynn took Gable's hand in his and squeezed it. "I know you feel protective of Calley, but you can't make her decisions. She decided to stay with Bill, despite of all the things they've been through together. There must be a reason for that, because she's not the dependent-wife type, so all I can think of is that she loves him. Despite of all of his flaws, she still loves him. And I know all about that."

Gable looked Flynn in the eye as if he was gauging if Flynn was joking.

"You're far from perfect, Gable, but I still love you. Don't ask me why, but I do. Calley probably can't explain her feelings for her husband either, but I have no doubt they're much the same."

Gable's face softened and Flynn felt warmth flooding his body. He did love this man and had stuck with him through the hard as well as the easy times, just like Calley had stuck by Bill. Flynn saw Gable look around and then pull him into a hug.

"You know I love you too, right?"

Flynn smiled.

"Let's go see how Calley and the babies are doing."

"Gabe, we can't just barge in there."

"Sure we can. Aren't you just a little bit curious?"

Flynn had to admit he was. He wanted to know what Gable's children looked like. "You know I am."

Just at that moment a doctor walked through the doors and they didn't close immediately. They were slowly shutting when Gable got up and dragged Flynn along. "Let's go, then." They slipped inside just before the doors closed completely.

Flynn was nervous about walking behind the sealed doors, but he was also amused to see this other side of his lover. They walked past the empty nurses' station and Gable pointed at the white board. "Calley Haines. Room 12." He winked at Flynn.

It wasn't hard to find the room. Gable knocked and slowly opened the door. The room was shaded and Calley looked to be asleep, so Flynn pulled him back. "Don't wake her, Gabe."

"I'm awake." Calley's voice sounded sleepy.

"Hey, girl. Everything okay?" Gable asked in a voice Flynn had only ever heard him use with Bridget.

Calley smiled. "Hi, guys. Did you see the babies?"

Gable shook his head. "We wanted to see if Mom was okay first."

Calley's eyes filled with tears. "I still can't believe it. The midwife said they were both doing well, but since they were born early they wanted to observe them for a little while. Oh, and to give me a bit of rest, since I'll have my hands full soon enough."

"We saw Bill on the way in," Gable said. Flynn could tell he was trying very hard to keep his voice neutral.

"He had to go see a cow," Calley replied flatly. "Don't know if that's a euphemism for 'girlfriend' or an actual farm animal, but hey…." Then she seemed to recover. "I know his mind is on work, so I told him to go."

To Flynn's surprise, Gable chuckled. "You know Bill."

"Sadly, I do," Calley said. Then she seemed to perk up. "Let me call the midwife and ask her to bring the babies. I want you to see them." Flynn was happy to see that she addressed both of them, although he was sure she only really meant Gable. "There's two of you here if they both start crying," she added matter-of-factly.

A few minutes later the midwife arrived with a bassinet containing two bundled-up infants, and Flynn could barely contain himself. He knew he had to be patient, though. He was last in line when it came to holding the children, and once he saw how tiny they were, he wasn't sure he wanted to anymore. The babies seemed quite content and warm, wearing a pink and a blue cap on their heads, respectively, the little girl sound asleep and the boy with open, searching eyes.

Gable looked into the bassinet and smiled, so Flynn moved behind him and wrapped his arms around Gable's waist so he could look over his lover's shoulder. "He's awake," Flynn noticed.

"You can pick him up if you want, Flynn."

Flynn gazed at Calley, who looked beautiful even with bags under her eyes.

"I can't. He's so small. What if I, I don't know, drop him?"

Calley laughed and stopped almost immediately, holding her belly. "If there's anyone I trust him with, it's you, darling. I saw you with the colts. You're so careful with everything, I'm sure you can manage. Help him, Gabe."

"They're a bit more helpless than a colt, Calley," Flynn replied. He couldn't keep his eyes off Gable, though, as Gable carefully picked the little boy out of his crib and handed him to Flynn. He then cleared the way so Flynn could sit down in the chair next to Calley's bed. Flynn was barely seated when he heard the other baby cry, but he couldn't keep his eyes off the child in his arms. The boy was looking up at him, his eyes still a little unfocused but searching anyway.

"Hey, baby," Flynn said, feeling a little silly. When he touched the boy's cheek, the baby turned toward his finger and tried to suck it. "You hungry?" Flynn had the feeling the baby liked his voice, so he continued talking in hushed, animated tones. "I'm sure Mommy will feed you soon. You're not crying, though, so it can't be that bad, right? You're nice and warm, got a clean diaper, and you like it when we talk to you, don't you?"

The baby seemed to doze off and Flynn looked up at Calley. His eyes wandered to Gable, who was sitting on the bed next to Calley holding the baby girl. She was quietly sleeping on Gable's shoulder. Seeing Gable sitting there, quite comfortably holding the baby, brought it home to him again how much he regretted not being able to have children with his lover. They'd closed the subject, though. This was as close as they would get, and if Calley kept her word, they'd get a chance to babysit and they'd see them grow up. He looked back at the baby boy and tried to see Gable in him. He recognized the beginning of a dimpled chin, just like Gable had, but other than that, he didn't really look like Gable, Flynn thought.

"So what are you going to name them, Calley?" Gable asked.

"Since both our fathers share the same name, I thought I'd name the boy Andrew," Calley said. "And the girl looks like a Vicky."

"Calley, you don't have to," Gable whispered.

Flynn looked up at his lover, whose face was rife with emotion, and then at Calley, who was smiling compassionately.

"I like the name," Calley said smugly. "And I think it suits her."

Gable kept looking at the little girl, his callused finger caressing her brow. Flynn looked from Gable to the little boy in his own arms and hoped fervently they'd see these children grow up.

Gable got up from where he was sitting. "Will you be okay, Calley? I think it's time for us to go."

Calley nodded and smiled. Gable kissed her on the forehead after he put her daughter back in the crib and Flynn saw her whisper something to him that made him smile. When Flynn placed the boy next to his sister, he saw they seemed quite content packed closely together in one crib. He kissed Calley on the cheek and then walked out with Gable.

"Vicky was your mom's name?" Flynn asked in the corridor outside Calley's room.

"Yes." Gable nodded. He didn't elaborate, though.

"That was thoughtful of her," Flynn continued, hoping to find out why Gable wasn't happy with Calley's choice of name.

On the way home, Gable remained silent, as if he needed time to process everything on his own. Despite the fact Flynn really wanted to talk, he knew it was better to give Gable some space. He'd hoped Gable would be happy to see the babies, but he also understood that it was a mixed feeling. Gable had never wanted to just be the donor and now he was. Flynn's one hope was that he could break the silent treatment before they went to bed and maybe entice Gable to talk about his feelings before they went to sleep.

Gable tried Flynn's patience, though. When Flynn walked in from the bathroom, Gable already seemed to be sleeping, so Flynn crawled under the covers quietly and tried to fall asleep himself. But his mind was racing too much.

"Gable? Gabe?"

With a soft moan, Gable acknowledged that he was awake.

"Are you okay?"

"Why wouldn't I be?" Gable asked gruffly. When he turned to face Flynn, though, he looked more hurt than angry.

"I just figured it was a really emotional day and that you might want to talk about it."

Although it was fairly dark in the room, Flynn could make out the short nod. He waited for Gable to say something, but no words came.

"Andrew looks like you," Flynn said softly, hoping to get Gable to loosen up.

"How can you tell?"

Urged on by Gable's words, Flynn moved a little closer and automatically Gable moved his arm to wrap around Flynn's shoulders.

"He's got the same dimple in his chin that you have," Flynn said, running his finger over the indentation on Gable's chin. "And your blue eyes."

"All babies have blue eyes," Gable replied flatly.

"He's got Calley's light hair, though."

Gable chuckled. "I was almost white as a child. With tanned skin, like those old Coppertone commercials."

"I hope he grows up looking like you," Flynn continued.

Gable didn't reply to that. They laid together in silence for a long time, neither of them sleeping, but simply savoring the quiet time together. Flynn thought they'd come a long way since their uncomfortable silences the first weeks after he came to the ranch.

"It's the best I can do, Flynn, and I'm sorry," Gable suddenly said, after which he sighed as if it felt good to finally say it. "I know you wanted to be a dad and the horses are a poor substitute, even the little ones. I know that."

Flynn looked up at Gable. Something was starting to dawn. "I thought the reason you'd changed your mind about donating was to help Calley? Because Calley wanted fair-haired children. I know we went through the whole charade with the four of us at the clinic for Bill's benefit, but I didn't realize you had different motives."

"Don't be mad, Flynn," Gable said softly. "I know you wanted our children and when you got the bad news that it wouldn't be possible for you... I know this is a poor substitute."

"I would have liked to have been consulted," Flynn replied softly, attempting very much to keep any recrimination out of his tone of voice. Deep down he was pretty happy about Gable's motives, though.

"Calley really wanted me to do it because it would make more sense to have blond children and all of you had dark hair. I asked her whether she'd consider having you as a donor, because I knew you wanted children and I didn't care that much, but I did sort of want to see what your kids would look like. So you see, I understand."

Flynn snuggled closer to Gable, needing to really feel him. How he loved this man! Flynn moved his head so their lips were touching and placed a chaste kiss on Gable's mouth that felt more intimate than the intense, invasive kisses they often shared while they made love. "I'm glad it was you." Flynn closed his eyes, wanting to savor just the feeling of closeness. Elation started to take over from the earlier melancholy and Flynn smiled. "And if Calley or Bill don't want to share them, we'll kidnap them and only bring them back when they cry too much."

Gable laughed. "That, I suppose, is the benefit. We can always give them back."

Flynn nodded, settling in closer to sleep in the arms of the man he loved.

—Epilogue—

THEY'D held on to some of the mares that were left after Gable's dramatic winter, but it took a few years for Gable to realize there was a reason for them to be there other than that Flynn wanted to breed horses as well as raise them.

After the first two colts, which had belonged to Hunter even before they were born, Flynn made sure they had about five or six little ones every year, and they slowly got the ranch out of debt. It was still hard work, but neither minded that very much. The horses Gable broke and trained were still eagerly sought, mostly by the neighboring commercial ranchers who needed riding horses for their wranglers, but the leftovers that were sold at auction brought in a nice dollar as well. Flynn wasn't really surprised that Gable had a reputation for turning out excellent horses, and at the end of the day that always meant extra money.

"How would you feel about having some more kids running around here?" Gable asked Flynn one balmy evening as they were sitting on their porch watching the sunset.

"What have you been up to?" Flynn asked, sitting up so he could give Gable the full benefit of a mock stare.

Gable smiled. "You know Craig scored a doctor, right?"

Flynn snorted. "Yeah. I don't know who was more surprised that it was a girl, you or him."

Gable chuckled. "Well, she works with disabled kids and she was looking into equine therapy, letting the kids ride horses to improve their balance and their confidence and such."

"And you think we should do that here?"

Gable shrugged. "I don't see why not. We have the breeding mares, which are docile enough to trot around the corral with a kid on their back, and then there are the older geldings. They're fully trained but not really the kind of horses that do well at auction because they seem a bit lazy, but you know they ride well."

"Yeah, I guess lazy horses are perfect for that. You can fire a cannon next to Mally and he still wouldn't budge," Flynn chuckled.

"I know we don't have a lot of time, but it would only be one afternoon a week and I thought…."

"I think it's a great idea," Flynn interrupted. "I mean, Hunter and Grant are well settled into their house, so we have more time now."

"You're right," Gable agreed. "Remind me that the next time Hunter comes up with a brilliant idea, like wanting to build his own house, we turn him down, okay?"

"Well, it did start as an excuse to have his own place without telling his mom he was letting Grant move in with him."

Gable smiled broadly. "You know, it's nice that we all get along so well. I even like the new Grant."

"Hey," Flynn said, poking Gable in the ribs with his elbow. "Don't get any fresh ideas."

"About what?"

"Grant," Flynn answered. "He may have morphed into a nice guy, but I think if you steal him from Hunter, Hunter will put you out of business. That is, if I don't kill you first."

Gable grabbed Flynn, pulled him close to his chest, and playfully bit his neck. "I wouldn't dare. Hunter can have him. Besides, I don't need anyone else but you."

"Is that so?" Flynn said, turning around so he could kiss Gable passionately.

"Oh, I almost forgot," Gable said, interrupting their kiss. "We have the twins next weekend. Calley wants a few days of leisure and she asked if we could babysit."

"Oh, great," Flynn sighed. "No sex next weekend." He rolled his eyes dramatically, but Gable knew he loved those kids to bits.

"I'll make it up to you," Gable teased. "Starting right now."

"Oh?" Flynn uttered, flashing his eyelashes.

"Water's been heating up all day. Want to take a shower together?"

Flynn pretended to think about it, but Gable could practically see his jeans grow tight before his eyes.

"Last one in the shower gets to bottom," Gable said, getting up and holding out his hand to pull Flynn up.

Just minutes later they were under the spray of the sun-heated water from their extra-large water tank. Flynn was leaning against the house with Gable on his knees in front of him, using his oral talents to the fullest until Flynn made him stop.

"Come here," Flynn beckoned, pulling Gable to his feet to invite him for a searing kiss. "How do you want it?"

Gable raised his eyebrows. "As long as I get to feel you inside me, I don't care."

"Want to ride me, cowboy?"

"Is the pony in the mood to buck?" Gable answered as he turned off the flow of water.

The position Flynn had hated so much in the beginning of their relationship had now become one of their favorites. Flynn could never get enough of seeing his cock disappear into Gable's tight body and witnessing first the restraint and then the total abandonment with which Gable rode him. The only difference now was that, after their more frantic movements, Gable would lean down to kiss Flynn as they caught their breath, and then Flynn would take over, thrusting up while Gable held himself over Flynn's body. It was much more about sharing than getting off, much more about making each other feel good than about feeling good themselves.

Then, as they both got tired, Flynn would knead Gable's buttocks while Gable ground his engorged erection against Flynn's belly.

"Pony's been doing a lot of running today and is getting kinda tired," Flynn murmured against Gable's mouth.

"Cowboy's got a bum leg and old knees," Gable replied, smiling without losing contact with Flynn's lips.

"Want to change around?"

Gable nodded and reluctantly pulled away. He hopped over to the shower again and turned on the water, holding on to the rail they'd installed there a while back so Gable could still use the outside shower.

Flynn followed suit and moved behind Gable, letting his hands run over the wet hairs on Gable's chest, now showing some gray among the dark ones. As Gable stuck his head under the spray, Flynn wiped a hand back over Gable's scalp and Gable turned around so he could do the same to Flynn. They stood close together as Gable grabbed the shampoo to wash Flynn's hair.

"You don't seem too eager to continue where we left off?" Flynn asked.

"I have no doubt we will," Gable said with a teasing expression on his face. "But I like to prolong the agony, ehm, ecstasy a bit."

Flynn gave him a mock-annoyed look, but showed his enjoyment of what Gable was doing by kissing him and mirroring his movements. Slowly, the way they were running their hands over each other's bodies was becoming sexual again and Flynn took both of their cocks in his hand and rubbed them together, bringing them back to full rigidity.

"Want to fuck me here?" Gable suggested.

"Mmmh," Flynn agreed. "Don't think we'll make it upstairs."

Gable turned around and rubbed his ass against Flynn's erection. They were both slippery from the water and shampoo and soap so Flynn slipped into Gable's body without any effort. It took them a few moments to find the right configuration, with Gable resting his knee on the bench, which was just the right height, before Flynn started thrusting in earnest.

"Fuck, that feels good," Gable moaned.

"You always say that," Flynn replied.

"That's because it always does."

Every time they made love, in whatever position, it never ceased to amaze Gable how well they fit together. It didn't matter how many false starts they'd had, how many obstacles they'd had to overcome; it was all worth it for those moments when the world could come to an end around them and they wouldn't even notice. It was at moments like these that Gable remembered how Flynn had stuck by him, even when he thought they'd never be able to make love again, or when Gable thought he could never be happy again, with or without Flynn. There was one constant in his life and that was the guy who had drifted onto his ranch and asked him for a job he'd found on a scribbled piece of paper at the post office. As Gable slowly felt his orgasm building, he thanked his lucky stars one more time that he'd said yes that day. Then all those stars erupted at once as Flynn cried out in his ear. He felt the heat of Flynn's release flood his groin and then seep out into the rest of his body as he too came with erratic spurts.

They stood under the spray, watching their combined release flow away along with the water, both catching their breath but reluctant to move, as if breaking their union would actually do some damage to their true bonding.

"I fucking love you so much," Flynn whispered into Gable's ear.

"I had no idea," Gable laughed.

"I almost didn't come here, but I was desperate to work on a ranch again."

"I almost didn't say yes, because I was a grumpy bastard who felt too old despite being instantly attracted to you."

Flynn giggled, his arms still wrapped firmly around Gable's chest and his chin resting on Gable's shoulder. "What do you mean, you were?"

"You're the bastard," Gable rebutted.

"Yeah, but you love me anyway."

Gable grew serious and let his head fall back. "More than life itself."

At that moment, lightning split the balmy evening sky, and almost immediately a loud thunderclap made them both jump.

"Guess we spooked Mother Earth," Flynn giggled.

"Mmmh, I suppose she just wants her own Clouds and Rain."

ZAHRA OWENS was born in Europe just before Woodstock and the moon landing and was given a much less pronounceable name by her non-English-speaking parents. Being an Aquarian meant she would never quite conform, and people learned to expect the unexpected. She started writing fairy tales in first grade; the same year she came into contact with her first group of English-speaking friends, a group which would eventually grow to include people from all over the world. On the outside she was a typical only child, accustomed to being with adults most of the time. On the inside, she sought ways to channel her wild imagination.

During the daytime she earns a living as a computer specialist, but it's her former career as an intensive care nurse that tends to seep into her fiction. Maybe this has to do with her weak spot for flawed characters and imperfect bodies, or maybe it's just her sadistic streak coming through. You be the judge.

Visit her web site at http://www.zahraowens.com/ and blog at http://zahra-owens.livejournal.com/.

Also by ZAHRA OWENS

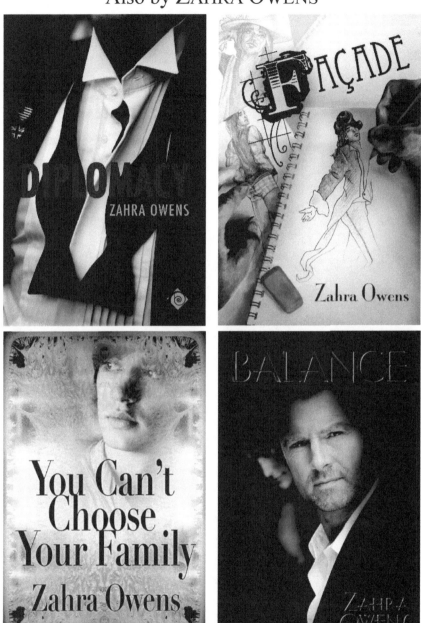

http://www.dreamspinnerpress.com

CPSIA information can be obtained at www.ICGtesting.com
Printed in the USA
LVOW01s0724051013

355511LV00007B/181/P